the red thread

Rebekah Pace

WITH TRACY LAWSON

Published by:
Level 4 Press, Inc.
13518 Jamul Drive
Jamul, CA 91935
www.level4press.com

Library of Congress Control Number: 2019944590
ISBN: 9781646300303
Printed in the United States of America

Other books by Rebekah Pace

ALL I WANT FOR CHRISTMAS

OPERATION SANTA

WALKING WITH THE PROPHETS

THE SANTA WARS

MIRACLE

Theresienstadt Ghetto, Occupied Czechoslovakia

June 1944

I sat between my parents on a hard bench while the orchestra tuned its instruments. In the violin section, Mira's chair stood empty. I'd been listening to her practice for weeks. She wouldn't have missed the performance unless something awful had happened.

When I turned to scan the crowd behind me, my mother nudged me to be still. Her face showed no emotion, but her eyes pleaded with me not to draw attention to myself. I knew I risked being singled out for punishment later, but at the moment I didn't care about myself—only about Mira.

As soon as my mother's gaze returned to the front of the room, I glanced over first one shoulder, then the other, trying not to be obvious as I craned my neck. When I caught the eye of one of our guests of honor, my heart jumped, filling my throat until it was hard to breathe. I gulped as he smiled and nodded at me. Cold, clammy sweat broke out all over my body, and I looked away.

"Peter." That one word, that whispered plea, stopped my fidgeting.

Everyone in the camp was ordered to attend this charade. Our four guests, a delegation sent by the International Red Cross, were the only ones in the auditorium who were not part of the show. The rest of us were performing as though our lives depended on it—because they did.

For months, the Nazis had used us as slave labor for their *Verschönerung*—the beautification project meant to prove to the world how well we were being treated inside this ancient walled fortress. As soon as the facade was complete, a German film crew had arrived to shoot newsreel footage and a documentary about the town Hitler had given as a gift to the Jews.

The Nazis used us to fool the rest of the world, and they carried out the deception with their customary cold efficiency. Before the film crew arrived, the camp director dispatched seven transport trains, bearing tens of thousands of people who were sent away to relieve the overcrowding. Mira's father was among them. A sudden stab of fear, like an icicle, pierced my heart. What if Mira had tried to speak to a member of the delegation about her father's whereabouts?

I clenched my fists in my lap and tried to keep my face from betraying my inner turmoil. Before the delegation arrived, we had been instructed how to behave, and Mira knew the rules as well as I. Our captors watched us constantly, and if one of us said too much, punishment would be meted out as soon as the delegation was gone—likely deportation to the east, and the unknown.

As the house lights dimmed, the Nazi officers took their seats. The conductor raised his baton in a hand that did not shake. As the first note sawed across my nerves, I blinked back tears.

I never laid eyes on Mira again.

Weequahic, New Jersey
2019

1

I moved my coffee cup aside and spread the newspaper on the kitchen table, but before I read the funnies or worked the crossword puzzle, I wrote several copies of the same coded message on different sheets of paper. The message itself was simple. Delivering it was the tricky part.

Leaving the notes on the table, I stacked my lunch dishes on the drainboard and ran water in the sink. My mother never liked to leave the dishes for later, and I guess that's why I did things the same way.

A knock on the door caught me off guard, scaring me so badly that I dropped the glass I'd been drying. It shattered on the linoleum, and I froze. In my panic, I forgot that whoever was on the other side wasn't going to break down the door and take me away.

There was another knock, and Benny called, "Pete? You in there, man? You okay?"

Benny owned the bodega on the corner where I did my shopping. With a sigh, I shuffled over to the door and checked the peephole. I didn't recognize the woman with him. She was holding a clipboard and looked young enough to be in college, but then again, everybody looked young to me.

"Who is that?"

The woman answered, speaking louder and slower than she needed to. There was nothing wrong with my hearing. "My name is Melody Richter, Mr. Ibbetz. I work for the county's Elder Services Department. May we come in?"

Richter. The judge, it meant in German. I took that as a bad sign. "What for do I need services?"

"This visit is just a courtesy, sir. We do it from time to time."

"Really?" I'd lived in Weequahic for more than seventy years, in this exact apartment for sixty-four of those, and most people would say I'd been "elderly" for a good twenty years. But I'd never had a visit from the county before. Something told me not to slide back the bolt or take off the chain.

Benny tried again. "It's all right, Pete. Let us in. There's nothing to worry about."

I trusted him, so I opened the door. Miss Richter stepped inside, looking around nosily. As I followed her gaze, I saw my apartment through her eyes. My portable transistor radio and the black-and-white TV with the rabbit ears antenna might be older than Miss Richter and Benny put together. There were scorch marks on the counter from the hot plate I'd been using since the stove stopped working about five years ago. The sagging sofa and the narrow bed had seen better days, that's for sure. So had the curtains. I think the woman who lived in this apartment before me bought them back in 1952, before she and her husband retired to Miami Beach. My worktable in front of the window probably looked like nothing more than a tangle of old electronic equipment—but I was familiar with every radio tube, wire, antenna coil, and transmitter.

Miss Richter's study of the apartment stopped at the broken glass on the kitchen floor. Embarrassed, I crunched through the shards to fetch the broom and dustpan from the corner, but Benny beat me there.

"Pete, you don't have to—I got it." He looked sad as he swept up the mess.

Miss Richter made a note on her clipboard. Though she was

smiling, it seemed like she was waiting for me to make a mistake. "Mr. Ibbetz, may we sit and visit for a few minutes?"

I gestured toward one of the vinyl-covered chairs at the kitchen table, and after she sat, I did too.

Benny lingered near the open door. "I'll get out of here and let you two talk. See you later this afternoon, right, Pete?"

Before I could protest, he bolted, and it dawned on me that this woman from the county was here because Benny had called her. I never should've opened my mouth and told him about my plans. I definitely never should've opened my door.

"Mr. Ibbetz." She kept smiling, but her friendliness was an act. "Do you have any health problems, sir? Do you take any medication?"

"No."

"That's remarkable for a gentleman of your age—which is ninety-one, am I correct?"

"Yeah." My mother used to say that a lady who would tell you her age would tell you anything. I'd admitted my age, but I wouldn't spill the rest of the beans.

"When did you last see a doctor?"

I shrugged. "Five, ten years. I can't remember."

"Do you cook your own meals?"

"Yes. Sometimes I am picking up a sandwich at the deli, but mostly I am cooking."

"And what was your profession?"

"Plumber and handyman. I am working as assistant super for apartment buildings in the neighborhood until I retire."

She cocked her head when she noticed the sheets of paper on the table, and I had to stop myself from slapping my forehead. *What a putz! Why did I leave the messages where anyone could see them?*

"How about friends? Do you socialize regularly?"

"I am shopping in Benny's bodega almost every day. In former times, back in the fifties, it was a deli."

"Yes, Mr. Martinez told me. He says you know a lot about the history of this neighborhood."

"I have lived here since seventy years. Benny, he is too young to remember half of what I can. So are you."

She made another note. "How about contemporaries? Other friends? People your own age?"

"I am the oldest guy I am knowing. All the others, they move away or pass on." I thumped my chest a little as I said with pride, "My ticker is still keeping perfect time."

"I see. That's very good. And do you have any travel plans?" There it was. She had waited to spring that question on me. She couldn't ask me right off the bat.

"Pssht! How does it look like I would travel? Where would I go?"

"You tell me, sir. Where would you go—if you were planning to go somewhere?"

"Home. I'd go home. But nothing is the way I remember when I was being young." *I can guarantee that.*

"Has anyone invited you to come for a visit? Anywhere, not just to your old home in . . ." The question hung in the air.

"Leipzig. After the war, it was no good for travel—was destroyed by the Allies. Then, it was being part of East Germany. But not anymore—not since 1991. I could have been going after that, but my relatives and the people I am knowing when I was a boy—they are dead. No one is asking me to come for a visit there."

"I see. So, no travel plans."

"No."

She stood up. "Do you mind if I take a peek in your refrigerator and your bathroom, sir?" I probably looked insulted, because she quickly added, "Just in case there's anything we can do for you, to make your life more pleasant."

You can get out, I wanted to say, but I didn't. Instead, I let her inspect the rest of my apartment. I had nothing to be ashamed of. The place was clean. Until recently, my life was orderly. Predictable. Now, I hoped she didn't sense the chaos inside my head.

In the kitchen, Miss Richter touched the scorch marks on the Formica, like she was letting me know she'd seen them. She smiled her fake smile again when she came out of the bathroom. "It all looks very pleasant and homey. Thank you for your time, Mr. Ibbetz."

I followed her to the door. Benny and Mrs. Simmons, my landlady, were waiting for her at the end of the hall. I acted like I was shutting the door, but I kept it open a crack. They were talking about me as they headed down the stairs, and they must've thought I was deaf because they didn't bother to lower their voices.

I tiptoed over to the stairwell.

Miss Richter said, "By law, there's nothing to be done unless you think he's a danger to himself. Are there any other causes for concern?"

Benny answered, "He's forgotten his wallet several times recently when he's come to get groceries."

"And does he remember to pay you later?"

"Yeah. Of course."

Then Miss Richter asked Mrs. Simmons, "Are you afraid Mr. Ibbetz will burn down the building while he's cooking?"

I suppressed a snort. *It was just the one time! With such a terrible cook as my landlady, Miss Richter should be more worried about her. Always with the smoke alarm going off. Oy vey.*

"No. He ain't never done anything like that."

"The scorch marks on the counter looked recent," Miss Richter kept on digging. "Does he wander off? Have you ever seen him step out into traffic?"

Benny spoke up. "Until recently, he was never confused, but a few days ago, he got lost in the neighborhood and was almost hit by a car."

It had been a mistake to tell him about that.

Then Miss Richter held up a piece of paper. "And what about this? It's nothing but gibberish. I find it concerning." She'd stolen one of the coded messages off my kitchen table when I wasn't looking.

Mrs. Simmons peered through her glasses. "Ain't that one of them Sudoku things?"

Benny shook his head. "No. Sudoku is numbers, not letters." He took the paper, looked at it for a moment, and shook his head. At least he had the grace to look uncomfortable before he spoke. "I've known Pete for about fifteen years, and I don't think he's losing his marbles or anything, but lately he's been talking a lot about his past. He's never done that before. Sometimes he speaks German and doesn't realize he's doing it until I point it out."

Miss Richter nodded like she had all the answers. "As people age, childhood memories can come to the forefront of their thoughts. Things that happened at the beginning of their lives seem clearer to them than what happened yesterday."

"It freaked me out when he mentioned he was planning a trip. That's why I called Elder Services." Benny ran a hand over his face. "He's got no relatives—no one but me, really. I don't think he's left the neighborhood in . . . ever. He's like a windup toy on a track. A creature of habit. He's a nice old dude, but I wouldn't call him adventurous or nothing. So why was he talking about going on a trip all of a sudden?"

Thanks a heap, Benny, my friend. The only person I trusted in New Jersey, and you turned out to be a collaborator.

But Miss Richter shook her head. "He denied having any travel plans when I spoke to him."

"What if he was lying to you?" As soon as the words left Benny's mouth, he folded his arms. "Okay, right? I don't think he's lying, either. I just think he's confused."

"Confused," Mrs. Simmons chimed in. "That's gotta be it. At his age, it's not unusual to get confused."

Miss Richter put her clipboard in her tote bag. "Of course, I'm most concerned about the incident when he was nearly hit by a car. I'll file a report recommending we seek an alternative living situation for him." She turned to Benny. "Do you know anything about his finances?"

"I don't think he's got much beyond his Social Security. You saw how he was dressed. He buys groceries every few days and never spends more than twenty or thirty dollars at a time. He told me he gets his place practically rent-free."

Mrs. Simmons nodded. "It's true. After Mr. Ibbetz retired, the new super let him stay on. His is the only apartment that hasn't been updated, so he gets a big discount on the rent." She walked Benny and Miss Richter out the front, and as soon as they were gone, I hurried back into my apartment and locked the door.

In the junk drawer, I rummaged around for my pocketknife, and then hustled to the bedroom. Stripping the bedding off my mattress, I lifted it up to expose the underside and slit the stitches that closed up the hole. I plunged my hand inside and brought out a fistful of cash.

Before the war, the Nazis had stolen my family's money and possessions. Even after I came to America, I never trusted banks—or the government. Because I had no wife, no family, and had never bought a house, I didn't spend much of what I earned, and I'd lived in this apartment rent-free when I was the assistant super. All the years I'd lived without Mira, I'd kept everything—including my money—to myself.

But Benny was right when he'd told Miss Richter how much I'd changed in the past few weeks. I had to leave right away, and it would take more than my landlady, the friend who ratted me out, and some well-intentioned buttinski from Elder Services to stop me.

When I said I never laid eyes on Mira again, that wasn't a hundred percent true.

2

I was born in 1928 in Leipzig, one of the larger cities in Saxony, in the eastern part of Germany. I lived with my parents on the southern outskirts of the city, in a two-story house with a garden in back.

Our ancestors had lived in Germany for generations. Both my grandfathers were decorated veterans who fought during the Great War. Though we were Jewish, we didn't go regularly to *shul*—not so different from Christians who attend church only on Christmas and Easter.

My father had gone to *cheder* as a boy, learned Jewish prayers, and became a *bar mitzvah*, but as an adult he'd abandoned the practices, which he considered old-fashioned. My mother, who had had no religious education as a girl, was even less inclined to embrace the old ways, and my father's parents would not visit us because we did not keep a kosher home. We were always welcome to visit them, though. We attended services at their synagogue during the high holidays, and when we had Shabbat dinner at their flat, I found the mystery and the ritual interesting, but more like a story or a play than anything that related directly to me.

Our neighbors were a mix of Christians and Jews, and when I was small, everyone was friendly to each other. A few mornings a week, after the men left for work, the women, with babies and young children in tow, would gather for coffee and gossip before starting on their housework. I remember playing with blocks and marbles with other little boys and girls. Our neighbors invited me to trim Christmas trees and hunt Easter eggs with my playmates, and in return, my family invited them to our house during Chanukah. That was before Nazi propaganda spawned the hate and fear that poisoned our neighbors against us.

The first concentration camp opened at Dachau in March 1933, less than two months after Adolf Hitler was appointed chancellor of Germany. At the beginning, only political prisoners were sent to Dachau, and most of them weren't Jewish.

That same year, Miriam, or Mira, as she was called, Schloss and her family moved in next door. Between Mira and Hitler, Mira had the greater immediate impact on my life. I was too young to understand politics or the changes that were sweeping the country.

Mira was my favorite among the girls in my class at Montessori school. Our mothers had been chums at university, and our fathers got on well, so naturally our families spent time together. Mira had curly brown hair, round, rosy cheeks, and blue eyes so dark they were almost purple. Her laugh bubbled up from deep inside her, and the sound of it made me want to do things to make her laugh more.

On the day the Schlosses were due to arrive, nothing could have coaxed me away from our front window. I clutched the curtains in my fists, opening and closing them like a camera's shutter. "Mutti, are you certain they're coming today?"

"Yes, Peter."

"But when?"

She joined me at the window, peeled the curtains from my sweaty fingers, and opened them wide. "Soon enough. Now leave these be, or I'll have to iron them again."

I obeyed, but without something to occupy my hands, my feet would not be still. When a horse-drawn cart came around the corner, I thought I might explode from the excitement. I pointed. "There! May I go out to greet them?" Then my shoulders slumped in disappointment, "It's only the dairyman."

The dairyman made his deliveries down the block, and a few moments later, a chimney sweep walked by with his long black brush over his shoulder, but these mundane occurrences couldn't hold my attention. Time inched along. Finally, I heard the rumble of a truck, and a shiny delivery van pulled into view. "Mutti!" I shrieked, "They're here!"

"All right, Peter. Calm yourself or you'll frighten Mira." Her words had the desired effect, and I held my exuberance in check as she opened the door. Once outside, though, I raced to meet the black taxicab that pulled up to the curb behind the van.

Mutti called, "Sylvia, you always know how to make an entrance. You couldn't walk from the trolley stop?"

Mrs. Schloss's husband helped her from the taxi, and she and Mutti kissed each other on both cheeks while he reached back and lifted Mira out. "Of course, we'd take a taxi, Elke. It's a special day. It's—"

"Mira Day!" I shouted, and the adults laughed.

Mr. Schloss set Mira down in front of me, and I grabbed both her hands and jumped up and down with glee. "Now every day is a Mira day!"

She jumped with me. "And every day is a Peter day!"

As the movers began unloading boxes and furniture swathed in blankets, Mr. Schloss fished a key from his pocket and hurried to unlock the front door. "Sylvia! Come here, my love." Mrs. Schloss giggled as he swept her into his arms and carried her across the threshold ahead of the first load of boxes.

Eager to take part in this moving-in ritual, I lifted Mira and trotted in after her parents.

My mother called after me, "Careful, Peter! Don't drop her." But I knew I wouldn't. In the empty sitting room, I set her down and we ran in circles, footsteps echoing, until Mutti and Mrs. Schloss shooed us out.

Mira started upstairs. "Come see my room." I followed her to the one painted a sunny yellow, with a bank of three windows that over-looked the back garden. "Mutti let me pick out a new coverlet and drapes. They're pink and yellow striped."

I nodded, though I had no real interest in home décor. "That will be nice. Come on! I'll show you the garden."

"Wait. I have to do something first."

I followed her into the smaller bedroom next door and watched as she pulled a sugar lump from her pocket, set it on the sill, and opened the window a few inches.

She gave a satisfied nod. "If I leave this for the stork, it will bring me a baby brother or sister. Gertie did it and it worked."

I shrugged— I had no interest in babies, either, and I wasn't keen to share Mira's attention. "Let's go."

We ran down the back stairs, dodging the movers and Mrs. Schloss in the kitchen. The Dutch door in the sunroom led to the back garden, where an ancient apple tree spread its branches across both our yards. "Mutti wouldn't let me climb the tree because she said it wasn't ours. But it's yours, so now we can. Do you want to?"

She nodded, her curls bobbing as she looked at the sky peeking through the network of boughs above us. One large branch dipped low enough to touch the crumbling stone wall that separated her gar-den from ours, and the whole tree seemed to lean on it, like a person propped up on one elbow. I climbed the wall and pulled her up after me, and together we sat on the branch, swinging our feet.

"Look!" She pointed. "There's a secret hiding place. Perhaps the fairies leave things for each other there."

I leaned across her to inspect the bowl-shaped indentation at the crux of two massive branches. "Like a post office?"

"Yes." Her laugh was pure delight. "A fairy post office!"

The next day, I left a shiny stone there for her, and the day after she reciprocated with a marble for me. Mira liked to pretend the trinkets arrived by magic, so we never admitted to giving the gifts. Though we believed our perch on that branch was our magical, secret place, we were not invisible to the rest of the world. My father snuck several good photos of us without our knowledge.

In most of my childhood memories, Vati was behind his camera. He took dozens of pictures at our birthday parties, of us wearing cone-shaped paper hats and blowing out the candles on our cakes. Flashbulbs popped at our evening Chanukah parties as, heads close together, we watched a spinning dreidel, the nuts and chocolates we'd won piled on the table. Backyard picnics, school concerts, hiking trips in the sandstone hills, you name it, he took pictures of it.

My mother left our photo albums with a neighbor for safekeeping when we had to leave. There's a chance they survived the war, but I wouldn't know where to begin to look for them now.

I didn't let myself revisit those early memories often, because once I started remembering happy childhood times, my thoughts inevitably turned to the things I wished I could forget.

If we had been born in another time, Mira and I might have lived next door to each other until we were grown, and our youthful infatuation might have ripened into something deeper. But we'd been neighbors for only a few years when things began to change in a way that would eventually seal our fate.

The Nuremburg Laws, passed in 1935, banned Jews from swimming pools, parks, skating rinks, public athletic fields, and cultural events. No more concerts, ballets, or movies. The government said the ban was to avoid the automatic disadvantage that the presence of Jewish children caused for German-blooded children, who suffered because the Jews were doing well.

Once the government was under Hitler's control and his propaganda machine began to shape thought and public opinion, few Germans of Aryan descent would stand up for their Jewish neighbors. No one protested when the government stripped Jews of their German citizenship. Without passports, we were trapped in limbo—unwanted at home, yet unable to leave.

Our families believed in biding their time until things got better. Shortly before Jews were banned from restaurants, the Schlosses invited us out for an evening of entertainment for Mira's seventh birthday. Mr. Schloss made a dinner reservation at one of the large hotels in the city center, where an orchestra played for the patrons.

My seldom-worn jacket and bow tie felt stiff and uncomfortable. The adults ordered oysters and champagne, and Mira and I drank ginger ale with a cherry in it, like a cocktail, and ate bread and butter before the main course. The meal took a long time, and my portion of rack of lamb was far too large for me to manage alone. Though I did not complain, I would have been happier eating *Wiener schnitzel* and fried potatoes in a wooden booth at the *gasthaus* in our neighborhood. I couldn't remember the last time I'd had to sit still for so long.

When the waiter cleared our plates and the adults had coffee and aperitifs before them, Mr. Schloss chucked Mira under the chin. "Someday, we'll listen to you play your violin here, *Liebling*." Mira had been studying the violin for almost a year.

"Don't go putting ideas into her head," Mrs. Schloss snapped, lighting a cigarette and casting him a disdainful glance, "She's likely not that talented."

Mr. Schloss's face hardened. "She's only been playing a short while. This is not the time to put limits on her." He downed the rest of his drink.

Mira, all smiles a moment before, now looked miserable.

When I was young, I understood little about relationships between men and women, and I could not fathom why Mr. and Mrs. Schloss bickered so much when they should have been happy together. Mr. Schloss owned a garment factory and claimed that Mrs. Schloss, who was very pretty, was the only advertisement he needed for his ladies' line. He often bought her jewelry, and they went out to restaurants and nightclubs nearly every week.

Though my mother was just as beautiful as Mrs. Schloss, she didn't wear as much makeup and favored simpler clothing. That was fine with me, because dresses like Mrs. Schloss's would have gotten mussed up when we went on adventures. My parents favored the outdoors and athletic pursuits over restaurants and nightclubs, and we had a grand time camping or skiing on holiday. Mutti and Vati rarely raised their voices to one another, and I could not imagine them saying disparaging things about me when I was listening.

My mother, in an attempt to smooth things over, said to Mrs. Schloss, "Mira plays beautifully for such a young girl."

But Mrs. Schloss only shrugged.

My father picked up his camera. "Gather around, now. Let's take some photos to mark this important occasion."

"Wait just a moment." Mr. Schloss pulled a small white box from his breast pocket and presented it to Mira with a flourish. "Happy birthday."

She opened it and cried out in delight.

I leaned over to see a heart-shaped gold locket nestled in the box. The design engraved on the front reminded me of a *springerle* cookie—a raised heart with crinkly edges surrounded by vines and flowers.

"Oh, Vati! Thank you!" Mira threw her arms around her father's neck and he kissed both her cheeks.

"That's a grown-up gift." My mother admired the locket as Mr. Schloss fastened the clasp around Mira's neck.

"Likely he spent too much," said Mira's mother, before taking a drag on her cigarette.

"What's too much for my Mira? Nothing. She's more precious than gold or jewels." Mr. Schloss put his arm around his daughter. "Now on with the photographs!"

As my father readied his camera, a waiter arrived with a large ice cream sundae, piled with whipped cream and alight with birthday candles. When he set it in front of Mira, I could see the flames reflected in her eyes.

"Say *Käsekuchen!*" my father called out.

The resulting photograph showed Mira, all smiles, holding her new locket against her chest as she leaned forward to blow out the candles.

Mira and I were not allowed to return to Montessori school after the spring term. We joined other Jewish children who had been in class with us at the new *Lehrhaus* school in the fall of 1936.

Jewish students of all ages who were prohibited from attending public schools or universities could go to *Lehrhaus*. My father, who had been let go from *Universitat Leipzig*, taught upper school and university-level mathematics and science classes there, and often walked with us in the mornings.

For a boy who had never felt close to my Jewish heritage, all of a sudden, I was unable to free myself from it. Every new restriction and decree made my world a little smaller, my opportunities fewer. Something that had not mattered at all before was now to blame for the bad things that were happening to me.

Perhaps I would have borne the changes better if I'd grown up in a traditional Jewish household, but I hadn't, and now I didn't know how to ask my parents to teach me about religion and my heritage. I began to question not who, but *what* I was, and the answer I received from my country's leaders and its so-called legitimate citizens was that I was *Untermensch*—less than human.

Had Mira and I lived in America when we were children, the coming madness would not have engulfed us and swept us away on its unrelenting current, and we would have led privileged lives.

Our fathers were both college-educated professionals. Our mothers had degrees as well and were accomplished in their own right. Mutti studied ballet as a child and had wanted a career as a dancer, but when she grew too tall, she attended university instead, majoring in art history. Mira's mother had studied French literature. After graduation, my mother had worked as an assistant buyer in an art gallery, while

Mira's mother had been a proofreader in one of the many publishing firms in the city.

In those days, most married women didn't work outside the home, and so our mothers poured their energy into us, taking us to the library, museums, galleries, and concerts—until it was no longer allowed by law.

Though we both did well in school, my marks were better than Mira's, only because I recalled everything I heard or read with ease and always got my lessons without having to study hard. It went without saying that my parents expected me to attend *Universitat Leipzig*, while Mira's future presumably lay at the famed *Conservatorium der Musick*.

The year we turned eight, we stayed closer to home, and our perch on that curved branch of the apple tree was the perfect place to dream.

My father had been reading a chapter of *Treasure Island* with me before bed every night, and I recounted the story to Mira during our playtime. Though she preferred *Grimm's Fairy Tales*, she was enamored with the thought of desert islands, buried treasure, and maps with X marking the spot. Once we were well into the story, she brought out her father's world atlas. Together we'd turn the pages, looking for the best place to bury treasure.

We chose an island in the Caribbean and Mira drew an X on it in red crayon. I was usually less careful with my possessions than Mira, and I was shocked that she would do such a thing to a book that didn't belong to her.

"Won't your father be angry?"

She smiled, playing with the locket on its chain. "He'll never notice it's there. Now it's our secret."

"Shall we go there someday? Bury your locket with our treasure?"

"Certainly not! I would never be parted from my locket. We'll have to bury something else. Besides, we'd have to go to the Caribbean by ship. Perhaps we should plan our first trip somewhere closer."

Heads together, we turned the pages, looking at Berlin, Paris, and London. Those were places we had heard of. Our mothers often spoke of the adventures they'd had visiting Paris together while they were university students, and Mira was drawn to the glamour of the City of Light. Mrs. Schloss always wore Evening in Paris perfume, and sometimes she'd dab a little behind Mira's ears, too.

I traced my finger along the route from Leipzig to Paris. "When we get there, what shall we do first?"

"We'll go to the Eiffel Tower and ride the elevator all the way to the top. Then we can see the whole city at once."

"I'd rather see the races at Le Mans." My finger diverted off in another direction on the map.

She frowned as she looked at the page. "That must be hours away from Paris by automobile."

"So?"

"So, I'm the one who's planning this trip."

"Well, plan an extra day or two or I don't want to go."

She sighed and rolled her eyes, then gave me an accepting smile. "All right, fine. Before we go to Le Mans, though, we must spend enough time in Paris to go to the Louvre. Of course, we'll stay at the Ritz and stroll along the Champs-Élysées. Mutti says that's the only way to see Paris. Vati will buy me an *haute couture* gown to wear."

Clothes were just as unimportant to me then as they are now, but because of Mr. Schloss's profession, of course Mira knew about such things. I snorted. "Whatever for?"

She giggled. "I can wear it when I play a violin concert at the Palais Garnier. You'll be my escort, so you'll need to bring a morning coat and a top hat."

"No thanks! I'll be your sound engineer and broadcast your concert all over the world on my shortwave." I gave my best imitation of a radio announcer. "Ladies and gentlemen, we proudly present, live from Paris, Miss Miriam Schloss, the best violinist in Germany—and all the world."

When we grew tired of making plans, Mira leaned over a branch to drop the atlas flat into the grass below. As she sat up, her locket's chain caught on some rough bark and broke. Mira made a grab for the golden heart as it slid off the chain. She lost her balance and nearly followed it to the ground, but I clutched her arm to steady her just in time. We watched it shimmer in the sunlight and disappear into the grass.

Her breath came in sobs as we scrambled down out of the branches. I'm not sure what worried her more—the damage to the necklace or her fear of being punished. We combed the grass beneath the tree until she found it, and her lip trembled as she cradled the locket and broken chain in her hands.

"I can fix it," I said.

She looked up at me with veneration in her teary eyes. "You can?"

"Of course I can. Come on!" I led the way to my father's workshop in the shed behind our house, and she hung anxiously over my shoulder as I turned on the lamp and laid out the chain. Though my father, who was always tinkering, had taught me how to use his tools, the chain was too fine for even the smallest needle-nosed pliers in the toolbox. Frustrated, I nudged her away, and my words came out gruffer than I'd intended. "Back up, you're blocking the light." When at last I shook my head in defeat, she reached for the chain, but I cupped my hand over it. "I'll say it was my fault."

"You don't have to do that."

"It was an accident. They can't punish me. I'm not their son. Besides, it can be repaired. I just don't know how—yet."

She moved my fingers aside and picked up the chain. "It's all right."

When we went inside, Mira's mother stubbed out a cigarette and regarded her daughter's tear-stained cheeks and the guilty looks on our faces. "What's the matter?"

Mira glanced at me before she answered. "It broke." She opened her palm.

"Careless girl!" When her mother slapped her, the necklace fell to the floor. Mira's father hurried into the room and stepped between them, looking down at his sobbing daughter.

"Here—what is the matter?"

"She's destroyed the gift you gave her. I told you it was too expensive for a child."

Mr. Schloss picked it up off the carpet. "It is nothing that cannot be fixed." He led Mira into his study. I followed and watched as he dried her tears and brought out a scrap bag. He rummaged for a moment and pulled out a narrow length of red silk cord. He wet one end in his mouth and twisted it tightly until it fit through the locket's bail and tied a knot at the ends. He hung it around her neck just as gently as he had when it was on its gold chain.

"Just the thing! Here you go, *Liebling*. All is well. We will have a jeweler fix the chain later, when we have the money, yes?" He kissed her and wiped away her tears. "There are cookies in the kitchen for you and Peter. I brought some of the lemon *springerle* you like from Frau Bressler's."

"Yes, Vati. Thank you." She rubbed the silk cord between her fingers.

The cookies were a welcome distraction and tasted delicious, but as we ate, we heard Mr. and Mrs. Schloss arguing.

"It was vain and stupid of her to wear it for roughhousing."

"She's a child. She will sometimes make mistakes, but she will learn."

Mrs. Schloss scoffed. "She shouldn't be allowed to wear it whenever she chooses—one day she will lose it altogether. It should be hidden away, so it can be sold."

After that, I never saw Mira take it off—until the day she left it with me for safekeeping. I'd held onto it all these years, and now it was stowed away in a box in my Weequahic closet. I had hoped to give it back to her someday, but at this point, my somedays were numbered. Whoever cleaned out my stuff when I died would have no idea what that necklace meant to her—or to me.

Not long after Mira and I planned our jaunt across Europe to Paris and Le Mans, I declared to my parents that I would marry her when we were grown up. I wanted to be with her all the time and make her smile, and in my childish way of thinking, this was enough of a reason to marry. I knew I could love her as tenderly as her father did, and I would grow up big and strong enough to protect her from her mother's harsh and unpredictable discipline.

It was traditional in Germany, especially in those days, for both the man and the woman to wear plain gold bands as engagement rings. I had seen a set in the window at the jeweler's and planned someday to buy it. Then I would put the velvet box in the fairy post office in the apple tree and get down on one knee when she found it. I didn't realize I'd never get the chance.

Six million Jews died in the Holocaust—and three and a half million survived. Those survivors who were strong enough to face the horrors head-on wrote books, gave speeches, and said things like "Never again" and "We must not forget." If the books and the speeches pushed their demons away and gave them enough space to breathe, then good for them.

I couldn't forget, either. But I wasn't that strong. I considered myself lucky to have come through the war alive and coped the best I could. Now that I was in my nineties, I wondered what would happen when I died a lot more than I had when I was young. In the camps, death hovered at our elbows every minute of every day. If I'd let myself think about it then, I would've gone crazy.

Some people claim love conquers all, but in my experience, love only leads to a broken heart. Fear is more powerful than love, because it steers people away from risk, and the person left standing in the end is not the one who loved the most, but the one who dodged the most risk. Benny once asked me whether fear kept me alive or kept me from living. I answered yes. And yes.

3

Most mornings when I woke up, I'd hear my neighbor's footsteps on the stairs and his apartment door open and shut. His name was Vashon Harris. He worked nights and came home every morning at 7:30, like clockwork. I tried not to disturb him during the day, because good for him if he could sleep when some people had insomnia.

Before Vashon, a guy named Napoleon Jones lived across the hall, and before that it was a lady named Shandra Washington. I remembered them all, back to Daniel and Flossie Zimmerman, who lived there when I moved in in 1955, even if I didn't get to know them personally.

I never slept more than five hours a night, ever, and I read in the newspaper that people need less sleep as they age. It's the truth. Lately I was lucky to get two or three hours. Even if I didn't need sleep, it was still hard for me to get out of bed in the morning.

Vashon's shower was running while I boiled water for my cup of Sanka and toasted a bagel on the hot plate. In the fridge, there was a bit of cream cheese left in the silver wrapper. Just enough for a *schmear*.

On nice days like this one, I opened the windows to air out the place, and that let in the traffic noise from Lyons Avenue. *Oy vey*, that stuff people played on their car radios didn't seem like music to me.

Music should soothe the soul, and let me tell you, there was nothing soothing about that garbage.

Sometimes a truck rumbled by and started my heart racing, and for a moment, before I got ahold of myself, I'd think the Gestapo was outside, coming to take me away. I always shut the window before I sat down to eat.

Ever since I retired back in 2004, one day has seemed pretty much like the next. After breakfast, I usually read the funnies and did the crossword puzzle. Sometimes, to change my routine a little, I'd do a jigsaw puzzle from the dime store. I liked to tinker with electronics and mechanical things, and usually had a couple of projects spread out on the table near the window. It was enough. I was content until I had to deal with other people—like Mrs. Simmons, my landlady. One morning, she came up and pounded on the door while I was trying to solder a broken tooth on the cylinder of an antique music box. She didn't wait for me to answer before she hollered through the door: "Mr. Ibbetz—the tenant in Four-A just moved out at the first of the month. I'll leave the door open today." She let me go through what people left behind before she had it carted off. As a matter of fact, I'd found the music box when a tenant in 1C moved out a few months ago.

I set down the soldering iron and opened the door. "Thank you. I am having to finish this before tomorrow and will be by to look later."

Uninvited, she stepped into the room and looked at the projects on my worktable. "Why you like all this junk so much? Can't watch nothing on that, can you? What is it, anyway?"

"Is radio. With vacuum tubes."

"They look like light bulbs."

"Is like this." I plugged in the set and fiddled with the tuner. The hum and the static nearly drowned out the local AM station signal that came through.

She scoffed. "Why you bother with that when you got a perfectly good radio right over there?"

"It reminds me." Before she could ask more, I pointed to a 1930s cabinet radio I'd rescued from a trash pile. "This one is being short wave. On it I am listening to broadcasts from China and India. Is fascinating thing to hear someone so far away."

"You speak Chinese?"

"Is no language Chinese. They are having many different languages for such a large country, right? But no, I am not speaking any of them."

She pointed at my telephone. "I know you like old stuff, but why you still using that relic? How you gonna reach it when you fall and can't get up?"

I studied the phone on the wall. "Is fine. It is not looking like a relic to me." It looks new. It's barely been used since I moved in here."

"You need to get a cell phone, or one of them life alert bracelets. Or both."

"What am I knowing about life alert bracelets or cell phones? This phone I got, I am knowing how to dial it. I am not needing a life alert bracelet." I didn't have a death wish. I was just being realistic. When I die, it's not going to matter to anyone, so why try to stop it from happening?

"You should quit wasting your time listening to languages you don't understand. If you had Wi-Fi, you could get Netflix."

It was my turn to scoff. "Netflix, shmetflix. Thank you for telling me I may search for treasures in Four-A. I am coming by later today." She left before I had to admit I had no idea what Netflix was. A few years ago, when the rabbit ears on my TV quit picking up the signal from the networks, the new super helped me rig up a digital antenna so I could watch *The Price is Right*. I liked the new fella they got as the host—the funny one.

Most afternoons, I walked down Lyons Avenue to Benny's bodega on the corner by the fire station. The kosher deli that used to be there had closed years ago, but Benny was good about stocking the foods I liked so I didn't have to take the bus to go shopping somewhere else.

The music box I was repairing was a wedding gift for Benny and his wife, Valeria. When I finished the last solder, I tested it to make sure all the notes played. Then I wiped the walnut cabinet with lemon oil and wrapped it in a clean cloth before putting it in my jacket pocket.

When I first came to Weequahic in 1948, I thought it was an all right place, but I didn't understand anything about New Jersey, or America. The only thing I knew was that I didn't want to stay in Germany.

Back then, you could buy anything you wanted in the shops on Bergen Street between Lyons and Custer—from fur coats to camping supplies to pianos. The good smells from the Bergen Bake Shop hung in the air a block away. Now, the bakery and the piano store were closed, and the furrier had moved out to the suburbs. The only people in this neighborhood who camped were the ones living on the streets. There were different names on the businesses that stuck around. Different faces everywhere, too. But I remembered exactly how everything used to be.

The neighborhood was a lot rougher at this time than it was when I moved here, but sometimes, when the weather was nice, I'd sit for a while on a bench down at Saint Peters Park and watch a Peewee soccer game or a few innings of Little League. The view across the street from the park made me sad. Too many houses sat empty and surrounded by overgrown shrubs, with weathered plywood nailed over the windows and doors.

Back in the old days, there were lots of Jewish families in Weequahic, and I didn't feel like I was taking my life in my hands every time I left my apartment. But there was still trouble. Once I had a run-in that frightened me so badly, I never forgot it.

It was 1950. I hadn't been in America that long, and I probably still looked and acted like a greenhorn. A group of young guys that hung around on the street corner made fun of me and would sometimes laugh as I passed. I didn't speak much English, but I understood enough to realize they were talking about me. I ignored them—until the day one of them called me a faggot.

I forgot I was headed out to a job. I turned and ran home and vomited in the alley before I staggered upstairs to my room in the Gittelmans' apartment. Shaking, I lay on my bed and clutched my stomach. Mrs. Gittelman, who was surprised to see me come home in the middle of the day, fussed over me at first. She brought me chicken soup and tea and demanded that I tell her what was wrong, but how could I? I was too embarrassed to repeat what they'd said. Finally, she shrugged and let me be.

I wasn't a homosexual—but I never went out with a girl after I came to America, either. I wondered if Mr. and Mrs. Gittelman assumed that about me, too.

When the Nazis were in power, simply being called queer was enough to get you arrested—and I'd seen firsthand what happened to men in the camps who had to wear the pink triangle on their uniforms. In my mind, I had no defense. I was so afraid I didn't leave the apartment for days.

I went out to the bodega that afternoon, eager to give the music box to Benny. On the way, I passed a couple of punks leaning up against the metal grate that covered a vacant building's window. They gave me the once-over as I approached, and I could feel the hair on the back of my neck stand up. I couldn't cross the street without looking like I was avoiding them, so I turned my eyes away as I shuffled past, clutching the music box inside my pocket and hoping they would assume I had nothing worth stealing.

The bell on the bodega's door jingled as I stepped inside. Benny was in his usual spot behind the counter.

"Hey, Pete!"

"Hiya, Benny."

"How's the weather out there?"

"Good." I placed the wrapped music box on the counter. "Gift for you and Valeria. For your wedding."

He unfolded the cloth. "That's real nice of you, Pete, but you didn't have to get us anything. You do know we've been married for almost a year."

"Yes, I am knowing. I am waiting until I find just the right thing. And then I fix."

He opened the lid. "Wow. How old is this?"

"My mother is having one like it when I am a boy, so is old, right?" I took it from him and wound the key on the bottom. "You play this for Valeria. Is romantic song, from my country, about a soldier who must leave the girl he loves but promises to be true to her until he is return." I set the box on the counter with the lid open, and as the song began to play, we watched the tips on the comb pluck the notes from the teeth on the rotating cylinder.

Benny nodded as he listened. "She'll like this. Thanks for thinking of us, Pete."

"Valeria, she is smart and pretty girl, and your little boy is gift from God, right?"

"Yeah." He ducked his head a little, smiling.

"When you love someone, you are doing everything to stand by them and love them. This is life. You are being lucky to have beautiful family."

Benny and I didn't usually talk about personal things. To cover my embarrassment, I picked up one of the wire shopping baskets and headed down the first aisle for a loaf of rye bread and the crackers I like. I always went up and down the aisles in the bodega in the same order, so I wouldn't forget anything. Next aisle, I added a jar of pickles, a couple of cans of soup, and a jar of Sanka to the basket. In the refrigerator case, some cream cheese, a half dozen eggs, and some turkey and pastrami. Swiss cheese, too. My favorite sandwich is turkey and swiss on rye.

He'd had a fresh delivery of bagels from the kosher bakery, so I got the tongs and put three in a plastic bag. Then I realized I needed milk, and as I turned back to the dairy section, the bell on the door jingled. I glanced over my shoulder in time to see those two punks come in. Why didn't I remember to warn Benny? As they stopped at the counter, I backed out of sight.

They all started shouting, and there was a big crash, like they'd knocked over one of the display racks.

I heard one of them yell, "Open the register! Gimme the money. All of it!"

Benny hollered back, "Get the hell out of here and run home to your mama before I—"

"We ain't playin'!" The other punk cut him off. "Do it!"

Another crash shook the floor, and I shrank against the wall, clutching my basket. There was nothing I could do to help my friend. Then a shot rang out, so loud that everything around me should have exploded. I cowered in the corner, squeezing my eyes shut, but that didn't erase the images etched on my brain—German SS pointing pistols at men and women poised on the edge of a pit. One by one, their knees buckled, and they crumpled and fell, their bodies piling on top of other bodies.

When a hand touched my shoulder, I jumped. Hot wetness flowed down my leg, soaking through the front of my pants. It took a second before I remembered where I was.

I'd never seen Benny look so worried. "Pete? Pete—you okay, man?"

My voice shook. "Are you killing them?"

"Nah. Just scared 'em off. The cops are here now. Everything's under control."

Ashamed of having soiled myself, I tried to pull the front of my jacket down over the wet spot.

"Don't worry about it. I about pissed myself, too. You ready to come out front now?"

"Yes."

"The cops want to talk to you." He must have seen fear in my eyes. "It's all right. Just to take your statement." He carried my shopping basket and held me by my arm. Even though I tried not to let on, my knees were shaking so badly his grip was the only thing that kept me from falling down.

In the front of the store, two cops were dusting everything for fingerprints—even the little potato chip bags that always hang beside the cash register. Benny's gun was on the counter. The music box lay on the floor, and one of the cops bumped it with his foot.

"Oh man." Benny let go of me and knelt to pick it up. The lid hung crazily on a broken hinge. "Pete, I'm so sorry. It got broken."

"Is no problem. I fix again."

"Really?"

"Pssht. What else am I doing?"

When one of the officers asked if I was able to identify the suspects, I hesitated. I'd been around long enough to know those kids would be back on the corner soon—maybe even today. How could I defend myself if they jumped me? "I was in the back," I said, "Didn't see nothing."

I could tell Benny was disappointed, but all he said was, "I'm going to walk Mr. Ibbetz home." He reached behind the counter for a couple of bags and loaded up my groceries, setting the music box gently on top. One of the cops unlocked the door to let us out.

As we walked toward my place, I tried to apologize. "You're a *shtarker*, Benny, that's what you are. Such trouble. Such trouble."

"Aw, come on, Pete. It's over now. Don't give it another thought."

"*Oy vey*. Also, I am forgetting to pay you."

"Seriously? Don't worry about that. Pay me next time you come in."

When we got to my building, my hands were still trembling so badly I dropped my keys. Benny picked them up and unlocked the front door.

"Which apartment is yours?"

"Second floor. Apartment Two-B."

He matched my pace on the stairs, and I let him unlock my apartment door, too.

"Wow. Cool place you got." His eyes roved over the room. "Love the retro vibe."

I tried to see it as he did. There weren't any family photos or personal stuff. The furniture he called retro is what the Gittelmans had left behind, thinking it was junk.

"My *abuelita* had a porcelain-top kitchen table like that when I was a kid, but hers was red and white. You could probably get about four hundred bucks for that if you wanted to sell it." Benny set the paper sacks on the counter and put the stuff that would spoil into the fridge. "I got lotsa good memories of her and her cooking. She taught me how to make tamales. You gonna be all right now?"

"Yes. I am fine." What else was there to say?

"See you tomorrow, huh?"

"You are being open tomorrow?"

"Yeah, I'll be there. You can count on it."

As soon as the door closed behind him, I turned the lock and latched the chain. I wished I'd asked him to stick around a little longer.

After I got cleaned up and put on a fresh pair of pants, I carried the music box to my worktable and examined it. Several of the picks in the comb were bent so badly they could not play their notes. When I wound the key, the gears made a grinding sound and the cylinder did not turn. I sighed and got out a screwdriver to remove the lid and started buffing out the scratches.

That evening, I listened to the Phillies game while I worked. Baseball was the first American thing that interested me, and back in the day, the Yankees won the World Series five years in a row, from '49 to '53. When the Dodgers were still in Brooklyn, I listened to their games, too. I most enjoyed the sport early in the season, when every team had a chance in the standings. Though I listened to that entire Phillies game, my mind was elsewhere. I couldn't tell you who won.

I delayed going to bed until I could scarcely keep my eyes open, but when I turned out the light sleep did not come. I lay awake for what felt like hours, but I must have slept some, because my eyes flew open at the rattle of a passing truck. Just like that, I was wide awake, heart pounding, every little sound amplified. Certain I had heard footsteps in the hall, I crept out of the bedroom and stood near the door, listening, until I felt safe enough to get back into bed. How would I cope the next time I had to leave the apartment? The last time I checked the clock, it read 3 a.m.

4

As I blinked back the sunlight streaming in the open window, a lilac-scented breeze set the curtains swaying. There was no hum of traffic, no noise from the street. No sirens. Just silence. The crack in the ceiling looked familiar, but I could've sworn it hadn't been there when I went to sleep. As I stared up at the ceiling, wondering how I could see that far without my glasses, my eyes fell on a hand-painted mobile of the solar system hanging by the window, and I realized with a start that I was in my childhood bedroom, in our house in Leipzig.

My head rested on a plump, goose-down pillow. I rubbed the sheet, crisp with starch, between my fingers. When I brought it up to my face, I breathed in the smell of the laundry soap my mother used. Mutti had always starched our sheets, because she said she didn't sleep well on anything less. When I was a bit older, I learned to sleep anywhere, on anything, and starch was the least of my worries. Now the sheet's coolness felt good against my skin. I put my arms outside the covers, on my red-and-blue plaid duvet. Remarkably, my brain had stored every detail of a room I hadn't seen in more than eighty years.

I sat up and swung my legs, which felt taut and muscular, out from beneath the covers, and the simple action was easy and painless. The hands before me that clenched and unclenched on my command looked like they belonged to someone else. I turned both palms up and stared at my inner arm, where the tattoo should have been. I probed the spot with my fingers, trying to find the numbers under my skin.

When I caught sight of my reflection in the mirror over the bureau, I stared back at a young man in his early twenties. Moving closer, I ran my hand through my hair and over the stubble on my chin. I'd never looked this good, even when I really was young. This guy, with his broad shoulders and trim waistline, was wearing my boxers and undershirt, and it was curiosity, rather than vanity, that led me to inspect him from all sides. It was like I'd borrowed a body from someone close to me, a nephew, or a son. Whoever he was, he was a handsome devil.

That's when I noticed that the picture books, toys, and mementos of my childhood were missing. Instead of my satchel and pencil box, there was a thick stack of university-level textbooks on my desk—calculus, physics, chemistry—and some German-language novels piled on the nightstand. Though it had been more than seventy years since I'd read anything in German, when I flipped through the books, I was able to understand everything on the pages.

A young man's personal possessions rested in the wooden tray on the bureau. In place of my jar of marbles and kite string, I found a signet ring, a fountain pen, a pocket watch—and Mira's heart-shaped locket, on its frayed red silk cord. I hung it around my neck and smiled at the sentimentality of placing her heart so close to mine.

At the window, I leaned out, hands on the sill, and took a deep breath, savoring the purity of the air and the warmth of the sun on my skin. The clipped lawn was too vibrantly green to be believed, and the low branch of Mira's apple tree still leaned on the garden wall. No one should be inside on such a beautiful day, and I was itching to go enjoy the weather.

But even if it was a dream, I wasn't going outside in my underwear. I flung open the wardrobe and, to my delight, found it full of clothes. Not little knee breeches and jumpers, but the kind of things a young man would have worn in my day. I dressed in a wide-legged pair of cuffed trousers, a sport shirt, and a leather belt. Spectator shoes, too. My clothes felt crisp and new and were the nicest ones I'd ever worn. The young man in the mirror held his head high. He knew none of the weight of my suffering—and carried no regret over the things I had failed to do.

Down in the garden, things I hadn't remembered until now were nonetheless there, like a marble statue my mother had placed among the flowering plants and my metal toy airplane, which was stuck high on a branch of the apple tree.

Though nothing was out of place, exactly, my father's workshop shed at the back of the garden was freshly painted. The window I'd accidentally cracked with an errantly thrown pebble was good as new. Were these anomalies significant? Some imperfections, like the broken window, erased, while the toy airplane remained abandoned on the tree bough?

With little effort, I climbed the apple tree to inspect the indentation where Mira and I had left trinkets for each other, but the fairy post office was empty. Perfect red apples hung within easy reach, so I picked one and polished it on my shirt. My teeth cut through the skin in the first luscious bite, and as I took another, juice ran down my chin. I wiped it away with the back of my hand, aware of the dampness and the prickle of my day's growth of stubble. My mind denied the truth of these sensations, whispering that it wasn't—it couldn't—be real.

Was this sanitized version of my lost childhood home some kind of one-day pass to heaven?

My appetites and curiosity swelled, and I experienced all kinds of wants with frightening ferocity. I wanted to be this young man. I wanted to inhabit this world and live his life. I wanted my family, and Mira. Where were the people who should have been here to greet me?

"Mutti? Vati?" My voice echoed across the manicured lawns. As I dashed back into the kitchen, I let the screen door slam behind me as I used to when I was a boy. The larder and the icebox were full of food, and a coffee mug rested in the drainboard. In the cabinets, the dishes and pots and pans were stacked neatly in place.

Perhaps my mother was down the street chatting with a neighbor, and my father—yes, my father had probably left to catch an early trolley to do some writing before his first lecture at the university. Because this was the life I should have had, wasn't it?

Upstairs in my parents' bedroom, my father's suits hung on his side of their wardrobe, his shirts starched and folded in a drawer. On the shelf above, his hats rested beside the leather satchel he carried to work, which had always bulged with his students' papers and a copy of the newspaper.

His personal possessions fascinated me—even the half-empty pack of cigarettes and book of matches on his bureau. I had to touch everything in his shaving kit: the brush, the china mug, and the straight razor with the leather strap. When I opened the jar of pomade and ran a dab through my hair, the scent was so exactly as I recalled that it brought tears to my eyes.

The tiepins, cuff links, and garters for his socks were of a bygone era, things I had never owned. Never needed. Never wanted until now.

I would not have gone through my mother's bureau drawers even in my wildest dream—which this likely was. Instead, I picked up and examined her favorite brooch and the silk scarf that lay on her dressing table. When I opened a metal tube of lipstick and spiraled it upward, I recalled she used to wear that shade of burnt orange with an emerald green dress.

Though my parents were not here, neither had they left. As I lingered in the doorway, I caught a whiff of my mother's perfume. Perhaps I was not truly alone.

Outside, I vaulted the fence into Mira's garden with confidence and ease. My brain might be old and confused, but my youthful body understood what it was doing. I ducked beneath the spread branches of the apple tree and tried the Schlosses' back door. When I found it locked, I knocked, and when no one answered, I pounded on it to vent my frustration.

With my hands cupped around my face at the window, I could see Mira's music stand in the garden room, and past that into the kitchen. Perhaps her family hadn't come down to breakfast yet. I scooped up pebbles from the flowerbed and tossed one at Mira's windows, waiting in vain for her to raise a sash and lean out to greet me.

"Hey!" I shouted to no one in particular. "Where is everyone? I want my parents. I want to see Mira."

I dropped the pebbles and closed my hand over her locket, squeezing my eyes shut and wishing on it as though it had mystical powers. But nothing changed. I was still alone, and lonelier than I'd ever been since I quit caring about whether I was lonely or not.

Maybe this wasn't heaven after all.

The silence was so loud that my heartbeat filled my ears. No mothers called to their children, no dogs barked, no horses clip-clopped while drawing peddler's carts, no automobiles rumbled past. The only sounds were ones I made myself. I scratched the toe of my shoe against the pebbles on the garden path and listened to them ricochet off each other like a kid's game of marbles. When I cracked my knuckles, they made a pop as loud as a pistol's report.

My mother used to say, "Better to be alone than in bad company," but after so many years of living a solitary life, I wanted noise. I wanted disturbance. I wanted to shout until someone, anyone, called out in response—even if it was to tell me to shut up, already. Covering my ears couldn't erase the void.

If only Mira were here to play for me.

We were six years old when Mira began studying violin. I waited outside during her practice time, wincing as she screeched her way through a simple folk melody, "Muss I Denn." After she'd worked on it for a week or two, it sounded much better, and I hummed along until the song seemed to underscore my daily tasks. The lyrics were very much like the promises Mira and I would later make to each other before we parted.

When I'm back, when I'm back,
When I finally return, finally return,
I'll come straight to thee, I swear.
Though I can't be always by thy side,
full of joy I'll think of thee.
When I'm back, when I'm back,
When I finally return, finally return,
I shall come home straight to thee.

Inspired by the way Mira took to her music lessons, my mother rented a piano and engaged a teacher for me. I had no desire to study music, but I did not wish to disappoint my mother by giving voice to my objection. I was as clumsy as Mira had been at first, but I failed to improve. After weeks of watching me fidget through my lessons and my halfhearted efforts to practice, my mother realized that forcing me to continue was a waste of time and money.

Even when Mutti admitted defeat and called me hopeless, she was not angry. She tousled my hair with a smile and turned me loose to my preferred outdoor pursuits.

As we grew older, Mira found a refuge from the hard times in her music. Maybe my life would have been different if I'd had something like that to cling to during my darkest days.

Though I could've sworn my mother had sent the piano back, it was there, in the sitting room, when I reentered the house. With a twinge of regret for missed opportunities, I pulled out the stool, opened the cover, and pressed a key. The note pleased my ear and filled up the silence, so I sat and amused myself by trying to pick out the tune of "Muss I Denn." To my great surprise, my fingers seemed to understand what to do, and I coaxed the melody out of the instrument with little effort.

Once the top line flowed like second nature, I brought my left hand up to the keys and added a few chords. Not half bad. I wished my mother could hear me now. By lunchtime, I had mastered the piece and could play it flawlessly. This unexpected accomplishment would have been more fun if someone had been there to listen.

Again, I struck a single note, listening to the reverberation that emanated from the string. I couldn't really be the only one here. I just hadn't looked hard enough. Perhaps I should explore farther than my own backyard.

As I set off toward the shop-lined street in our neighborhood where I'd often gone with my mother, the rhythm of my shoes striking the cobblestones echoed off the buildings. At every turn, flowers overflowed from window boxes on freshly painted half-timber houses.

Every vista looked like a picture postcard, but instead of taking in the beauty, suspicion rose in my chest. This perfection felt too much like the *Verschönerung* at Theresienstadt.

I scoured the area for a stray leaf, a dead blossom, or a gum wrapper, and relief flooded over me when I rounded a corner and spotted a bicycle lying against the curb in front of the bookshop. Finally, something was out of place—like it had been touched by a human. Whose bicycle was it? How long had it been there? I ran over and tried the bookshop's door, but it was locked, and the store was dark inside.

"Hello? Is there anyone here?" I pounded on the door.

My joy at finding everything as I'd remembered it faded. I already knew there was little happiness to be found in a solitary existence—and in my dream, the solitude was unbearable. I should be surrounded by family, friends, and neighbors. Why dangle the illusion of this life in front of me and then pull it away? I clawed inside my shirt and clutched the locket's red cord. "Mira!" My voice broke as it echoed across the square. "Mira, where are you?"

There was no answering call.

On the bicycle, I could explore beyond my neighborhood. I picked it up and swung one leg over.

I spent the afternoon searching every street in our district for signs of another human. Even when I ventured into the rolling hills outside the city, it was the same—as if frozen in time, void of any living thing, save vegetation. I thought I was done being angry about things I couldn't change, but the younger version of me was hot-blooded. It was his rage that flooded through me until my brain was like an inferno roiling with questions.

What had I done to deserve this kind of torture? Why was this place being shown to me now? Was I missing some sort of message? Was I dying?

By the time I coasted into the alley behind my house, I'd reached a decision. If being here meant being alone, I wanted out. I dropped the bicycle and shouted at the skies.

"Somebody—show yourself or I'm leaving. Last chance."

When there was no response, I pinched my arm. It hurt, but I didn't wake up. I slapped my cheek so hard the blood rushed to the marks left by my fingers. That turned my rage to panic and my throat constricted until I thought I would suffocate. Why couldn't I wake up? Why was I trapped here in the memory of my childhood home?

The image of my father rose to my mind. Gentle. Patient. Kind. Vacant. He had spent too much time inside his own head, ignoring what was happening around us.

Why didn't my father get us out of Germany before it was too late? He was supposed to protect us. How could he let such awful things happen to Mutti and me? I picked up a stone and threw it with all my might, shattering the workshop window.

Chest heaving, I picked up another stone and ran a few steps toward Mira's, but I couldn't bring myself to damage her home. Instead, my anger turned inward. Just like Vati, I had failed. I hadn't protected

Mira and hadn't done enough, after the war, to build the kind of life I should have had. I knew that.

Casting the stone aside, I jumped up on the garden wall and began to climb the apple tree. I was higher than the rooftops when I shook free my toy airplane and watched it coast gently to the lawn.

I'd once heard someone say that it was impossible to die in one's own dream. It was time to test that theory. Near the top of the tree, I slipped and scrambled for a foothold. My arm grazed the jagged bark, and as I clung to the branch, heart racing, I watched the blood trickle down my arm.

High above the rooftops, I shouted one last time to rouse someone. "Mutti! Vati! Mira!" When there was no reply, I swung out, feet dangling above the network of branches between me and the ground. I let go.

5

Threadbare sheets. Age spots on the backs of my hands. Faded numbers inked on the inside of my arm. This was reality. I was old, but I wept like a little child over the young man I would have liked to be, thinking even as my tears fell what a *putz* I was. It had been many years since a dream had left me so emotionally drained. Then, I had dreamed that I saw my parents walking on a city street. They were young and dressed in the style I remember from my childhood, before we were taken away. I ran to catch up, calling out to them, but I could not make my way through the crowd fast enough, and it swallowed them up.

My parents had been lost to me nearly my whole life. Maybe my subconscious never accepted it. Maybe it hurt so much to remember them because I hadn't honored them the way I should have. I imagined how disappointed they would have been by the course my life had taken.

I rolled over and something slid across my neck. I grabbed at what I feared was a cockroach, but instead, I clutched the hard metal of Mira's locket. I didn't have to look at it, because I knew it by touch. When had I put it on?

There was a scab on my arm where I'd scraped myself on the rough tree bark. At my age, a cut like that would take a week or more to heal, but this one was half-mended already. Strange. I couldn't remember scraping myself on anything else in the past few days. Maybe it happened during the bodega robbery. Did I have other injuries as well? A concussion? I sat up and pressed all over my head, checking for a bump or bruise.

The clock read 9:30, and I hadn't heard Vashon come in. I felt rested, like I'd had hours of uninterrupted sleep. With my thoughts still half in the dream world, the routine of boiling water for coffee and toasting a bagel seemed lacking. I wanted my mother to cook me breakfast. I wanted to see my father off to work.

Mira's locket hung heavy against my chest, and I clutched it again. I always kept it safely put away, never lying around. How did it get to be around my neck?

In the closet, I rummaged on the shelf until I found the right shoebox and brought it to the kitchen table. Inside, a piece of silver cloth lay folded, just as I'd left it, but as soon as I picked it up, I could tell it was empty. Maybe I got up in the middle of the night, put on the necklace, refolded the cloth, and put the shoebox back on the shelf without waking up. Maybe I was completely *meshuggeneh.*

Someone familiar with the old ways, like either of my grandmothers, might have been able to interpret the dream for me. They probably would've had a theory about how the necklace came to be around my neck, as well. My parents would have scoffed and insisted that messages delivered in dreams were the stuff of fairy tales, and fairy tales were not logical or real. They would say I had simply forgotten I had put the necklace on.

Long before lunchtime, thoughts of the dream drove me out of my apartment. Outside, it was noisy. It was real. Cars, buses, and people crowded the street, streaming past me as I headed for the bodega at an old man's pace.

As the bell on the door signaled my arrival, Benny looked up, surprised. "Pete—what are you doing here this time of day? You all right?"

"Yes, I am thinking so." I took out my wallet. "First I must be paying you for the groceries."

He shrugged. "I don't want you to worry about that."

"I will be worrying if I am not paying you. How much?" I handed two twenties across the counter and he gave me back my change. An awkward silence fell as I shoved the bills into my wallet and put it back in my pocket. As much as I wanted to talk about the dream, I didn't know how to explain it to him. "Was I hurt yesterday during the robbery? I am not remembering when this happened." I showed him the scrape on my arm.

He peered at it. "Gee, I don't think so. That looks pretty well healed."

"I have thought so too. Was I getting a bump on the head, maybe?"

"I don't know, but if you think you did, you should probably visit your doctor."

"Yes, maybe. Benny, are you having a grandmother or someone who knows about the meaning of dreams?"

He shook his head.

"Are you ever having dreams that seem real, even after you are waking up?"

He shrugged. "I don't usually remember my dreams, but I don't think it would be unusual if you had a nightmare last night."

"Was not a nightmare—but is not leaving my brain now that I am awake."

"I'm all ears if you wanna talk about it."

"Well, I was waking up in my bed—at home."

"But you were in a parallel universe, exactly like this one?"

I knew he was kidding me. "No, it was my bed in the house where I was living when I was a boy. Everything was being perfect—but not so perfect, right?"

"You were upset after the robbery. Maybe your brain needed to show you someplace safe, so you could get away from what was bothering you."

"The dream was nice, but it wasn't, also. My family, they should still be alive in this place, but they were not there. I wanted to leave. But now all I am thinking about is to go back."

"I'm sorry, Pete."

"Is okay. I should be paying attention to what is here, in front of me. Still I am needing to fix the music box."

"It's all right. Don't feel like you have to."

"But I am wanting to."

"Then no rush, all right? Promise me."

"Yes, yes, all right, I promise."

The damage to the inner workings of the music box was much worse than when I'd first found it, and I worked into the evening, peering through a magnifying lamp as I shaped new tips to replace the broken ones on the cylinder. Though I had hoped the delicate work would require all my attention, still I couldn't put thoughts of my old home out of my mind. When I turned off the lamp, leaving the job unfinished, I went to bed hoping to have the dream again. I laid my hand over Mira's locket and cradled it against my chest.

I could tell before I opened my eyes that I was back. The air smelled too clean for it to be my Weequahic neighborhood. Just as I had the first time, I bounded out of bed with ease and stuck my head out the open window. When I heard violin music, my heart swelled until I thought it would burst out of my chest.

I dressed in record time and ran my hands through my hair. There was no time to find a comb. Such thick, wavy hair I never had in my life.

Dashing downstairs and out the back, I vaulted the garden fence. This time, the Dutch door and the windows in the Schlosses' garden room were thrown open, and I held my breath in anticipation as I drew near.

Mira stood in the center of the room, violin tucked under her chin, eyes closed as she drew the melody from the strings. The soft breeze carried out the notes like a long and satisfied exhale.

Somehow, I had wished her into my dream. Without disturbing her, I let my eyes feast on the woman I'd longed to see for so many years.

She was young, like me, and lovelier than I could have imagined. Her skin glowed with good health, and her hair, darker now than when she was a child, fell in glossy curls that brushed against her shoulders as she worked the bow over the strings. Tears welled up in my eyes at her blissful smile. She looked as though she'd never known an unhappy day in her life.

"Mira." When I tried to speak, a hoarse whisper was all that came out.

She stopped playing and laid the violin on the table. "Oh, Peter! I was hoping you'd come by today." She ran to throw her arms around my neck, and we laughed as we clung to each other over the half door.

"Is it really you?"

"Of course, it's me."

"You look so happy." As she opened the door and joined me in the garden, the gold locket on the red silk cord sparkled at her throat. I brushed my hand across my own chest. The locket I'd been wearing was gone, but I didn't take the time to puzzle that out. I was only interested in Mira. "And you're a knockout! Gorgeous. I was afraid you wouldn't be here. Oh, Mira, you don't know how good it is to see you and hear you play. It's been so long."

The ground rumbled under our feet like an earthquake, but with the answers to the questions that had been burning inside me for seventy-five years within reach, I wasn't about to let a little tremor get in the way. "What happened to you?"

A look of alarm crossed her face as the earth trembled again. "Nothing happened. I'm right here."

"No, I mean the day you disappeared from Theresienstadt. Where did you go? I never stopped looking for you…."

This time the earth tilted so violently that I lost my balance. She reached out, but as I tried to take her hand, a swirling wind, like some kind of reverse gravity, sucked me away and I grasped empty air. Her voice, calling my name, echoed in my head as everything faded to black.

I woke with a start, like I'd been dropped from midair and landed on my bed. I was back in Weequahic, tears on my cheeks and Mira's name on my lips. The pain of losing her seared as hot as if it had been real, and not just a dream. Even worse, the last thing I had said to her was a lie.

Could I go back into the same dream? I glanced at the clock. I had hours until sunrise. I took a deep breath and held it, closing my eyes as I consciously relaxed the muscles in my face, my arms, my legs. *Don't think . . . don't think . . . don't think . . .*

The violin's last note faded away as I opened my eyes.

"Oh, Peter! I was hoping you'd come by today." Mira set the instrument on the table and ran to throw her arms around my neck. We laughed as we clung to each other over the half door. Her surprise at seeing me was genuine. Did she not remember I'd just been there minutes before?

I stuck to the script. "Is it really you?"

"Of course, it's me."

"You look so wonderful. And happy." As she opened the door and joined me in the garden, the gold locket on the red silk cord sparkled at her throat. I took both her hands in mine and looked her in the eyes. "Where were you the night you should have played in the concert at Theresienstadt?"

No sooner had the words left my lips than the world tilted again, and I awoke back in my bed in Weequahic.

Undaunted, I took another deep breath, settled back against my pillow, and started over. *Don't think . . . don't think . . . don't think . . .*

Again, when she rushed to greet me, nothing in her manner indicated that I'd been there—and disappeared—a few moments before.

Assuming I was about to make another hasty exit, I took a moment to appreciate the warmth of her hands in mine before I spoke. "Where were you when you heard Hitler had committed suicide?"

This time when I found myself back in bed, I got a pen and scratch pad out of my nightstand drawer and wrote a list of the questions I had asked. Then I lay down and tried again.

Don't think . . . don't think . . . don't think . . .

"Where did you live after the war?"

"Did your hair turn gray when you got old?"

"Did you have any pets?"

"Where were you when the Berlin Wall came down?"

"Where are you now?"

She met every question with the same bemused expression, which melted into a look of concern as the world tilted and spat me out of the dream.

Everything I'd asked pertained to things that took place after I last saw Mira. And it all got me banished back to my present.

I'd had to fight my way out of the dream when I was there alone. Now I couldn't stay for more than a few minutes—unless, it seemed, I stopped asking questions.

But why?

Perhaps Mira was what I imagined she would be, no more, no less. Maybe she couldn't answer questions *I* didn't know the answers to.

I'd never had dreams in which I realized I was dreaming. Now I would continue the experiment. If I could avoid speaking about anything that occurred during the seventy-five years since I'd seen Mira, would I remain with her as long as I liked?

It wasn't a difficult choice. I'd rather be with her than know the answers to any of those questions. *Don't think . . .*

Mira set down the violin and ran to the door. "Oh, Peter! I was hoping you'd come by today."

I threw my arms around her and buried my face in her hair. "I'm here."

6

When Hitler became chancellor in 1933, there were more than eleven thousand Jews living in Leipzig—the sixth-largest Jewish population center in Germany. Leipzig was somewhat insulated from the increasing sanctions against Jews because its international trade fair brought people to the city from all over Europe. In the early days of his regime, Hitler was not ready to let other countries know how badly the Nazis treated Jewish people.

That Germany's Jewish citizens had made significant contributions to the nation's success in medicine, banking, education, commerce, and the arts no longer mattered. As part of Hitler's Aryanization of Germany, the government confiscated Jewish businesses, including Mr. Schloss's garment factory, and transferred them into German hands. The new manager was one of Mr. Schloss's long-time employees, and a family friend. He relied on Mr. Schloss's advice to run the business and paid him under the table.

After my father was barred from teaching at the university, he was able to find steady work doing odd jobs and repairs for other Jewish families, in addition to his role at the *Lehrhaus*. On the days he did not accompany Mira and me to the school and teach class, he left for work in coveralls, with the leather strap of his toolbox slung over his shoulder.

I was ten years old when Mira's father's factory burned to the ground during the pogroms known as *Kristallnacht*, the Night of Broken Glass. Mr. Schloss had kept up the payments on his insurance policy, but when he filed a claim, the government confiscated the money, saying that as a Jew, he owed reparations for the riots. Without the insurance money, neither he nor the new manager had the funds to rebuild. Once the business closed for good, Mr. Schloss took in tailoring jobs. Though he struggled financially, he insisted Mira continue with her violin lessons.

After *Kristallnacht*, one of Hitler's advisors recommended Jews be required to wear the Star of David on their outer clothing, since it was hard to tell on sight who was who.

It was true of my family. If you'd seen us in a park or at a museum, you wouldn't have immediately recognized us as Jewish. We all had fair complexions and light brown hair. My father and I didn't wear yarmulkes or prayer shawls. My mother dressed in the same style as other young German housewives.

European Jews had been forced to wear distinguishing badges or clothing as far back as the thirteenth century. The practice had been abandoned in the 1800s—until the Nazis brought it back. The yellow Star of David was meant to set us apart, but for the first time, I experienced solidarity with other Jews.

When deportations began in the weeks following *Kristallnacht*, those who could bribe government officials to get visas fled the country. My father applied for us to immigrate to Palestine, but we were so far down the queue that there was no hope. Jews were being turned away from America. Poland and Czechoslovakia had fallen to the Germans. We could not escape Nazi-occupied territory.

These were all things I could have talked about with Mira in the dream—but I did not want to.

Earlier that same year, my father had been elected to serve on the

Judenrat, or Jewish Council. As Jews from all over Leipzig were forced into ghettos, the *Judenrat* took responsibility for reestablishing the social services that were now denied to Jews. Without their intervention, the burgeoning ghetto population would have been without food distribution, clinics, orphanages, schools, and care for the elderly. Though the council's purpose was to serve the Jewish community, the German administration pressured its members to enforce anti-Jewish laws and regulations.

Even with his position on the council, I heard my father tell my mother we were not safe. It was just a matter of time before the Gestapo came pounding at our door. I lay awake most nights, listening for the inevitable rumble of trucks, the tramp of boots, and shouting. But when they finally came for us in April 1939, it was without any of the expected warning signs.

The knock sounded normal, like a neighbor calling. My father and I didn't even look up from our chess game when my mother went to the door. When she called my father's name, he rose immediately at the note of panic in her voice, and I followed him into the foyer.

He put a hand on her shoulder as they faced the uniformed officer at the door. His voice was calm. "It's all right, Elke." Then he glanced back and saw me standing behind them. "Why don't you take Peter into the sitting room?"

With a dancer's poise, my mother held her head high as she led me away. She kept her arm around me while we waited on the sofa, but her trembling only increased my anxiety.

After a quiet conversation with the Gestapo officer, my father closed the door and, face ashen, joined us in the sitting room. He had to take a moment to compose himself before he spoke. When he did, he managed a watery smile. "We are not being deported."

My mother's grip on my shoulders relaxed, and the panic that had squeezed my heart began to ebb away. Then he spoke again.

"But we will no longer live here. Our home has been reassigned to a German family."

"What? How can they do that? This house belongs to us!" My mother clenched her fists in her lap.

"That doesn't matter. There is no way to fight this. We have three days to vacate."

I found my voice. "But Vati, where will we live?"

"We are moving to a neighborhood for Jewish families. We will have a furnished apartment."

"Furnished?" My mother looked around. "We already have furniture."

My father shook his head and put a comforting hand over hers. "We are allowed to bring what clothing and personal items we can carry."

I thought of my books and toys upstairs. I didn't want to leave any of them behind for some other boy to use.

My mother blinked back tears. "The dining room table—the dishes. They were my grandmother's."

"It will be all right. Possessions don't really matter, do they? It's more important that we will be together."

His voice should have reassured me, but the look on his face said he did not believe it would be all right. We sat on our sofa for a long time. Then my mother went upstairs to decide what we should pack. My father stood and ran his hand over the varnished wood on the radio cabinet.

"Will you be able to carry the radio?"

He shook his head. "We are not allowed to bring it."

Three days later we left, and my father signed over our house. From then on, the *Reichsvereinigung*, the national association of Jews, was the property manager. His fountain pen scratched on the form, and as he completed his signature, he wrote with such violence that he punctured the paper.

"We'll be back soon, right?" I took my father's hand and looked up at him for reassurance.

"As soon as we can." He did not smile down at me as he usually did.

When we reached the corner, I looked back and saw some of the neighbors come out of our house, their arms full of items we'd had to leave behind.

"Vati! Are they stealing our things?"

He put a hand on my head to turn my gaze away. "Come, Peter. It does no good to look back."

In the *Judenhaus*, two, sometimes three families were crowded into each apartment—but my father's position on the *Judenrat* allowed him some say over our circumstances. We were assigned to share space with just the Schlosses. I considered this a stroke of luck—at first.

Our new neighborhood was near the city center, far away from our old one and nowhere near as nice. After we left our house, I wondered if there was an Aryan boy or girl now living there, sleeping in my bed, playing with the toys I'd had to leave behind. Did they have a friend who lived next door? Had they discovered the fairy post office in the apple tree? I didn't want any other children to have the home I'd been denied.

The grownups were reeling from the rapid changes too. Though my mother and Mrs. Schloss had been friends for many years, their differences in temperament became apparent once we were all living under the same roof. In their worry over our safety and our futures, their differences came to define them, like they had been assigned roles to act out in a drama.

My mother had always been house-proud and placed a high value on the arts and beautiful things, but as our situation worsened, her practical side won out. She never once complained about our shabby flat or mourned for the heirlooms she'd left behind. Instead, she approached the privations with good humor and a sense of adventure that made it seem like we were camping out.

While my mother focused on the bright side of things, Mrs. Schloss tended to see our collective glass as half empty. Had we not been forced into such close quarters I might never have known that my mother took a more liberal view of sex and relationships than Mira's.

The day we moved in my mother opened the door off the sitting room. "One bedroom and two twin beds for the six of us? They said we'd have two bedrooms." She looked around, puzzled. "Where's the other?"

Mrs. Schloss set her suitcase on one of the beds and opened a door on the far side of the room. "Here—I found it. *Oy veysmere*. We might as well be in one room." Whoever occupied the small second bedroom would have to pass through the other family's sleeping space.

My mother looked over Mrs. Schloss's shoulder and shook her head. "And twin beds. In both rooms." Though many married couples slept in separate beds at that time, I could tell my mother was thinking about the wide bed she and my father had shared at our house.

"What does it matter?" Mrs. Schloss took a drag on her cigarette. "Which room do you want?"

My mother's determined cheerfulness dimmed. "I suppose we should take the back room. Do you think Avram will need to stay up later than we do? If so, he can come to bed when he has finished his work for the night, without worrying about disturbing us."

"Yes, that's probably best. For now, anyway."

The day after we moved in, our fathers had orders to report for work at Hugo-Schneider-Aktiengesellschaft Metallwarenfabrik, or HASAG, which was originally a manufacturer of lamps and metal goods that began producing armaments in 1933. Our fathers worked on the assembly line, creating the *Panzerfaust*, a hand-held anti-tank weapon.

I read later that at the Leipzig HASAG headquarters alone, more than ten thousand civilian forced laborers, prisoners of war, and internees of concentration camps from all over Europe worked to produce ammunition and anti-tank warheads. Even at the time, the irony of the situation was not lost on any of us: Vati and Mr. Schloss were being forced to make weapons that would hobble attacks by Great Britain and France—the nations that were now at war with Germany—and delay our liberation.

Many of the laborers were housed in large camps near the factory grounds. Because our house was close enough that our fathers were able to walk to and from work, they were permitted to return to us each night. Sometimes they smuggled home extra food or clothing. Though we had ration cards for food, there never seemed to be enough to feed the six of us, and Jews were not allotted a clothing ration.

Perhaps my father hoped serving on the *Judenrat* and acting as though he was cooperating with the Germans would afford us a measure of safety. But instead, he had made a deal with the devil. Guilt tormented him when the local officials forced him to make lists of the people who lived in the *Judenhauser* and their property and recommended who should be deported. Though he had no choice but to obey the government's orders, resentment grew against him and all the members of the *Judenrat*. They were perceived as collaborators and traitors against their fellow Jews. My mild-mannered father, who would never have willingly hurt anyone, seemed to age overnight. He lost his hair, and the worry lines that furrowed his brow deepened. People shunned him on the street, and muttered *shpyon* and *vizele* under their breath.

Mr. Schloss, on the other hand, was considered a *mensch*, and was in demand for his skill as a tailor. In the evenings, as soon as the dinner dishes were cleared away, he would spread fabric on the kitchen table and set his sewing kit on a chair, and work to make over clothes for people whose old ones had worn out. He was clever about using scraps to add panels and sections to my clothes and Mira's as we grew.

One evening, he was working on a pair of my father's trousers. I put aside my homework and watched as he sewed a little pocket into the inside of each trouser leg.

"How do you reach whatever's in that pocket?"

"It's not meant to be that kind of pocket, Peter. This pocket is to conceal things you don't want anyone to find."

I nodded. "Could you make me one, too?"

"I suppose. What do you have to hide, my boy?"

"Nothing yet. But I might, someday."

"Indeed."

True to his word, he made me a pocket for my knee breeches and told me to button it closed before I put my pants on. Then he showed me how to clip the stitches that held it in place so I could transfer it to another garment myself.

It's funny how something so simple can become so significant.

7

Mira felt warm and soft and real in my arms. As we embraced through the open upper half of her back door, I could hear the soft whoosh of her breath near my ear, feel her chest rise and fall against mine. She smelled faintly of Evening in Paris perfume.

Somewhere nearby, a car horn honked, and I opened my eyes with a start. Sunlight streamed into my bedroom in Weequahic. Across the hall, I heard the water running in Vashon's shower.

All day long, I couldn't concentrate on anything. I messed up the crossword, and the single solder I made on the music box was going to have to be redone. My hand strayed to Mira's locket around my neck so many times that I took it off so I could see it without having to look in the mirror. I polished it on my shirttail, even though I knew the nicks and scratches on the golden heart wouldn't rub off. The red silk cord was frayed and close to breaking in a couple of spots. On the kitchen table, I made loops and coils with the cord and framed the locket inside a larger heart. Such a silly, sentimental gesture.

Twice I started out the door to visit Benny, but I was afraid he'd think I was crazy to make such a big deal over a dream. That evening, I went through the motions of dinner, dishes, and settling down to listen to the ballgame in bed, but after sitting around the apartment in a stupor all day, I worried I wouldn't be able to fall asleep.

Before I opened my eyes, I could feel the rough bark of the apple tree's trunk against my back. My legs dangled into space, and the scent of fruit and flowers hung in the air.

Mira sat on the branch a few feet away, legs crossed at the ankles, the sunlight that shone through the leaves dappling her skin and hair. Her lips moved, but her voice sounded faint, like I was underwater. I had the sense that she was much farther away than she appeared.

"Peter? Did you hear me?" This time her voice came through loud and clear, as if someone had turned up the volume. Startled, I almost lost my balance on the branch, and she reached for my arm to steady me. "If you don't pay attention, you could fall." She laid a cool hand on my cheek. "Are you all right?"

I took her hand and as I pressed her palm to my lips, I again caught the scent of Evening in Paris. "Yes. I'm all right. How are you?"

"We're here, and we're together. There's nothing to worry about—and a lot that doesn't matter anymore."

I nodded, and said, more to myself than to her, "It doesn't matter what is true."

"The strangest things are true, and the truest things are strange." She said it in a singsong voice. "Look around. Everything's perfect. We're in a fairy tale."

"Or perhaps we're like Adam and Eve, in our garden. We even have our apple tree."

She nodded. "Maybe the Adam and Eve reference makes more sense, since there's no one here but us."

"No snakes in our garden, either?"

"Not a one."

No matter what I said, she was agreeable. "Good." I swung one leg over the branch and sprang to the ground. "Come on. Let's go explore. Maybe today someone else will join us." I put my hands at her waist and helped her down.

Hand in hand, we covered every street in our district. Everything was just as it had been on my first visit, but this time when we got to the square, the door to Bressler's Café stood ajar.

Mira dropped my hand as she ran across the street to the café, calling, "Frau Bressler? Hello, is anyone here?" I followed her inside, and she looked back at me and shrugged, and then went behind the counter and ducked through the curtained doorway to the kitchen.

A table in the center of the café was laid out for afternoon tea, with little sandwiches, a plate of *springerle* cookies embossed with flowers and wreaths, and a china teapot. I laid my hand against it, only half surprised to find it hot.

In a moment, Mira returned. "There's no one else here."

"But someone thought we might be hungry."

"Oh, I am! Aren't you? Remember how our mothers used to bring us here?"

As I pulled out Mira's chair, unexpected tears welled up in my eyes. What had become of the café's owner during the war? "Frau Bressler was always jolly, wasn't she? And she had a ginger cat."

Mira smiled. "Yes. Her lemon *springerle* are my absolute favorite cookies in all the world. And everything's laid out, like she was expecting us."

I sat across from her. "But what if Frau Bressler comes back and finds out we've eaten food meant for someone else?"

Mira poured the tea. "Let's not think too hard about it. Just enjoy it."

This was my first taste of food in the dream world, and the flavors and textures were even better than I remembered. We both ate with the appetites of young people.

Afterward, we strolled through town, hand in hand, like any couple who had eyes only for each other. A light shone out from the synagogue on the far side of the square. Mira paused and asked, "Should we go inside? Adam and Eve were on speaking terms with their Maker." She glanced at me from under her eyelashes. "Until they fell out of favor, that is."

"No." I had no relationship with God and didn't care if I was in his favor or not.

"Then let's go home."

As we walked, she snuggled closer. It occurred to me that she had subtly offered herself to me. Suddenly I was nervous at the thought of doing more than kissing her. I hadn't kissed anyone since I was sixteen.

In an attempt to stop my racing thoughts and remind myself that none of this was real, I changed the subject. "It was wonderful to hear your violin again. When we were children, you played very well for your age. But now you play like an angel."

"It's always been easy for me."

"Remember how my mother would hound me to practice the piano—but I never improved, no matter how much I tried?"

At that, she dimpled. "You were hopeless. And I don't think you tried all that hard."

"You're right about that. But I recently learned how to play. I'm not as good a musician as you, but I'm all right."

"Really? We should try a tune together when we get home."

It seemed as though I was going to be out of my comfort zone no matter what. "I don't know if I'm ready for a duet."

"There's only one way to find out." She pulled at my hand, turning me homeward.

To my relief, we played together as though I'd been accompanying her for years. She only had to name a tune and the notes were in my head before I ever touched the keys. I expected to stumble, but I played with nuance and feeling—and no mistakes. At the end of our duet of "Waldeslust," Mira drew the bow slowly over the strings to prolong the final note. As the sound faded away, tears welled up in my eyes at our synchronicity.

As I tried to wipe my eyes without being obvious, she nodded to show she understood. "That song always makes me sad."

"*Love of the Woods?*"

"Yes—not the first verse, but the part about the lonely girl who doesn't want to live anymore. I always want to comfort her."

"Sing it for me." I turned back to the piano and played the introduction.

"*My father does not know me; my mother does not love me, and I do not like to die I'm still so young. Waldeslust, waldeslust, oh how lonely beats my heart—*"

She was singing about herself, and my heart ached for her. "Mira," I stood and wiped away the tears that coursed down her cheek, "Would it be all right if I kissed you? I mean, really kissed you?"

"Of course it's all right. We've kissed before."

"Yes, but when we were kids. That doesn't count, does it?"

"It does. First kisses are important. Our story should pick up again where it started, don't you agree?" She led the way outside with a teasing smile and climbed up into the tree as easily as she had when we were children.

As I landed beside her, my shyness returned. I wasn't sure how to start, or how to hold her, or anything. She giggled at my hesitation and laid gentle hands on either side of my face. Teasingly, she kissed me first in greeting, one cheek, then the other, before she pressed her lips to mine. My arms encircled her, and as I held her close, my body awoke. The kiss went from being the kind you'd give to a friend to something more, and the need to possess her thrilled and frightened me in equal measure. We kissed in the tree until I nearly lost my balance and toppled us both off the branch.

We climbed down and resumed kissing lying on the grass beneath the spread branches. When I rolled on top of her and felt her beneath me for the first time, she sighed with pleasure and ran her hand down my back and over my hip. Her perfume mingled with the outdoorsy scents of lilacs and fresh-cut grass, and when she guided my hand to her breast, my body was screaming all systems go and I could barely breathe for the anticipation. But I pulled away.

There was no doubt Mira understood the power she wielded over me. She rose and took my hand, and we kissed every few steps as she led me across the garden to her back door. But when she stepped over the threshold, I stayed on the porch, seeing not the woman, but remembering the little girl who had tearily looked to me to fix what she had broken.

"Aren't you coming inside?" She kept hold of my hand.

"Maybe this is happening too fast."

"Are you afraid of me?"

"No."

"Then what's stopping you? My mother and father aren't here. There's no one to see or to judge us."

"I know. But shouldn't we get to know each other better first?"

She laughed. "You don't need to get to know me, Peter. You always knew me better than anyone."

It was like being in an argument with myself. "That may be, but I'd like to take you out for an evening. Just as if this were—" I didn't say real, but she understood.

"If that's what you want." She gave a little shrug as she let her fingers slip through mine. "*Gute Nacht*, Peter."

"*Gute Nacht*." After she shut the door, I waited on the porch. "Aren't you going to lock the door?"

I heard her laugh again. "And lock you out? I'd rather not."

The darkness, expansive and foreboding, enveloped me as I stood on the porch until I wished I had followed her inside. When at last I heard the click of the lock, I vaulted the stone wall and hurried to my own house, where I secured the doors and windows and inspected every room, even under the beds. I hadn't been aware of the silence when I was with Mira, but alone, it pressed on my eardrums again.

Maybe I was a fool not to stay with her. But the thoughts that had flooded my mind when we'd kissed weren't all happy ones. I couldn't forget the time long ago when my affection for her had devastating consequences.

8

My family and the Schlosses had had plenty of personal space when we'd been next-door neighbors. But in our cramped, dingy two-bedroom flat with the bathroom down the hall, the tension and discord festered.

My mother tried to smooth over little hurts and make light of our privations, but Mrs. Schloss rejected my mother's well-intentioned good cheer. Her fear and depression left her unable to offer comfort or accept it from anyone. She isolated herself until she did not seem to be a part of our household, leaving my mother as the functioning adult in charge.

Our fathers, my two closest male role models, were both barred from their professions and stripped of their dignity. Mr. Schloss fared better socially than my father, but they were both frustrated, distracted, and exhausted. I stepped up to fill a role in the household that neither had the energy to take on. I became Mira's protector.

Though we learned to live with the tension, we were like a bundle of sticks held in someone's hands, bending under the forces we could not control, until finally, one by one, we would snap. Mrs. Schloss broke first.

Besides the two bedrooms, our flat in the *Judenhaus* had only a sitting room with an alcove and a kitchen. None of the rooms were spacious. Our parents, still clinging to the vestiges of privacy, decided that we children would sleep in the sitting room, where no one would trip over us in the night. Mrs. Schloss hung a curtain across the arched doorway to the alcove and made up a pallet for Mira on the window seat. I slept on the sofa and rolled up my bedding every morning and put it in my parents' room. I tried to be a good sport when my mother insisted it was like camping, but the novelty soon wore off. I longed for my own bed in my room at home.

The *Judenhaus* was never quiet. Even late at night, there was always a baby crying or people arguing. Often, it was Mr. and Mrs. Schloss. It felt awkward, pretending I hadn't overheard.

One night, when their bickering was worse than usual, Mira crept out of her bed and gently shook my shoulder. I could see the tears on her cheeks as she held out her hand, and I let her lead me behind the curtain. She moved her pallet to the floor, and we huddled there in the darkness, swathed in her blankets with our backs against the window seat.

Her parents' room was just a thin wall away, and we heard every word.

"The money is gone? All of it?" Mrs. Schloss was angry. "I thought you said you trusted him."

"I did." Mr. Schloss sounded miserable.

"Then where are the papers you paid him for?"

"They would do us no good. His work has been spotted as forgery."

"Then get the money back."

"I cannot get it back. My contact has been arrested. He has not been at work for the past few days."

"Fool! Avram, now we have nothing. We cannot get by on just the ration cards. What will we do?"

"Hush! Everyone in the building will hear you."

Mira shuddered. I put my arm around her, and she whispered, "I don't want to run away. I'm glad we're not going."

"Where do you think you would go if you did?"

"I don't know. But it would be someplace far from here."

"The farther the better. You'd have to get out of Europe. Maybe you could go to China—or Australia."

"Maybe I'd go to that island in the Caribbean. But I don't want to be anywhere unless you're there, too." She took her locket off over her head and leaned close, trying to hang it around both our necks, but the red silk cord wasn't long enough.

"Here." I took the necklace from her gently and pulled it back down over her hair, smoothing it as I did so. Then I drew her down beside me and pulled the blanket over us, spooning her back against me. She took my hand and laid it over the locket. I let my fingers tangle in the cord, and my thumb stroked her delicate collarbone. She shuddered again and put her hand over mine. Soon the tension ebbed out of her body, and her regular breathing told me she'd fallen asleep.

The next day I felt strong and powerful because I'd been able to comfort her. Every night after that, she beckoned me back to her pallet. We were still children, and despite everything that was going on around us, I was an innocent. I didn't know anything about touching her in a sexual way. Sometimes the sounds we heard coming from our parents' bedrooms made us giggle softly, and even though I didn't understand what was going on, I knew it had something to do with being married. I also had a vague sense that our parents wouldn't approve of Mira and me sleeping in the same bed, but I couldn't refuse her. I always crept back to my blankets on the sofa before the adults were awake—until one morning when I overslept.

Mira's mother found us curled up together on the pallet and grabbed Mira by the arm, pulling her away from me so forcefully that I awoke in a full-out panic. I watched in horror as she dragged Mira to her feet and dealt her a resounding slap. Mira's cry of shock and fear brought my parents and her father running to see what was wrong.

"You took him to your bed? Little *hur!*" Mrs. Schloss clutched Mira by the shoulders, shaking her until her head lolled. My parents hustled me away and sequestered me in their bedroom.

"Stay here and don't worry. Everything will be all right." My mother put a reassuring hand on my shoulder for a moment before she closed the door. She and my father went back to speak with the Schlosses, and I pressed my ear to the door. Mira and her mother were both crying, and there was so much shouting that I had trouble following what was said. We were in a lot of trouble.

Soon my father came back. "Go get ready for school or you'll be late."

I grabbed my clothes and toothbrush and ran past the Schlosses to the bathroom at the end of the hall. On my way back, Mira passed me, face blotchy from crying, her gaze fixed on the worn carpet. I could hear Mrs. Schloss railing at my mother before I got back to our flat.

"*Shanda.* He must be punished for what he's done, or else he'll do it again."

"Sylvia, you're blowing this out of proportion. They're children. Do you really think they—"

"Who knows what they've been doing right under our noses? The last thing we need is that kind of trouble. You must cut Peter's rations to punish him. That will teach him a lesson."

"I'll do no such thing!"

At breakfast, Mutti set a bowl of oatmeal before me and glowered at Mrs. Schloss as though daring her to take it away. I shoveled in huge spoonfuls until my mother put a hand on my shoulder. "*Geyn slouli,* Peter." After that, I took the time to swallow between mouthfuls.

Mutti and Mrs. Schloss were too busy glaring at each other to say goodbye when Mira and I followed our fathers out the door. We did not dare speak on the way to school, and even though our fathers did not seem angry, they offered us no words of comfort. Perhaps they were as shaken by Mrs. Schloss's reaction as we were.

After school, Mira went to her violin lesson, and when I returned home alone, the smoldering silence between Mutti and Mrs. Schloss confirmed that they had not yet resolved the issue. When Mira came in, she kept her eyes cast down and did not speak to anyone, cowering in her mother's presence like a dog beaten by a once-trusted master. I tried to catch her eye, but she would not look in my direction.

That night, my mother served herself deliberately small portions at dinner and put the extra on my plate.

Mrs. Schloss moved Mira's pallet into their bedroom, and after that, I occupied the alcove alone. From the next morning on, Mrs. Schloss walked us to the ghetto school and back to assure we would not speak to each other on the way.

After a week of searing silences and suspicious glances from Mrs. Schloss, my mother called me into her bedroom when I returned from school. As soon as the door closed behind us, I asked in a furious whisper, "Why is Mrs. Schloss still treating Mira and me like we've done something horrible? We just fell asleep."

"I know. I think Mrs. Schloss is being too harsh in her efforts to protect Mira."

"But Mutti, that's all I'm trying to do, too. It upsets Mira when her parents fight. She was frightened and sad, so I stayed with her."

My mother kissed my forehead. "You are a good friend, Peter, but you and Mira aren't children anymore. That kind of close contact isn't appropriate. She's becoming a young woman, and you'll soon be a man."

I looked away. "What does that have to do with anything?" Now I was sure Mrs. Schloss's reaction had something to do with the noises we'd heard coming from our parents' bedrooms. My cheeks grew hot as I wondered what I'd have to do to Mira to make her sound like that.

The whole thing should've blown over quickly. When it did not, Mira let her violin express the sadness and confusion she could not voice.

Mira had never minded me being around while she practiced, but since any sign of my presence upset Mrs. Schloss, I retreated behind the curtain in the alcove to listen. The window faced the courtyard, and I could see people in flats on the other side of the building.

As Mira played, a number of women paused in their tasks and leaned on their windowsills, wiping away tears as they listened to the plaintive tunes drifting through the dingy courtyard.

When the final note was stilled, I parted the curtain to make sure the coast was clear. Our mothers were preparing dinner in the kitchen. "Mira," I whispered, and when she turned, I beckoned to her, opening the curtain so she could see too. "Look."

Her audience was still there, waiting expectantly, hoping for another song. Someone blew their nose, and Mira bit her lip as she saw the melancholy on their faces. Then she set the violin back under her chin and it was like she had stepped onto a stage. I retreated out of the way.

She struck the bow across the strings with a verve that I hadn't seen since before her mother had chastised her so harshly. She launched into a sprightly folk tune—a complete change from her last selection. The children down in the courtyard began to dance and clap in time, and right away the women at their windows joined in. Long after her practice time was up, Mira stood at the window and played. She reluctantly put the violin away when we were called to the table for dinner.

After that, Mira spent the afternoons sharing her gift with the inhabitants of our *Judenhaus*, giving of herself to heal their hurts. My pride swelled every time I listened to her play.

Though I'd barely spoken to Mira since the trouble started, Mrs. Schloss continued to watch me, trying to catch us doing something we shouldn't. But she never thought to examine our homework.

Like any boy my age, I enjoyed reading stories about spies and secret agents, and for my last birthday, my parents had given me a book on ciphers and codes. Though I'd been unable to bring the book with me, I remembered some of the simpler ones and decided to use one to communicate with Mira.

I practiced a transposition code until I could read it without having to unscramble the message with a pencil and paper. Each pair of letters was reversed, so the word "four" appeared as "ofru." I wrote in the code: *My mother says everything comes out in the wash.* I included the key to decipher it and slipped the sheet of paper into the top book on the stack Mira had brought home from school. It was a storybook of Chinese folk tales she'd borrowed from the school's library.

Since she played every afternoon until dinner, she did her homework at the kitchen table in the evenings while her father sewed alongside her. Mr. Schloss had never chastised Mira or me, but neither had he spoken to his wife in our defense. I did not consider him an ally.

I usually spent the evenings playing checkers with my father in the sitting room. He worked long hours in the factory, and without enough to eat, he tired easily and went to bed early. That night, his hand shook as he moved the pieces, and after I had beat him three times in a row, I stood and stretched. "I'm tired, Vati. Is it okay if we stop for tonight?"

He smiled, not fooled. The strain he was feeling showed in the worry lines on his face, but his voice was both kind and teasing, just as it had always been. "You played well, son, but you'd best be on your game. I'll beat you next time."

"Yes, Vati. I wish . . ."

"What, Peter?"

"I wish you still had your camera."

"Someday I shall have another. Perhaps it is best not to record this chapter in our lives, eh?" He stood and kissed my forehead, tousling my hair as he walked past me. The bedroom door opened and closed, and a few moments later, the bedsprings squeaked.

A kitchen chair scraped the linoleum, and when I heard Mira bid goodnight to her father, I retreated to my alcove. The next morning, my arithmetic book lay on the floor just outside the curtain. I opened it and found my note. She'd written her reply in code: "*Then hand me the soap.*"

With our line of communication reestablished, Mira pretended complete obedience to her mother while slipping coded notes into my arithmetic book every evening. Most were short and concerned with her resentment of her mother, who, she said, could not really understand what Mira was going through, because her own growing up years had been so very different. How could her mother deny her daughter happiness, since who knew when things would grow worse for us all? When *she* had children someday, she'd be a mother more like mine. Worst of all, her mother had bullied and broken her dear father until he had no pride left.

In the months after the incident, I noticed my mother had been right. Mira was becoming a young woman. I was changing, too, and my feelings for her ripened into something I couldn't explore in my waking hours. In my dreams, Mira came to lie with me on my pallet. I could smell the fragrance of her hair and feel the warmth of her skin. She felt and tasted so real that when I woke up, pajamas and sheets wet, I wondered how in the world we had known how to do what we'd done. With no one to talk to, I faced the agony and the embarrassment alone.

As Mira and I left our childhoods behind, we both learned how to act a convincing lie. It was a skill that would prove necessary to our survival.

Now, I tossed and turned in my childhood bed alone. Though Mrs. Schloss had once terrified me, she was not here, and she had never been able to control my thoughts or my dreams. Was it irrational to deny myself this specter of a physical relationship with Mira? It was true that nothing stood between us now, but I'd still be alone in the morning, just as I had been when I'd had dreams about her before. And I hated to admit it, but in this fake-perfect alternate reality, where neither of us could fully be ourselves, I felt lonely even when I was with her.

9

Late in 1941, Nazi authorities began deporting Jews from Bohemia and Moravia, and transport trains full of the exiled came through Leipzig's central station. As the trains arrived more frequently and our neighbors began to receive notices to report for deportation, my parents and the Schlosses should have set aside their quarrels and grown closer, but they never truly reconciled.

One by one, the flats in the *Judenhaus* emptied. No new families arrived to take their places, and our footsteps echoed in the empty halls. In September 1943, my father's position on the *Judenrat* was no longer enough to keep us from being deported. We received six pink slips giving us three days' notice to report to the Leipzig train station. We were allowed to bring one suitcase each weighing fewer than fifty kilograms. As we left our flat for the last time, Mira carried her suitcase in one hand and her violin case in the other.

Crowds thronged the Leipzig station. To my surprise, other Jews supervised us while we waited to board the transport train. I whispered to my father, "How can our neighbors help the Nazis send us away?"

He would not meet my eye as he replied. "Someone must keep order at the platform. Members of the *Judenrat* have taken turns at this duty since the deportations began."

"Have you done such a thing, Vati?"

He gripped my arm. "Yes, because I had no choice, Peter. The Nazis do not tell us where the transports go. It is possible our situation wherever we're going will not be so bad."

"Do you believe so?"

"I must. How else can I stand it?"

We waited at the station for a day and a half. I slept that night with my head pillowed on my mother's lap, her coat over me. There was no food or water, and we were all hungry and thirsty by the time the transport train arrived. But otherwise, the *Judenrat* staff treated us humanely. I believed that my father, sensitive to people's fears, would also have tried to set everyone at ease when he supervised departures.

German guards herded us outside to the platform and onto the waiting train. I heard someone behind me in the crowd murmur, "They say we're going to a Jewish settlement—a resort town."

But the trains didn't look like anything that would bring us to a resort. The guards ordered us into boxcars without seats, toilets, or windows, and we were crammed in so tightly we could not sit down. The journey took more than a day. Later, I learned that the distance was fewer than two hundred kilometers—a two-hour trip by car—and to this day, I wonder why it took so long.

By the time we arrived, my mouth felt furry and my tongue stuck to my palate. I craved water, but I was no longer hungry. The stink of waste from the overflowing buckets we'd had to use as toilets clung to my nostrils, and the thought of food turned my stomach.

Shouting and confusion met us when the doors slid open at the station. The guards pulled us from the cars, not caring that our muscles were stiff and sore from standing and absorbing the jolting and swaying of the cars. Many of the adults stumbled, fell, and lost their grip on their luggage. Numb with fatigue and disoriented from emerging from the dark railway car into the sunlight, I tried to stay with my family as I was jostled by the crowd.

In front of us, a man stopped to relieve himself at the side of the road. A guard hit the man with his rifle butt and kicked him when he fell to the ground. Then he shouted at the rest of us. "Everyone move! Get going! *Schnell!*"

My father held my mother under the elbow as they shepherded me ahead of them. I stayed right behind Mira, who was stumbling along after her parents. Her mother, who had believed the rumor that we were going to some kind of resort where we'd wait out the rest of the war, kept looking around, dazed. She seemed to have forgotten she'd vowed never to let Mira out of her sight again.

A guard shoved in between us and tried to take Mira's violin, but she clutched it against her chest.

"No." Her voice was just above a whisper.

I didn't know if the guard heard her, but her body language was clear enough.

The guard raised his rifle to strike her, but Mr. Schloss, my father, and I quickly closed ranks to shield her. A second guard stepped in and pushed the raised rifle aside.

"What do you think the little girl has in there? A Tommy gun? This is Chicago and she is Al Capone, *ja*? *Dummkopf.*"

He turned a fierce glare on us. "Go on! March. Don't push your luck."

My stomach rumbled as we walked the four kilometers from the train station at Bohušovice nad Ohří. Our destination was Terezín, or Theresienstadt, as they called it in German, a transit camp and sorting station. There they separated the men from the women and assigned us to barracks within the walled fortress.

The Nazis had encouraged us to bring money and valuables, which they were all too glad to confiscate upon our arrival. Mira saved her locket by hiding it inside the secret pocket in the hem of her coat sleeve.

In the men's barracks, there was just enough room for our one suitcase apiece. We were to sleep on bare wooden bunks set into the walls, three tiers high. At least six men slept in each ten-foot-long bunk. My father's and Mr. Schloss's feet hung over the edge when they lay down.

In our first weeks at Theresienstadt, I learned that the camp commandant was strict about hygiene, but not so concerned with whether we had enough to eat. We were not guests. We were prisoners.

Our parents received work assignments—our fathers, to do manual labor, and our mothers, to tend to the elderly members of the community. For the first time in over a year, Mira and I spent time together without one of them looking over our shoulders. I think Mira was happier than she had been since before we came to the *Judenhaus*, because within the fortress walls, she found solace. The many artists and musicians there nurtured her spirit and her talent, and she soon found an excellent violin instructor among our fellow inmates. Out from under her mother's thumb, her confidence grew, and she became too headstrong for her own good. Though men and women prisoners were not supposed to mingle, she sometimes took my hand when I walked her home from her lessons. I, of course, could find no fault with her.

She and I attended informal school a few hours a day, and while she was at her music lessons, I began my spiritual journey. For the first time in my life, people who understood how to cling to their faith and their identity even in our troubled situation surrounded me. Searching for a glimmer of hope in our situation, I decided it was time I knew more about the Jewish faith. I studied the Torah and learned to pray.

Both our fathers sought a seat on the *Judenrat* at Theresienstadt. When my father won the election and Mira's did not, the tension and unease that had festered while we all lived together caused both Mr. and Mrs. Schloss's jealousy to flare into open animosity.

Though I couldn't recall the last time I'd thought about our arrival at Theresienstadt, that morning when I woke up in my Weequahic apartment, memories lingered until the walls seemed to close in on me. When I headed out to get some air, I went to Benny's. He was busy with a customer.

The bell on the door jingled when I was in the back of the store, and I ducked behind the freezer case again, fearing those punks had come back. After a minute, Benny called, "You okay, Pete?"

I picked up a carton of ice cream on my way to the counter, though I didn't really need it. "All this thinking, it is driving me *meshuggeneh*—crazy."

"Are you still that upset about the robbery?"

"It is not so much the robbery, but I am thinking it has made me to remember other things that are not so pleasant."

"Could be. I'm really sorry you're having a hard time."

"Yes, it is coming back to me all the time now. The Nazis are telling us there is nothing to fear—as long as we follow their rules. Work will make us free. But this was lies. There is always something to fear. Always. The robbery is making me think of this, right?"

"You're still having dreams?"

"These dreams, they are so real, but at the same time I am knowing I am dreaming. It is making me remember the real things that I would be liking to forget."

"It sounds like you have post-traumatic stress. If you had it from long ago, the robbery could have triggered it. That happens a lot to people in the military."

Benny was wearing an olive drab army jacket with his last name, 'Martinez', printed on the left chest pocket.

"Were you being a soldier, Benny?"

"No. This belonged to my *abuelo*. After the robbery, I got to thinking about how he must have felt when he was in combat and all the stuff he must've seen. I was a little nervous about coming back to work. Wearing his jacket gives me courage."

"When I was being a boy, I am never thinking about soldiers having fear. They are the ones with the power over us, right? But now I understand that the guards in the camps, they were bullies—cowards. Did you know when they are hearing the Allies knocking on the door, they are running off fast. We prisoners are thinking the Russians who liberated us are heroes. They are never seeming scared. Sad, horrified by what they are finding, yes. But not scared."

Benny nodded. "People show fear different ways. Some guys I know push back when they're scared, and it makes them reckless. Channeling fear and using it when you're scared can make you a hero, but it can also get you killed."

"Were you having fear during the robbery?"

"Plenty! Valeria and Benito, and you, somewhere in the back—all flashed through my mind in less than a second." He was silent for a moment. "*Abuelo*, he fought in Vietnam—two tours. *Abuela* told me he always hated the Fourth of July because of the noise from the firecrackers. You know, like how they have those compression shirts for dogs?"

"Huh?"

"They like, hug the dog, make them feel safe when they're frightened of loud noises."

"No kidding? What will they come up with next?"

"I wish they'd had something like that for *Abuelo*. My dad told me that when he was a kid, he learned not to sneak up on his father, not to make sudden moves or loud noises. My dad said *Abuelo* wasn't like that before the war, and no one ever did anything to help him. Now they got shirts to calm down dogs with anxiety. Don't seem right."

"No, it is not. Every war is leaving a lot of broken people behind."

"*Abuelo* blew his brains out the night after my youngest aunt graduated high school. Guess he figured his kids were all grown up and able to take care of themselves. His memories must've haunted him until he couldn't take it anymore. Back then, they never got veterans the psychological care they needed."

That I understood. "It was same for us who were being in the camps. No one was knowing how to deal with us. The soldiers, the Red Cross, the aid societies, they cannot be understanding what we'd experienced. They gave us medical care. But counseling? Talking about my feelings? Nah. It was enough to be surviving, right? We are just trying to put it behind."

"Pete, how long have we been friends?"

"I am thinking since you start working here, before you are buying the business. You were stock boy, right?"

"Yeah. In all that time, you've never talked about your past. It's not good to keep what's troubling you bottled up."

"Bottled up was how I am surviving. I am learning not to call attention to myself. The Nazis during the war are taking away so many things. Home. Family. Education. Careers. Freedom."

"That's what I mean. This is heavy stuff and you've been carrying it alone. Have you got another friend—someone from way back, maybe? A better friend than me you can open up to?"

"It is not good to be talking about it. I am making peace long ago and am putting it out of mind. What is the good of rehashing?" I was lying and he knew it.

He put my ice cream in one of those paper bags that help keep frozen foods cold. "I think my *abuelo* felt the way you do—but the memories he kept inside ate away at him until they destroyed him. I don't want to live like that, and I'd hate for you to let your memories keep you from living."

"What is keeping me from living? *Oy vey*, I been living so long I am not stopping. Fit as a fiddle." As I walked out of the shop, I looked back. "If I was going to be talking about this, I am doing it seventy years ago. Not now."

At home, I scooped myself a bowl of ice cream. I didn't want to think about what happened after Mira disappeared, but I couldn't stop obsessing about the past. At the moment of my death, if my life passed before my eyes, I wouldn't want to see it all again.

10

The five hundred Danish Jews that arrived at Theresienstadt in late 1943 caused a stir in the camp. We were not allowed access to radios or newspapers, and as 1943 passed into 1944, transfers who came through Theresienstadt from other camps had whispered rumors that all the Danish Jews had escaped the Nazis and made their exodus to neutral Sweden. We'd also heard rumors that Germany was losing the war, but we did not know whether to believe it.

Though the new arrivals had not managed to flee to safety, their homeland did not forget them. The deposed Danish government inquired after them and sent them care packages. This made me resent my home country even more.

The Nazis called Theresienstadt a Jewish Residential District. It was touted as a resort town, good for families, and also a place where the elderly would receive excellent care. My family and Mira's had arrived nearly a year before the camp fell under the scrutiny of the International Red Cross.

Children were considered an inconvenient but necessary part of the charade, but as there were no schools for us, some of the adults who had been teachers and professors took turns giving us our lessons when they were not at their work assignments.

My father pulled strings to get me a job fetching tools and sweeping up at the box factory. Before I went to work the first day, he took me aside. "You must work hard, Peter, but not so hard that you draw attention to yourself."

"Yes, Vati."

"Useful hands are less likely to be sent away. Do not speak unless you are spoken to. Do not smile or laugh."

I heeded his words. A few months later, I helped clear the factory away to make room for a marquis tent on the same site and assisted a crew of carpenters who were refurbishing a café in the town. Down the block, another crew repaired and painted fences, and still more workers cleared away years' worth of garbage generated by too many people crowded into inadequate housing.

I wasn't supposed to know why we were doing these things. Again, my father spoke to me in confidence and treated me like an adult. "A delegation is coming to inspect Theresienstadt on behalf of the Danish government, to make sure their citizens are not being mistreated."

"We will be lying if we make it look like everything is fine here."

"Yes, we will. But the Nazis believe they must do this to save face. So you must continue to behave as I asked you."

I'd forgotten what it felt like to be treated well and wondered how we would fool anyone into thinking we were happy to be living at Theresienstadt. But once the *Verschönerung* beautification project was in full swing, our prison came to resemble a town, and it seemed that the deception might work.

The camp commandant designated the community hall as a school and ordered a playground built on a square where, just a few weeks before, we had been forbidden to tread. We had never had a real football to play with—just one made of rags tied together. But a shipment of new balls arrived ahead of the delegation, to be used in the scheduled exhibition matches.

The camp commander appointed one of the men from the *Judenrat* to act as mayor, and outfitted a troop of prisoners with uniforms so they could pretend to be the Jewish police force. We were supposed to be self-governing in Theresienstadt.

A commissary sprouted overnight in an empty storefront. With newly issued camp money in hand, the women shopped for used clothing and sundries.

When truckloads of flowers and shrubs arrived, groups of women and girls went out armed with trowels to plant them. Others wielded paintbrushes and brooms. Soon even vacant storefronts resembled thriving businesses, with curtains hung in the windows so our visitors would not see through the guise.

About a week before the camp beautification project was complete, my father pulled me aside outside the barracks. "They're bringing in a camera crew to shoot newsreel footage and a documentary. When they arrive, I want you to stay away from them and the filming. Take care not to appear on camera. Don't act interested in what's going on."

"Of course, Vati." I would have liked very much to watch the film crew at work, but I obeyed him.

Just before the delegation arrived, we were briefed on what to do and how to act. We were to work together to keep up the charade, so we went about our business and tried to look happy. One afternoon, the whole camp sat outside in the sunshine to watch a football match. I was sure the delegation noticed that all the players had been shaved bald. Did they not wonder why?

Other men gave demonstrations of the skilled trades set up in the shops in town, but no matter what lies the Nazis told our guests, we did not live here as free people. No one paid us. We labored under the threat of execution.

A swing band—comprised of Jewish musicians, of course—played in the new café every evening of the delegation's visit.

The camp commander ordered that children's rations be increased, but even the littlest ones understood enough to say, while members of the delegation were within hearing, that their tummies were too full to eat any more bread and butter. When the children sang and gave recitations, their performances helped convince the delegation they were not being mistreated. Although they probably thought children were truthful, often to a fault, at Theresienstadt, even the littlest children were taught to lie. Outsiders would not understand, for how could they conceive of the horrible things we children had witnessed since we had first been taken from our homes?

I was tired of the lies. I wished to tell our visitors how the Nazis regularly forced the men who sat on the Jewish Council, like my father, to decide which of us would be transported to other camps. We heard rumors that prisoners were treated far more harshly at the camps in the east. I worried that the strain of making decisions that sealed the fates of others would cause my father to suffer a nervous collapse.

My father was far from the only one in anguish. Now that I was working with a crew of young men, I heard the kinds of rumors that had not reached my ears in the schoolroom. Some older girls and women were being forced into sexual relationships with guards. I was now old enough to understand why the men with sisters and wives in camp despaired over their inability to protect their loved ones.

Relationships between Aryans and Jews violated the Nuremburg Laws against mixing the races, but the officers who sought favors from prisoners did not care. Some female prisoners granted favors for food or protection. Others did it for fear of reprisal against themselves or their families if they did not.

Though we lived in separate barracks, Vati and I spent as much time with Mutti as possible and took our evening meal together in the cafeteria. Sometimes the Schlosses joined us.

The adults always looked tired and worried, but one evening when it was just me and my parents at dinner, my mother leaned close to my father and whispered, "Sylvia's afraid to come out of the barracks. She says she will not work tomorrow. Samuel, is there any way you can intervene?"

He shook his head. "It would do more harm than good to step in."

Tears welled up in her eyes. "I wish this was happening to almost anyone else. I fear for her sanity whether she gives in to him or not." My mother picked at her watery soup and stale bread and sipped a little of the hot beverage that passed for coffee. Then she pushed her plate over to me and left.

I took a bite of the bread before I asked, "Vati, what's the matter?"

"I tell you so you'll understand, but you are not to repeat it, yes, Peter?"

"Of course, Vati."

"Mrs. Schloss, she is a pretty lady, yes? One guard noticed how pretty she is, and he, well—he wants her to visit him and keep company with him alone."

I could not tell him I'd already heard about that kind of thing happening. "But she's married. What about Mr. Schloss?"

He sighed. "That does not matter to the guard, who expects her to obey. Of course, this makes Mrs. Schloss very nervous and sad because she did not ask for that kind of attention. And you are right, it is not proper for a married lady to keep company with another man. But we don't have choices here. We have no laws to protect us. No matter how unpleasant, we must choose to either do as they tell us or suffer consequences."

I nodded, thinking perhaps it was better for a woman not to be pretty in such a place as this. But Mrs. Schloss couldn't help how she looked—and Mira resembled her. Mira was nearly sixteen. Had the guards already begun to notice her? How would I protect her when grown men were unable to protect their wives?

The next afternoon, both my parents were waiting for me when I returned to the men's barracks. My father had seen Mr. Schloss's name on the latest transport list. They had sent him farther east, though to where, Vati did not know.

Panic seized my chest. My breath came in gasps until my vision blurred, and I feared I would pass out. When I could speak, I choked out, "What about Mira? Is she all right?"

My mother wiped away tears as she answered. "She and Mrs. Schloss are devastated. What else would they be?"

I broke away and ran to the women's barracks. Even though men were not allowed inside, boys my age often visited their mothers. I found Mira and Mrs. Schloss on their pallet on the floor. Mrs. Schloss wept and clung to Mira while a small group of women clustered around them.

One woman said, "Sylvia, you must compose yourself. If you don't report to work, you won't get your ration. Avram would want you to be strong, for Mira's sake."

Mrs. Schloss wiped her eyes and gulped. She said to Mira, "From now on, you and I must go everywhere together. You'll come to work with me. I cannot have you leave my sight."

Mira stifled a sob. "But what about my lessons? What about the concert?"

"No more lessons. You attract too much attention to yourself, carrying that violin around."

I opened my mouth to protest, but then I remembered my father had told me about Mrs. Schloss's problem with the guard in confidence. I wondered if the guard had put Mr. Schloss on the transport list. If Mrs. Schloss kept Mira too close, the guard could not fail to notice her. Would he want Mira more than Mrs. Schloss? No matter what, Mrs. Schloss's plan to keep Mira close to her was a bad one.

As I racked my brain for a better solution, Mira sat up, brushed back a lock of Mrs. Schloss's hair, and kissed her cheek. "Mutti, listen to me. We can't help Vati now. As long as I have music, I am not *Untermensch*. I will not quit my lessons. I will not let them dehumanize me, Mutti. This is how I choose to live."

I wanted to hide Mira away and keep her safe. But she had already made her choice.

When I was not needed on the construction crew, I worked a few hours a day as a messenger boy, carrying documents and communiques from one office in the camp to another. When I passed the kitchens, I sometimes stole part of a potato or a crust of bread that had been thrown in the trash.

The afternoon of the concert, I had found a piece of bread that was just a tiny bit moldy, and I looked forward to sharing my good fortune with Mira when I walked her home from her violin lesson. As I waited outside, the strains of music that came forth from the practice room's open window mingled with the shouts of the children on the new playground. If I'd closed my eyes, I could have been outside any school in the world.

Mira had practiced hard, and she was the only young person in the camp selected to play in the adult orchestra for the Red Cross delegation's visit. While she was excited, I dreaded the thought of her being on display before the camp officials. I didn't want them to watch as her fingers danced across the strings. I cast a sidelong glance at her. Her hair, which had once shone like the varnished wood of her violin, looked brittle and dull, but she was still pretty enough to attract attention.

When I produced the bread and broke it in two, she took her half and we ate quickly, before someone saw us. She swung her violin case just a little as we walked, to rid herself of her nervousness. "Finally, I will play in a real orchestra."

"But aren't you afraid to play for them?"

"No. I'll do my best and prove that I'm just as good as any of the German violinists. Maybe even better."

As we turned the corner, we passed a young guard. He winked and spoke under his breath, "*Guten Tag*, Mira."

To my horror, she smiled in return.

I whispered, "How does he know your name?" We were known only by our numbers in the camp. I took her arm and kept walking, not letting her slow down, but the guard turned and followed us.

He was right behind us when he spoke again, a little louder. "Maybe I'll come see you later when your brother isn't around."

My anger and my jealousy flared—at both of them. When the guard had turned a corner and was out of earshot, I turned on Mira. "Why do you look at him and acknowledge him when he speaks to you? You know he's only after one thing."

She tossed her head. "You sound just like my mother. Having a guard who thinks well of me is a good thing. Someday we might need a favor."

"But do you know what you must first do to deserve a favor?"

Her face hardened. "Yes. Do you?"

"You don't have a father to look out for you right now."

"I don't need anyone to look out for me. I can take care of myself."

I didn't answer.

In front of her barracks, she glanced around to make sure we were alone before reaching into her pocket and handing me something wrapped in a scrap of cloth. She whispered, "Don't look at it here."

"What is it?" I quickly stuffed the tiny package into my own pocket.

"The locket Vati gave me. It's the only thing I have left of him now. I always wore it for recitals, but this time"—tears brimmed in her eyes— "I want you to hold on to it for me. Please—for luck."

"You should keep it." I shoved my hand back into my pocket and pulled out the locket, wishing I could hang it around her neck where it belonged. When she remained silent, my stomach twisted with dread. "I have nothing to give you in return—but I have a secret." Lifting her chin, I fixed her with my most earnest gaze. "I was going to ask you to marry me someday when we were old enough, but I want to ask you now. Will you, Mira?"

"Yes." She smiled brightly and a tear threatened to fall. "I will marry no one but you, Peter."

I pulled her around the corner into the shadow of her barracks and she stretched up on tiptoe to kiss me. As we clung together, that kiss sealed my fate. She was the only one I would ever love. "We . . . we should have a plan in case we ever get separated—all right?"

"Yes." She glanced around, and her voice faltered as she echoed, "Separated."

"As soon as you can, go home. I'll meet you there at our apple tree."

When she nodded, a single tear slipped down her cheek. "I promise. I have to go get ready now. I'll look for you in the audience."

"I'll be front and center . . . " I put the cloth-wrapped necklace back in my pocket and squeezed her hand, " . . . for all your performances."

She kissed me again and pressed her forehead against mine. "Everything will be all right. We just have to stand it until we can go home." At the door, she looked back. "*Wir sehen uns dann,* Peter. See you then."

But the orchestra performed that evening without Mira. No one knew where she was or what had happened to her. I was numb with shock, blaming myself for not having stayed with her until she was safely in her seat on the stage.

The delegation, satisfied, left the following day to report their findings to the Danish authorities in exile. With them went any restraint our captors had shown.

Frantic to learn what had become of Mira, I went to the office that made up the transport lists.

The clerk was a young woman who lived in Mira's barracks, and we had sometimes spoken during our free time. Now she looked at me with sympathy. "One of the supervisors is late turning in his report. I will go see if it is ready to be sent out. Just a moment, please." She stood, and with a backward glance, left her desk unattended.

As soon as she was out of sight, I craned my neck to look at the papers on her desk, hoping to see the recent lists. If Mira had been sent to another camp, I meant to volunteer to be sent there, too. When the clerk did not return, I moved around to the side of the desk and lifted the top page on a clipboard.

"Here—what are you doing?" It was the office supervisor.

I put my hands behind my back. "Nothing."

He struck me across the face and dragged me out of the office into the street. He shoved me so hard I went sprawling, and then he shouted for a guard. When I heard running feet, I curled myself into a ball and covered my head, expecting to be shot.

Instead I heard a familiar voice. "Please. What has happened here?" It was my father.

I uncovered my head and saw him standing between me and an armed guard, his hands raised in a gesture of surrender that nonetheless held the guard at bay.

The office supervisor spoke. "He was riffling through private documents."

My father gave me one stricken glance before addressing the office supervisor. "I am certain he meant no harm. This is my son. My only son."

The supervisor gazed down at me as though he couldn't have cared less. "Then he should know better."

"And he does. He will not do such a thing again. Will you, Peter?"

"No, Vati."

The office supervisor nodded to the guard. "He will join that work crew." He pointed to a group of men who were headed past.

My father drew a shuddering breath. "Thank you, sir. I was on my way here to submit these reports." He handed over a sealed folder, and the office supervisor accepted it with a nod and went back inside.

The guard hauled me to my feet and hustled me to the end of the line. This was a much rougher crew than the carpenters I'd been with during the *Verschönerung*. Once we arrived in the field where we were to work, I understood that this detail was meant as punishment. Our job was to move rocks from one side of a field to the other. Then when we were done, we moved them back again.

I had no gloves, and the rocks were sharp and heavy. I came home the first night barely able to walk from exhaustion, my hands raw and bleeding. My mother bathed my wounds and wrapped them well, but there was not enough time for them to heal before I had to report for work the next day.

Gone was the freedom I'd enjoyed as a messenger boy. There was no time to attend school. There was only a pile of rocks.

In the evenings, I was so weary I could barely keep my eyes open, but my parents insisted I go to the dining hall. At dinner, my mother spoon-fed me my rations while she and my father caught me up on the happenings in the camp.

Mrs. Schloss, now the last member of her family at Theresienstadt, refused to eat and would not leave her bunk for roll call, unless my mother forced her to come out and literally held her up in the line.

Within days of the delegation's departure, the camp commandant sent the crews who had worked on the *Verschönerung*, as well as the musicians and everyone who had appeared in the propaganda film, away on transports.

Except me—I was busy moving rocks and they overlooked me.

This, for Mrs. Schloss, was the final straw. Leaning on the arm of another woman from the barracks, she moved slowly up to our table in the dining hall, a ragged shawl clutched around her shoulders and a shaking finger pointed at my father.

"You." Her mouth twisted in anger. "You had Avram sent away, and now Mira, to protect your precious Peter." Her gaze came to rest upon me where I sat, my hands swathed in bloody bandages. "He is the one whose name was on the list—but he is still here."

My father rose to his feet. "Sylvia, this is not true. I had nothing to do with what happened to Avram and Mira. You must believe me. I hope you will come to see that your accusation is baseless."

My mother stood beside him. "Sylvia, you've let your grief cloud your reason. You must see that Samuel has done nothing to hurt you. We grieve for the loss of your family, just as you do."

But Mrs. Schloss only sniffed. She raised two fingers to her lips like she used to when taking a drag on a cigarette, and spit three times through her fingers in my parents' direction to ward off the evil eye. Then she slowly turned and walked away.

Everyone at the tables near us had watched Mrs. Schloss's accusation and gesture of contempt in silence. One by one, they turned their backs on us. To this day, I'm not sure if it was Mrs. Schloss's false accusation or my carelessness in reading prisoner lists that ultimately sealed our fate.

The Nazis began emptying Terezín in late September 1944, and in October, my father, mother, and I were packed into a train car with just the clothes on our backs. I tried to stay close to my parents. Once we were underway, several men pushed through the crowd and surrounded my father, separating him from my mother and me. "Hey!" I shouted and tried to wedge myself between them to stay with Vati, while holding on to Mutti's hand. But other men prevented us from following. As the crowd swallowed him, Vati called back to us, "Don't worry. Everything is all right."

When we arrived, my father was nowhere in sight. My mother clutched my arm until guards started shoving the women into one line and the men into another. As we were ripped apart, Mutti's fingers clawed the air trying to hold on to my hand, her eyes wide with terror. "Peter!"

There was no time to say goodbye.

I never saw either of my parents again.

One of the Czechs who remembered me from my work at the construction site caught my arm as I was swept along in the crowd and pulled me into the line with the young men chosen for slave labor. I emerged with my prisoner number tattooed on my arm, and the guards marched us to barracks. This place was Birkenau, a sub-camp of Auschwitz.

Without my family or Mira, I had nothing to cling to. The prayers I had learned at Theresienstadt had no meaning. Though I searched for God, at Birkenau, he was nowhere to be found.

The only thing I had to remind me of my former life was Mira's locket, buttoned into the secret pocket on the inside of my pants leg. Three months later, when the Russians liberated the camp, I carried it out with me, just as I carried the hope that I would find Mira in the post-war chaos.

11

The Yankees game had just gone into extra innings when someone pounded on my door. Heart in my throat, I looked out
the peephole. It was Vashon, my neighbor from across the hall.
When I opened the door, he handed me my keys.

"Here, sir. You left these in the lock."

I nodded as I pocketed them. "Thank you. I am such a *forgetsik*
these days."

"You need to be careful about things like that."

"Yes, I will be." I replaced the chain and turned the deadbolt. When
the ball game ended, I climbed into bed and took deep, slow breaths.
I had to relax if I was going to get back into the dream. Even though
these nights with Mira made me feel lonely in a new way and left
me no closer to resolving the questions that had plagued me most of
my life, it was still better to be with her than to be here, where I was
truly alone.

I opened my eyes and found myself on the sofa in Mira's parents' sitting room. Late afternoon sunlight slanted in through the windows.

"Don't you remember?" Mira was asking, as she turned the crank
on the phonograph.

She and I must have been in the middle of a conversation, but about what? I shrugged. "Yeah?"

"Well, get up, then." She held out her hand.

I thought fast. "No, you go ahead."

She set the needle on the spinning record and the tinny strains of an old jazz recording filled the room. "Don't tell me you can't remember our mothers doing the Charleston?" As she kicked, shimmied, and twisted, a vision of our mothers when they were about the same age of Mira and me now formed in my mind. Before stress and worry caused the discord between them, they had danced on that very carpet, laughing as they mimicked the American dance craze they'd seen in the movies.

"Come on, Peter, you have to try!"

I shook my head. "You're too good for me."

"Didn't you ever learn to dance properly?" She lifted the needle and put on a different record— "Lustig ist das Zigeunerleben"—a waltz. This time when she held out her hand, an excuse about my knees not being what they used to be nearly escaped my lips.

She tilted her head to the side and quirked an eyebrow, waiting expectantly. Hoping I'd catch on to dancing as quickly as I'd learned to play the piano, I faced her and let her guide my right hand to her waist. She put her left hand on my shoulder and then clasped my left hand and raised it to the proper position out to the side. "Don't worry. There's nothing to it. Just let yourself move to the music." As we swayed, she nestled closer, and my hand slid from the curve of her waist around to her back. She smiled up at me. "See, it's easy once you have the rhythm. Now for lesson two: the box step."

Soon my feet and body moved through the pattern with ease. We box stepped around the living room. Just as I was getting comfortable enough to stop mouthing, "back-side-together, front-side-together," she lifted our arms up and added a simple turn. When the record ended, we started it over. By the third time through the song, I was leading, reveling in the feeling of being in control while I held her in my arms.

"Peter, I don't know why you were worrying. You're a lovely dancer."

I pulled her closer. "I have a lovely teacher."

When the song ended, neither of us made a move to change the record. I closed my eyes. Her hair smelled like flowers. As I held her, I ceased to exist in the moment, and I sighed as both longing and loss threatened to overwhelm me. When she sensed my pensive mood, she stepped back and turned under my upraised arm, and then spun in until I was holding her close again. "Lesson three: the jitterbug. It's impossible to be sad when you're dancing the jitterbug."

Mira never seemed to tire of dancing, and finally, I collapsed on the sofa, protesting, "That's enough for now. I'm starving."

She relented. "I could eat. Let's go out."

We strolled through the silent city in search of the *gasthaus* we remembered for its *Wiener schnitzel*. When we arrived, the door was ajar, and in a corner booth, two plates of *schnitzel*, heaps of golden fried potatoes, and two mugs of beer were ready and waiting.

It was just getting dark when we left the pub, and streetlamps flickered on as we passed. A few blocks away, the movie house, its marquee bordered with bright neon tubing and lit by hundreds of bulbs, was like a beacon. I asked, "Fancy a movie?"

She giggled. "Sure. I wonder what's playing?"

There was no title on the marquee. "I guess it's a surprise." Inside, the lobby smelled of fresh popcorn. "Do you want some?"

"I know we just ate, but it wouldn't be a movie without popcorn. Let's share a bag."

I scooped the popcorn while she opened soda bottles.

In the theater, thick carpet muffled our footsteps as we headed down one of the aisles. Crystal chandeliers and sconces gave off enough light for me to see and admire the flocked wallpaper and the fringed velvet drapes that framed the screen. I started toward the middle of the theater, but Mira hesitated. "Let's sit in the back row. I never liked the feeling that someone could come in behind me." We settled into seats in the center of the back row and waited, but nothing happened.

She took a handful of popcorn. "When does the newsreel start?"

I turned around and peered up at the projection booth's window. "Guess I'd better go look."

Narrow stairs led to the projection booth, where I found a film reel in its metal can. I flipped a switch on the side of the machine, and through the window in the booth, I saw a huge rectangle of light appear on the screen below. It took a minute to figure out how to thread the projector, but as soon as I got it humming, I hurried back downstairs to Mira.

"What's the feature?"

"I didn't notice. Does it matter?"

"Honestly, no. Not at all."

I put my arm around her, and she snuggled against my shoulder as the title credits for *Somewhere I'll Find You*, starring Clark Gable and Lana Turner, emerged and the music swelled. German subtitles appeared at the bottom of the screen.

Even after living in America for most of my life, I often struggled to find the right words when I spoke English. But I'd had no trouble expressing myself when I talked to Mira.

When I saw the German subtitles, it all made sense. In this ongoing dream, I'd been thinking and speaking in German—the language we'd learned first when we were children.

I didn't need the subtitles, as I understood English perfectly well, so I turned to look at Mira. As our eyes met, a blazing smile swept across her face. She set the popcorn aside, and when she kissed me, everything but her faded into the background. I couldn't tell you anything that happened in the film, but when the lights came up, kissing had left her lips swollen and her hair mussed. She was so beautiful that even Lana Turner couldn't hold a candle to her.

We held hands as we went out through the lobby, where a flicker of movement down the hall past the projection booth caught my eye. By the time I got a proper look, there was nothing there. Believing I'd imagined it, I kept walking, but as I held the door open for Mira, I heard the click of a latch, like a door closing, somewhere in the recesses of the theater. The skin on the back of my neck prickled. Had someone been in there with us? Mira seemed not to notice anything, so I didn't mention it and told myself there was nothing real in this dream except me. There was no reason to worry.

But on the walk home, I couldn't shake the sensation that I was being watched. We were about a block away from the theater when the lights on the marquee went out, plunging the street behind us into deep shadow. I put my arm around her, glancing behind us as I picked up the pace. Our footfalls on the cobblestone street were the only sound, but my ears strained to hear more.

The warm night air was redolent with lilac—a perfect romantic end to our evening—but still I shivered. I didn't want to ruin the mood, nor did I want to go back and investigate, so I babbled to break the ominous silence. "This was great. One of our favorite meals at one of our favorite places, plus popcorn and a private film screening. Being here is—"

She touched her fingers to my lips. "Don't say it. Don't even think it."

"I was just going to say it's too good to be true. I could look at you all night."

She gave me a sidelong glance. "Then come home with me. Stay the night." She stopped and put her arms around my neck, pressing the length of her body against mine.

There was a hiss and a pop, like fireworks, and the streetlamp nearest us exploded in a shower of sparks. The flash of light burned into my retinas, and as I tried to blink away the afterimage, I saw a man's shadowy outline. By the time I rubbed my eyes and looked again, he'd disappeared. But I knew who it was.

It was me—the old me. Though he had pined for Mira all his life, it was I, not he, who belonged with this youthful version of her. In this place, Old Peter was an interloper.

My skin prickled again. He and I should not both be here.

12

When we reached Mira's house, I locked us in, and as I turned away from the door, she reached up to brush a lock of hair off my forehead. Her fingers trailed down my jawline, and my shiver jump-started my heart.

"You don't have to sleep on the couch." She drew me toward the stairs and stood one step above me, so we were the same height. She leaned in, and just like that, we were back to what we were doing at the movies. "Come upstairs, Peter. Nothing bad comes from showing someone you care about them."

I cradled her face in my hands and kissed her closed eyelids. This time, when our lips met, she drew me into the depths of the kiss, her tongue a feather-light touch that set the nerves on the roof of my mouth tingling.

Then I made the mistake of opening my eyes. Over her shoulder, Old Peter was looking in the sitting-room window, hands cupped around his face. Talk about ruining the moment.

She put a finger on my chin to bring my attention back to her. "You are literally the last man on Earth. You win by default. Don't worry. Don't think."

Mind reeling, I realized I was not the last man on Earth—I was actually the last two. My eyes darted to the window again, but my older self was gone. "If I was the last man on Earth and there were a million girls to choose from, I wouldn't give the other nine-hundred-ninety-nine-thousand-nine-hundred-and-ninety-nine a second look. It's always been you I cared about." I took a step back and held both her hands in mine. "But I wouldn't pressure you if you weren't ready."

Tears sprang into her eyes and she looked at me for a long moment before she spoke. "No, you wouldn't. That's what makes you—you." She kissed me on my forehead. "You win. *Gute Nacht*, Peter."

"*Gute Nacht.*" I watched her ascend the stairs and then I hurried to the window and peered into the street, but no one was there. I shut the blinds, but could I shut out any unwanted visitors? I had entered this world through abnormal, supernatural means, and I assumed Mira had, too. Did the laws of physics apply here, or could we walk through walls?

I crossed the sitting room, moving at a steady pace toward the door. I focused on passing through it as if it wasn't there, but then my body connected with solid wood and I banged my forehead, hard. The resulting thud echoed in the quiet space.

"Peter? Is everything all right?"

"Yes. Fine." I rubbed the sore spot, thankful for the consistency of physics. Turning out all but one light, I stretched out on the sofa. As I listened to her going-to-bed sounds—water running, the soft click of her door closing—I felt content knowing she and I were in the same house.

Though I meant to stay awake, at least for a while, the next thing I knew I awoke to the traffic noise of Weequahic.

It seemed like I wasn't sleeping at all, yet every time I opened my eyes, whether I was at home or with Mira, I felt refreshed. It was the opposite of the insomnia that had previously plagued me. As I made breakfast and puttered around the apartment, I wondered if time passed at the same rate in the dream as here. Did it continue for her when I wasn't there, or did it pause when I was away and resume when I returned?

Missing her company, I turned on the radio to find some music, but a talk show caught my attention. The guest was a psychiatrist; the topic was how stress and trauma affected people. I knew from personal experience that stress could take a toll on a person's mental health, but I did not know trauma could invade the genes people passed to their children.

While I sat at the worktable and soldered tips back on the music box's cylinder, I wondered what kind of traits I would have passed along to my children if I'd had them. Would my children have been afraid all the time, like me, even when there was nothing to fear, or would they have been impervious to high-stress situations?

The soldering iron started to smell like it was burning. Even though it got very hot, I had never known it to smell like that. I quickly turned it off and opened the window, but the odor of burning plastic grew stronger. I sniffed the air that flowed into the room, but the smell wasn't coming from outside. I turned back toward the room and saw flames dancing from the hot plate. How could I have left it on?! I rushed across the room to unplug it, then grabbed a towel to move it off the scorched counter, but I burned my hand and the hot plate fell into the sink, where the towel ignited with a whoosh. I dodged the flames to turn on the water with my uninjured hand, and the hot plate and the fire expired in a hiss of steam and smoke.

Panting, I cradled my throbbing hand against my chest. What a *forgetsik* I was getting to be.

When I woke up on the sofa in Mira's sitting room it was morning. My hand showed no sign that I'd burned it on the hot plate. Mira poked her head out of the kitchen. "Peter? Oh, good, you're awake. Come have breakfast."

I stood and stretched before I joined her at the table, where she'd set out bread, butter, and jam. As I sat, she poured hot cocoa into mugs. "Are you always this quiet in the morning?"

"Usually." I took a sip of cocoa. "When did you get up?"

"Hours ago."

In the dream, she could be awake when I wasn't. Did that mean I was leaving her alone and vulnerable whenever I transported back to Weequahic? "Did you hear anything last night?"

"Besides you banging around? No, I slept very well." She gave me a quizzical look as she sat down across from me. "Are you worried that you snore or something?"

"No."

"Then what's bothering you? Are you afraid of me? Have I done something wrong?"

"Kissing is one thing. Talking presents its own challenges."

"Oh." Her face fell. "You don't like me. Is that it?"

"I do like you. I've always liked you. You're perfect."

She laughed. "That I am not."

"I want to get to know you: what you think, what you like, what drives you nuts. And there's so much I can't—"

She wrapped her hands around her mug. "The universe is full of questions that have no answers."

She was still talking in riddles. I couldn't tell her I wanted to get reacquainted with the real Mira, not make small talk with a facsimile.

When I didn't answer, she said, "Fine. I'll go first. Why is it considered good to respect the dead more than the living?"

"I don't know. Maybe because the dead aren't here to defend themselves." I started to get angry as I thought about it. "The living can change. They can stop doing things that hurt or disappoint us. The dead leave us stuck with the hurt and the damage. So why shouldn't we speak ill of them?"

"No one is perfect."

"You always were, to me."

"But I'm not." She looked down in her mug before she went on.

"Although maybe if we're to reconcile whatever damage people—alive or dead—have caused, we have to focus on the good things about them so we can forgive. Now you ask a question."

"All right." This was kind of like playing chess with myself. "Is the future pre-determined?"

"Like fate?"

"Yes. If something terrible happened"— I caught a warning glance from her— "could we have prevented it, or did it have to happen that way?"

"I'm going to answer that question with a question: do we have free will?"

"Of course we do. We can choose good or evil. Animals aren't evil because they can't make reasoned choices. A cat can't decide to stop hunting mice and birds and become a vegetarian."

"Fair point."

"So then why doesn't God intervene? Shouldn't He step in before the evil gets out of control?"

"Because we're not puppets. The freedom to make bad choices has been a problem since the Garden of Eden." A mischievous smile played at the corner of her lips. "Do you really think that was an accident?"

"But wait—what if the Garden of Eden was a setup? Did God mean all along for Adam and Eve to eat the apple?"

She leaned forward. "Ah, but then some outside force would still be predetermining the future. Do we only assume we have free will when we do not?"

I held up my hands in surrender. "Got it. Everything is out of our control." That was more in keeping with what I believed.

"That's not what I'm saying. Adam and Eve gained awareness. Our sense of awareness ties into our concept of passing time: that the past is fixed, and the future unknowable."

"Time runs out for everyone."

She got up and refilled her cocoa. "You have a narrow and fatalistic way of looking at things, Peter. Some people believe that everything there is, and all that ever will be, goes through cycles, percolating and recycling souls into different lives, over and over."

"One life might not be all there is?"

She laughed and glanced around. "Do you seriously have to ask that?"

Hope welled up inside me at the thought of a do-over. My spotty religious training had offered me nothing on this topic, but perhaps what I was experiencing was another chance. Maybe it was one of many chances. "But do we remember our experiences? Would you and I remember each other if we met again?"

"I don't know. Maybe deep inside. Haven't you ever met someone and, within an hour, felt as though you've known them all your life? To remember everything—especially the saddest things—might be too heavy a burden for a child to bear."

"Agreed. Okay, I've got another question."

"Go ahead."

"How do we know when something is real?"

Her face was unreadable. "What do you think?"

"In the heat of the moment, we can't rely on our senses. We're too easily fooled. But photographic evidence and sound recordings—"

"Those are just things we collect and treasure to remind us of what we think is real. Have you ever looked at a photograph and thought the people in it looked happy? You don't know what they were really thinking. We remember things in the way that serves us best. Does it matter if it's real or not?"

"Yes." I took her hand. "Mira, are you—"

"Am I what?"

I wanted to say *real*, but I couldn't. "Happy. Are you happy?"

"So happy, Peter. Aren't you?"

"Yes. I'd rather be here with you than anywhere else." When I leaned across the table to kiss her, her lips tasted like cocoa.

She stood and reached for my hand. "Come see what I found." She led me into the sitting room and brought out her family's brown leather photo album. We sat on the sofa and she opened the album across our laps. "The photographic evidence, as you say, is what keeps my memories alive."

I stared at her for a moment, expecting her to disappear. But she didn't.

"Like this one." She pointed. "We were five, almost too young to remember, but Mutti told me the story of the day we moved in so many times."

The photo was of us standing by the garden wall. "I remember it all perfectly. Your family came in a taxi. You left a sugar cube on the windowsill for the stork before we went out to play. I thought you were the most beautiful little girl in the world."

"You, my dear friend, are very biased." She smiled as she caressed my cheek, then looked back at the album. "I treasure photographs so. When I look at us together when we were children, it's as though no time has passed at all."

Her mother had arranged the photos on the black pages with little triangle-shaped holders at the corners. My gaze lingered on one of our mothers and Mr. Schloss. My father was behind the camera. Their young smiling faces only saddened me.

This was all that remained of our parents. I couldn't pretend that their lives didn't end in tragedy. Though Mira was right beside me, I felt so alone that I had to leave the room to hide my tears.

13

Of the estimated 1.3 million people deported to Auschwitz between 1940 and 1945, approximately 1.1 million died there. Auschwitz, though among the worst, was just one of around 15,000 concentration camps in occupied Europe. The idea that civilians did not learn what was happening at the concentration camps until after the war was a lie. Other world leaders knew of the camps, too—including President Roosevelt, but he claimed he did not believe the United States should intervene in the domestic affairs of another country. On the international stage, winning the war took priority over rescuing those of us being held in bondage.

When the Russians arrived to liberate Auschwitz-Birkenau on January 27, 1945, the soldiers were unprepared for what they found—a stinking slice of hell populated by living skeletons. So many of them cried when they saw us. Then they gave us little bits of chocolate and cookies, the kinds of treats we hadn't had in months or, for some of us, years. They treated the younger inmates like little brothers and sisters and gave us hugs. Their doctors administered medical treatment, and they fed us small amounts of food until we could handle more. But the Allies didn't know what to do with us—so they contained us again.

Some of the liberated who were brave enough to venture forth left the camp and began walking wherever they chose, but that was dangerous, with the war still going on. I was among a group loaded on a Red Cross train. We rode in a real passenger car with seats and windows that carried us to a displaced persons camp outside Leipzig. Relief workers set up housing for us in a school and some apartment buildings. Though I no longer feared dying at the hands of the Nazis, I was still behind barbed wire, with guards at the perimeter. Food was still inadequate, but at least we were no longer treated cruelly.

Some of the children had not been called by their names for so long, they had to be taught to respond to them, as well as to simple pleasantries like "Good morning." Together, survivors and relief workers reestablished religious services and cultural, educational, and social programs, and tried to make our daily routine resemble what we'd had before the war. Slowly, we came back to life.

Though I could have attended secular school in the DP camp, I was sixteen and I hadn't seen a book in over a year. School sounded like a waste of time, and so did the religious classes that were offered at *yeshiva*. My thirteenth birthday had come and gone without me becoming a bar mitzvah, but after what I'd been through, I had no doubt I was a man. I was too old to sit in class with little boys of ten.

My future might have taken a different course if my parents had been there to encourage me after the war. Without their guidance, I seemed as unlikely to attend university as I was to fly to the moon. I enrolled in a vocational course and learned to be a plumber, deciding it was as good a trade as any. I didn't realize I would end up being one for sixty years.

After all, I was nothing special. Thousands of other young men like me had been orphaned and displaced by the war. I saw no point in complaining or talking about what I'd been through. No one was handing out medals for living day to day.

Other survivors might have felt differently. Maybe they believed their survival and future successes would redeem the lives of their lost loved ones. But I wasn't like them. There was no fire inside me. I felt no responsibility to do great things on behalf of those who would never have the chance. All I felt was lost and alone.

In the DP camps, we were supposed to work to find a permanent home. With many of the great cities of Europe in ruins, New York and Palestine were considered the best places to build a bright future. Both were tough tickets. Though the refugee situation in Europe was dire, the United States did not increase immigration quotas above what they had been in years past, and the British restricted immigration to Palestine.

Relief organizations helped feed us, but their task was overwhelming, and food often ran short. Young people, especially, grew frustrated waiting for travel visas. The young men who weren't afraid to trade on the black market got better food, clothes, and cigarettes. They were also the ones who got the girls.

The privations and horror of the war years had hardened many of those young women, and just like the guys, they were bursting at the seams to be on their own. The boldest of them frightened me. There was nothing soft or flirty about them, and they pushed and demanded and henpecked even the men they were trying to attract.

No way was I ambitious enough to date one of those girls. Without Mira, I wasn't interested in anything, not even myself. I expended the least amount of energy and functioned at the lowest level. I wasn't even excited when my visa was approved. I couldn't remember what it felt like to have ambition or plans.

I hadn't pushed to go to America. I was so used to hiding that I couldn't draw attention to myself to ask for anything. Without the unexpected sponsor in America who came forward to claim me, I cannot imagine where I would have gone.

And then there was my promise to Mira, which I had not forgotten. When we'd agreed to meet at home at the war's end, I had imagined a joyous reunion. After just three months in Auschwitz, I saw how few survived, but still I clung to the hope that she had also lived. Every week, I read the survivor lists in the newspaper and listened to radio programs for bulletins about people searching for missing loved ones. I wrote to some of the German families in our old neighborhood hoping they'd survived the air raids and had come back home. I asked for news—especially news of Mira—but received no replies.

And was there anything to return home to? Since late 1943, the Allies had bombed Leipzig on multiple occasions, and most of the city, including the southern suburbs where we had lived, lay in ruins. Though I was only a two or three days' walk from home, I found excuses not to go. I convinced myself it was too risky to leave the safety of the DP camp, but in truth, I couldn't face my growing fear that Mira was gone forever.

I woke up in my apartment with a young man's appetite, craving a Reuben sandwich so badly that it was the only thing that would do for lunch. I remembered they made a great one at a place about ten blocks away, so I double-checked to make sure I had my wallet and headed out just before eleven.

I got turned around once or twice on the walk over, and when I arrived, I found the windows boarded over and a "For Rent" sign on the door. Maybe it was on a different block. I wandered around for a while, but there was no restaurant nearby. When I ended up back where I started, I decided they must have moved, and I had forgotten. In the pawnshop next door, I asked the guy behind the counter, "Are you knowing what has happened to the deli?"

"What deli?" The guy was no spring chicken, so he should remember.

"The one that was being next door." I pointed. "They are making a great Reuben."

The man shrugged. "I been here twenty years and there ain't never been no deli."

"You are certain?"

"I'm sure, man. That was a print shop for as long as I been here."

"Maybe I am thinking of the wrong block. Sorry to bother you."

When I left the pawnshop, I figured I'd go one or two more blocks farther before turning back. As I stepped into the street, a blaring horn made me stumble backward, and I caught my heel on the edge of the curb.

As I fell, everything seemed to happen in slow motion. My hands grabbed empty air. I had time to think about Mira, about what this fall would do to my aging body, and about where the hell that restaurant had gone to before I felt my head strike the pavement and everything went black.

14

When I opened my eyes, Mira and I were strolling through our neighborhood. She was wearing a flowered yellow dress, her hair tied back with a matching ribbon. It made me think of a song that probably hadn't been written yet, so I didn't bring it up.

"I always loved that house." She pointed at a large two-story home with half-timbered gables, and we slowed so she could bury her nose in the honeysuckle that grew near the front walk. "It seems lonely, don't you think?"

"Every house in this district but yours and mine are empty. They're all lonely."

"Which one do you like?"

"I never thought about it."

When we arrived at the trolley stop, a car was waiting. We stepped aboard and took seats, and though there was no driver present, the trolley started and rolled past the industrial district that lay between our neighborhood and the city center.

Mira asked, "Do you remember going into the city like this with our mothers?"

"Yes. I loved taking the trolley. When I was five, my dearest ambition was to be a trolley conductor."

She giggled. "A lofty goal."

"I certainly thought so at the time."

The trolley car stopped in front of the zoological garden's entrance, where the gate stood open to invite us inside.

"Do you remember going to the zoo?"

"Tell me." I remembered very well, but I wondered if she would remember something I did not. We wandered through the park, where, though it was devoid of animals, the landscaping and the flowers still made for a lovely stroll.

Mira viewed the empty cages and enclosures a bit wistfully. "Oh, once there were so many animals—the big cats and the elephants, bears, monkeys, penguins. You liked the tigers best."

"What about you?"

"I cried because the elephant looked big enough to smash through his barrier and escape. The animal kindergarten was my favorite."

"The what?"

"I can't believe you don't remember. They had a petting zoo for the baby animals. You fed one of the tiger cubs out of a bottle. We only came here together once. That was the summer they changed the laws." She was silent for a moment. "It's a gift, to experience the life our families wanted for us here. When I was young, I wanted to travel, but I didn't expect to settle down and live anywhere but here, at home."

"What about the sad times?"

"I don't remember the sad times."

"How can you not remember people holding their noses as we passed and calling us dirty Jews? They spit on us. We had to walk in the gutter."

"But none of that matters now."

I shook my head stubbornly. "That doesn't mean it didn't happen."

She was silent for a long time, as though searching for how to say what she was thinking. "But everything's perfect now. Our time together can be anything we want it to be—you can be anything you want to be. If nothing bad had happened when we were young, what would you have done with your life?"

"I don't know."

"I do! You would have become a pioneer in broadcasting."

"I was too young to know what I wanted then—except you. I always wanted to be with you."

"You had to want more than just me. If I wasn't here, would it be the worst thing in the world?"

I reached over and took her hand. "You have no idea." I was not the kind of man Mira or my parents—or I—had expected I would turn out to be.

"Peter, it's safe to say things are not always as you perceive them. You've been treating me as if I'm made of glass. You seem surprised when I react to what happened to us in a way you don't understand. Don't you believe I can think for myself?" Before I could respond she startled me with a harsh laugh. "What if this isn't your dream at all? Don't dwell on the past, Peter. In fact, don't think at all. While you're at it, please stop assuming you know what I'm thinking and let me come down off my pedestal."

I was too stunned by her outburst to answer. I was the one who was experiencing a lucid dream. I was in control—wasn't I?

As we left the zoo, I noticed two bicycles parked near the entrance that had not been there when we arrived. By now, I knew to take the hint. "Would you like to bicycle over and have lunch at the market?"

"Yes. That would be nice." If she was still frustrated with me, she didn't let on.

At Augustusplatz, in the city center, the market stalls were full of produce, textiles, and crafts, but the vendors were nowhere in sight. Mira wandered up and down the rows, basket on her arm, selecting food for a picnic lunch. Our footsteps echoed off the buildings as we crossed the cobblestone plaza to a bistro table topped by a red umbrella, where we spread our lunch and ate with a view of the Gewandhaus concert hall. That gave me an idea, and I took her hand. "You made me learn how to dance. Now I'll pick something for you to do. I think you should play a concert on a real stage."

"A concert for one?"

"Sure. Who wants to hear you play more than I do?"

At that she smiled, and as we went back to eating, I could tell she was thinking about what selections to include on the program.

On this public square, I missed the sounds of other people almost as much as I had when I'd been in the dream alone. I longed for the sight of ordinary things, like children playing, old men engrossed in a chess game, and women shopping at the stalls. Then a flicker of movement caught my eye, and I turned in time to see a curtain fall closed in a shop window. I got up so fast I knocked over my chair and dashed across the square. I could hear her calling behind me.

"Peter? What's the matter?"

There was no time to answer. Keeping my eyes trained on that window, I watched for more proof that he was here. I don't know what I was planning to do if I found him. Ask him to get lost?

The shop door rattled in its frame as I rammed my shoulder against it but did not yield. I looked around, grabbed a rock out of a flowerbed, and raised it to throw through the window beside the door.

Mira shouted my name again. Before I could decide whether to break the window or turn back to her, a gale of wind slammed me against the building so hard I saw stars. I sagged against the wall, rubbing my head. In those few moments, the sky darkened to grayish-yellow and daylight turned to dusk. Storm clouds rolled in ominously fast, and another strong gust of wind sent bistro chairs skittering across the cobblestones.

Staggering out of the shelter of the building, I held up my arm to ward off the dust and debris that swirled through the square. Mira was nowhere in sight. When I shouted her name, the force of the wind drove the words back down my throat. Our bicycles blew over with a clatter, and as lightning flashed, I spotted a glimpse of yellow on the ground, beneath a table. The rest of the square looked like an overexposed negative.

I ran to her, stepping over the scattered remains of our lunch. Her market basket blew away, and when I pulled her to her feet, the wind whipped her skirt. As we fought to stay standing, an updraft caught the umbrella on a nearby table.

"Look out!" The umbrella's pole missed her by inches as it took flight, and the table turned over with a crash. She covered her head and I bent my body over hers.

She clung to me. "I told you not to think!"

"What?" I wasn't sure I'd heard her correctly. As we ran for the shelter of the market house, the heavens opened, and rain fell as though someone had dumped it from the world's largest bucket. We were soaked by the time we reached the entrance, but when I pulled at the doors, they would not yield.

She shivered as she pushed her dripping hair off her face. "How will we make it home in this?"

I took her arm, and as we rounded the corner in search of another entrance, another gust nearly blew us off our feet. She fell against me, and I righted her and pulled her into the next doorway, but that door was also locked. "We'll have to wait it out here." We huddled beneath the canvas awning, watching as more market umbrellas and bistro chairs blew across the square, scraping over the cobblestones and crashing into buildings. Trees bent double in the wind.

As the storm raged, the awning sagged lower under the rain that pooled in it. When it reached the tipping point, cold water gushed over the sides and doused us anew. Had my attempt to come face to face with Old Peter unleashed the wrath of the storm?

I muttered, "All right. I get it. This isn't mine to control." If Mira heard me, she didn't react.

Right away the wind died down and the rain slackened. I raked back my hair. "Well that was something else, wasn't it?"

She lifted the soaked hem of her skirt and tried to wipe the rain from her face. "Yes, it was. I guess the storm ruined our lunch."

"It ruined the whole market." I looked around. The stalls, decked so prettily just a short while ago, had all blown over. The produce and handicrafts were drenched and scattered across the square. "It must have been some kind of cyclone."

She pulled at my sleeve. "Let's go."

We retrieved our bicycles, shivering in our wet clothes as we pedaled home through the puddles. We were both spattered with mud from head to toe when we arrived at her house.

Straightaway, Mira went upstairs to take a hot bath. While I waited my turn, I shed my wet shirt and wrapped a blanket around my shoulders. Outside, where storm clouds still threatened, one house on the next street was ablaze with light.

"Peter? I'm finished with my bath. I'm drawing water for you."

I shivered as I turned away from the window and made sure to lock the door before I started upstairs. When I headed to the bathroom, I heard her humming in her room as though nothing was wrong.

The sky lost its grayish-yellow tinge, but the rain continued into the late afternoon. Mira stood with me at the window. "We'll just get wet all over again if we go out for dinner. We missed lunch and I'm hungry. I'm going to cook dinner now."

"Sounds great. Can I help?"

"You can set the table." She opened the cupboard and handed me plates, then busied herself in a way that indicated she had the situation under control, and I need not linger to keep her company. After I'd done my part, I got out the world atlas that had belonged to Mira's father. The boundaries and the countries on the maps dated from before the Great War, before our parents were born. As I flipped through the pages, I thought about the trip Mira and I had planned when we were children and traced my fingers over different ways to get from Leipzig to Paris.

I turned more pages and found the route I'd traveled from Hamburg, through the North Sea, the English Channel, and across the Atlantic to New York. When I turned the page to New Jersey, my vision grew blurry. The floor tilted, and I slammed the book shut. Was just thinking about my home in that other plane—or wherever it was—enough to send me back there?

Again, I entertained the possibility that this was more than a lucid dream. I existed both here and there simultaneously. My geriatric alter ego was here somewhere, too. Mira had proved herself capable of independent thought, and she didn't always agree with me. What if Mira was also alive somewhere in what I, for lack of a better term, thought of as the real world?

"Peter? Come taste this and tell me what you think."

Shaking my head to clear the cobwebs, I went into the kitchen. She held a wooden spoon to my lips.

"You made *Eintopf*." I savored the rich broth. "It's perfect. Just like my mother used to make." I took the spoon from her hand and wrapped my arms around her. "Thank you."

"It sounded good for a rainy night." She smiled up at me. "Everything will be ready in a few minutes."

"Then I'll be right back."

When I returned the atlas to the shelf, I thought of our time in the *Judenhaus* and wondered if there was a way to get around the rules of the dream and communicate with Mira.

If she was real, she would remember our secret code. On a sheet of paper, I printed, *sihtsiomerhtnadaerma? rayeuoerla? Is this more than a dream? Are you real?*

The wind swirled in the open window, lifted the note from the table, and blew it across the room. I grabbed it just before it disappeared out the opposite window, but the wind blew harder, tearing at the paper in my hand as if someone was trying to take it away from me.

In the kitchen, Mira was facing the stove. If she saw me leave the note on the counter and weight it down with the sugar cannister, she gave no sign.

After dinner, when I cleared the table, the note was gone. I tried to catch Mira's eye, hoping she would give me a signal if she'd found the note, but just like when her mother had tried to keep us from communicating with each other, her face revealed nothing.

As soon as I heard her run water to do the dishes, I slipped out the front door and headed back to my parents' house. Upstairs in my old room, I found the physics textbook.

I was coming up the walk to her front door when I hear her cry out. I dashed inside and met her coming out of the kitchen, a dish towel wrapped around her hand. Blood soaked through and spread like an opening blossom.

"What happened?"

"I cut myself on a knife."

"Is it deep?" A mixture of guilt and panic clutched at my insides.

Her face crumpled as she nodded. "It's on my index finger."

I took her hand and applied pressure over the cut.

She drew a sobbing breath. "If it heals badly, I won't be able to play."

When the bleeding slowed, I unwrapped the towel. A deep, inch-long cut split the skin and tissue over the joint. It should have had stitches, but I shrank from attempting such a thing. There would be Mercurochrome in my parents' medicine cabinet. I shuddered, remembering how much it stung when my mother had used it to treat my cuts and scrapes.

Upstairs, I found her medicine cabinet similarly stocked. She sat on the edge of the tub and didn't cry when I ministered to her. Once I'd disinfected the cut and wrapped her finger in gauze, I settled her in bed with her hand resting on a pile of pillows and went down to brew a pot of tea.

Alone, my hands shook so much I could barely fill the teakettle. If I'd brought on the storm that afternoon because I'd pursued the secrets of our dream world, I had caused Mira's injury, too. While I waited for the water to boil, I searched the kitchen for the note, but it wasn't in the waste can, in a drawer, or even between the pages of the cookbooks.

Tea things assembled on a tray, I tucked the physics book under my arm and hurried back upstairs, forming another plan to get around the rules. I almost changed my mind when I saw her looking so pale. I set the tray in the middle of the bed and poured two cups. "No more cooking until you're healed. Agreed?"

"All right." She took a sip.

Settling back against the headboard next to her, I opened the book.

She smiled. "Are you going to read me a bedtime story?" Then she looked at the cover. "That will put me to sleep in no time."

"Just hear me out. It turns into a love story." I cleared my throat. "Once upon a time, time stopped moving forward in a straight line. It looped and coiled and touched other points in time."

She wrapped the red silk cord of her locket around her uninjured hand and wove it through her fingers.

I remained silent for a few seconds, and when the earth failed to rumble beneath us, I took a sip of tea and pressed on. "Once it did, the bureaucrats at the Ministry of Time Management realized that time, manipulated in this way, could reunite people who had been separated—but clearly belonged together—"

Too late, I felt the tilt and pull of the reverse gravity. As my teacup fell from my hand, the amber droplets hung motionless in the surrounding air, as if together the tea and I had gone weightless. As the room grew smaller, darkness gathered around Mira, spotlighting her on the bed. Then I was gone.

15

"Are you all right? Can you hear me?"

Mira's voice sounded far away. As I struggled to sit up, a man's voice cut in.

"You should take it easy, sir. That was a nasty fall."

Confused, I squinted into the bright sunlight and peered up at the two strangers who knelt over me. The man took me by the arm and helped me sit up.

The woman twisted the top off a water bottle. "Here. You're probably dehydrated. Drink this." She didn't sound all that much like Mira. She was lots older than Mira, too.

But still, it was nice of her, and I felt better after I'd taken a sip. "What happened?"

"You tripped on the curb." She leaned down to check the back of my head. "You're not bleeding or anything, but I think you blacked out."

The guy pulled out his cell phone. "Do you want me to call you an ambulance?"

"No. I am just wanting to go home."

"You could black out again. We'll walk you."

"You are not needing to do that. It is not far. I will be fine." But when I tried to stand, I couldn't support myself. There was no way I was getting up off the sidewalk without help. They each took one of my arms and pulled me to my feet.

"Maybe is better if you are walking with me a little way, right?" It was slow going. When I got woozy, they made me stand in the shade until I felt better. By the time Benny's bodega came into view, I was wiped out.

At my building, I fished out my keys, and I thought I'd give the nice couple a few bucks for their trouble. But when I put my hand to my back pocket, my heart sank. "*Oy vey.* I think I lost my wallet."

The woman bit her lip. "It wasn't on the sidewalk. We'd have seen it when we helped you up."

"Yes, yes, okay. But I am having it when I left home. I was going to a restaurant for lunch."

The guy's attitude went from helpful to defensive. "I don't know what you're trying to say, but we didn't take your wallet. We walked you, like, eight blocks out of our way. If you wanna call the police, go ahead. But we're not sticking around. We did our good deed for the day."

He took the woman by the arm, and she looked back once as he pulled her away. I guess I should've explained. There wasn't much to lose in that wallet. Maybe twenty bucks in cash. No credit cards or checks. I never had a driver's license. But it was better not to let strangers into the building anyway, right? My hand shook as I unlocked the door, and I took the stairs slowly. When I went inside my apartment, there was my wallet, on the kitchen table.

I came to New York on a steamer ship in 1947, and when I arrived, I met with an agent at the Hebrew Immigrant Aid Society office at Ellis Island. I never would have ended up here without my uncle Saul, who was my father's older brother. He located me through the HIAS and sponsored me.

For a refugee kid like me, education wasn't as important as the will to work hard. My caseworker at HIAS had asked me questions to test my employable status, and he was glad when I said I'd had some vocational training to be a plumber. I bet he could tell I was so emotionally beaten down that I'd take any job without complaint and work like a draft animal—hard, but with no thought of rising above my position.

When I was finished with the processing at Ellis Island, my caseworker gave me a voucher for discount train fare and sent me on to New Jersey. My uncle lived in Weequahic, the Jewish section of Newark. He and my cousin, David, who was seven or eight years older than me, met me at the train station.

Uncle Saul resembled my father, and when I saw him, my heart surged. I had known my father would not be there, but for that one moment, I thought it was him. My brief elation was overtaken by sorrow. My father would never be there to meet me, not at this station or any other. I'm sure I looked like a scared rabbit. Uncle Saul cried as he embraced me and kissed me on both cheeks, but it was awkward for me, as we had never met before. The first time I heard them speak, I wondered, *So this is English?*

At first, I stayed with David, his wife, Ruby, and their little boy, Aaron, in their one-bedroom apartment on Elizabeth Avenue. It wasn't a lot of space, but it felt like a palace after the way I'd been living. Ruby, who wasn't that much older than I was, made up a bed for me behind a curtain in a corner of their bedroom.

I spoke very little English, and though Uncle Saul spoke German and David did a little, Ruby and Aaron did not. I communicated with them mostly in broken Yiddish and gestures.

In the evenings after he came home from work, David liked to listen to Dodgers games on the radio. Even though I knew nothing about baseball, I'd sit in the room with him, listening and trying to pick up the language. Eventually, I could understand most of what the announcers said.

About a week after I arrived, Aaron turned four. When I watched him blow out his candles in his paper-cone hat, memories of my own childhood parties came rushing back, like I was looking at my father's snapshots of Mira and me blowing out our candles.

Instead of applauding for Aaron like David and Ruby did, I drew a long, choking breath and ran from the room. I had barely closed the bedroom door before the torment of my own memories left me lying on the floor, sobbing and howling like an animal caught in a trap. It humiliated me that something as normal as a birthday party could devastate me that way.

That night, I heard David and Ruby arguing in fierce, low tones. I couldn't understand much of what they said, but I knew it was about me.

The next afternoon, Uncle Saul came to the apartment to take me to Brooklyn for a Dodgers game. I stumbled getting on the escalator at the train station, because I'd only been on one a few times before. Crowds thronged the platform, jostling me, and while we waited for the train, I broke out in a cold sweat. I felt a little better when I saw it was a real passenger car with seats and windows, but still I was so nervous I could barely step on.

Seeing a baseball game in person differed from what I'd imagined, and I found I understood and enjoyed the game. Uncle Saul and I each had a hot dog and shared a bag of peanuts. I had a soda and he, a beer. A couple times, out of the corner of my eye, I thought Uncle Saul was my father, and that tinged the otherwise pleasant afternoon with sadness. I could never do things like this with my father. Yet Saul had David, and David had Aaron.

Though I had made it to America, I still did not belong. The established families in Weequahic were mostly German Jews who'd settled the area a hundred years before I'd gotten there, and some of them acted like they were too good to associate with penniless greenhorn refugees like me.

But other newcomers to the neighborhood saw the established families as role models. They didn't keep to themselves the way I did. They married, started businesses, went to temple, and sent their kids to the public schools. Their kids grew up speaking English without accents, moved out to the suburbs, joined country clubs, and sent their kids to college.

I lacked the confidence to try to fit in. I told myself I'd never belong to the country club set. But as long as people in the neighborhood spoke Yiddish, I figured I could get by.

The following week, Uncle Saul took me to meet Mr. Gittelman, a rotund, hairy man with a stout wife who stood a good three inches taller than him.

My uncle explained that now that I'd had some time to get used to living in America, I was to work for Mr. Gittelman as a plumber's assistant for ten dollars a month plus room and board.

Mrs. Gittelman showed me to an alcove off their sitting room. It was very much like the one I'd had at the *Judenhaus*. Inside, with the curtains drawn, I felt every bit as lost as I had when Mrs. Schloss had kept Mira and me away from each other.

With no confidence or reason to go anyplace else, I plodded through my daily tasks, and in the evenings, I stayed in the flat. I didn't care for amusements, and I didn't try to make any friends.

For a long time, my only regular purchase was stamps and writing paper. I sent weekly letters to the Red Cross, requesting information about Mira and my parents.

Mrs. Gittelman resented my presence. She fed me grudgingly and badgered me to venture outside the apartment in the evening to give her and Mr. Gittelman some privacy—just so she could holler at him for his own good without me listening in.

One afternoon, when I came home from work, she took me by the arm and walked me across the street to a storefront with a "For Sale" sign in the window. "You should buy yourself a little business, Peter. Like this laundromat—you can take one of the upstairs apartments for yourself and rent the others. Build up a nest egg and find a nice girl. Settle down. What are you waiting for already?"

At that I'd shrugged, casting down my eyes. I didn't want to find just any girl and settle down, and I refused to defile Mira's name by speaking it to Mrs. Gittelman. Mira was mine and mine alone. Other young men flirted and kept company with the girls who worked as store clerks and secretaries, but I couldn't do that. Instead, I relived every moment of my friendship with Mira. I would imagine what it would be like to live with her instead of with the Gittelmans until it felt as though she were just in the next room.

For years, I held out the hope that I'd find Mira and we would be together. Then one month, I did not send my usual letters to the Hebrew Immigrant Aid Society and the Red Cross. I don't know why I stopped. Maybe I figured if I quit making inquiries and never learned the truth, then Mira would never truly be dead to me.

Instead, I envisioned her out there somewhere in the world, living an exciting life. Yet for most of mine, I was only marking time. If God had ever had plans for me, I am sure I fell short of His expectations.

16

I didn't dream the night of my fall.

My head felt better the next morning, and by afternoon, I was ready to make a trip to the bodega. As I trudged downstairs, my landlady was piling boxes in the foyer near the front door. She set down a box of books with a thump and wiped her brow.

"You never came down to go through the stuff the tenant in Four-A left behind. You never saw such a mess! I'll be moving boxes for weeks."

"Apartment Four-A? I was thinking it was another apartment."

"We're having a lot of turnover this month. Don't you remember me telling you?"

I did not. A book caught my eye. "Is okay if I am looking now?"

"Yeah, sure. Take whatever you want. Otherwise it's going to the junk hauler." Mrs. Simmons went back into the unit for another load.

The cover and the edges of the pages showed signs of wear, but looked very much like Mira's father's copy of the *Peerless Atlas of the World*. I pulled it gently from the box, careful of the broken spine as I opened the cover. It was the same edition. I sat down on the stairs, book across my knees, and turned the brittle pages. When I got to the maps of the Caribbean islands, my breath caught in my throat. The X, drawn in Mira's red crayon, was there. It was the same book. Somehow, it had survived the war and ended up here, in my neighbor's apartment.

Who was the tenant who had moved out of 4A? Why did they have Mr. Schloss's book?

I cradled the book in my arm as I hurried down the hall, seeking Mrs. Simmons in the vacant apartment. "Who was this person? What was their name?"

My landlady jumped and dropped another box. "For crying out loud, Mr. Ibbetz, you just took ten years off my life. Are you telling me you don't know your own neighbor's name?"

"I do not, but she is having this atlas, and it is very familiar to me. I am wondering to ask where are they getting it?"

"She won't be able to tell you. She's dead."

I clutched the atlas. "What was her name? How old was she? Where was she from?" Even as my voice grew hoarse with questions, I told myself there was absolutely no possibility that Mira had been living in the apartment one floor below me. None.

The landlady tossed me a magazine off the coffee table. "Here."

The name on the address label read Mary Towers.

I carried the atlas and the magazine to the bodega. Benny looked up from his phone as I came in.

"You're late today, Pete. Everything okay?"

I rubbed the back of my head. "Yes. I am getting in a little accident. But all is okay now."

"Accident? What happened?"

"Was stupid. I was not looking both ways, and almost a car—"

"Seriously? When? Why didn't you tell me?"

"Was all right. I am feeling foolish. No need to cause trouble."

"Pete, you can always call me if you need me, or if you need food, all right? I'll make a delivery for you."

"I am needing some food now, but also to find out more about a lady. Perhaps you are also helping me with this?" I handed the magazine across the counter. "This is her name."

"What's this all about?"

I laid the atlas on the counter. "This I think is the same atlas that was belonging to my friend, in Germany, before the war." I turned to the map of the island. "When we were children, she makes the mark of the X for buried treasure here. Now, this book is out for the trash. It was my neighbor's. She died." I clenched my hands to stop them from trembling. "What if she was the same person? What if I never knew she was here, too?"

He stared at me. "Did you ever meet this neighbor or talk to her?"

"No."

"Wow." He inspected the address label. "I wonder what we can find about her online." He pulled out his phone. "You go shop. Give me a minute, okay?"

As I walked the aisles in the same order as always, I kept looking back at Benny as, brow furrowed, he worked his thumbs over his phone.

When he called out, "Found her!" I stopped deliberating over which flavor cheesecake I wanted and hurried to the front.

"What does it say?"

"This is her obituary." He held out the phone and I squinted at the photo.

"That is her?"

"Yeah. Does she look familiar?"

"No." *Thank God.* "This is not my friend."

"Says in the obituary she owned a second-hand store not far from here. She could've picked up that atlas from an antique wholesaler or an estate sale. There's no way to know."

"Is all right. I wondered if perhaps my friend had changed her name. Mary Towers is sound more English, but is similar to Miriam Schloss, which is meaning 'castle' in German. But this Mary, she is not old enough to be my Mira. May she rest in peace." I glanced heavenward for a moment. "I am all my life never finding Mira. But still I do not believe she is dead."

When Benny packed my groceries, he put the atlas into one bag so it would be easy for me to carry. "Do you want the magazine?"

"No. Is fine to throw it out."

When I got home, I spent hours looking through the atlas. Mira was still out there somewhere. I could feel it. But should I be asking where in the world she was—or when?

17

When I returned to Mira, I found her in bed, examining her hand.

"How is it today? Is it bad?" I asked as I came into the room.

"No." She flexed her fingers. "It's healed. Just a little white scar that looks like it's been there for years. How can that be?"

I sat down next to her, gathered her into my arms, and kissed her forehead. "Magic. And there were lights on in a house down the street last night."

"Why didn't you say something?"

I shrugged. "You made that fantastic *Eintopf*—then you nearly sliced your finger off."

She threw back the covers and went to the wardrobe. "Let's go see if someone's home. The storm has passed."

"Maybe I don't want to share you."

She tossed me a smile over her shoulder. "You'll still be the only man on Earth for me, Peter. Now hurry—go get dressed."

When we were both ready, she grabbed my hand and nearly pulled me out the front door. "Which house was it?"

I pointed and we set off down the cobblestone street. The porch light was still shining like a beacon.

"That's the one I said I liked yesterday." She ran lightly up the steps to the porch and rapped her knuckles on the door. Then she looked at her hand in surprise. "I forgot about the cut when I knocked, and it didn't hurt at all." When no one answered, she pressed her nose against the window beside the door. "Look!"

"What is it?" I came up beside her and shaded my eyes to peer inside at empty rooms.

"It's perfect." The front door opened at her touch, and I followed her inside. She stood in the middle of the sitting room and turned in a slow circle. "Look at all the light in here. What do you think of Delft Blue and yellow upholstery, with cream lacquer on the furniture? And silk portieres?"

"I guess so. What for?"

"For us! We'll live here together."

She looked so delighted that it was easy to get into the spirit of the game. "Only the best for you, my dear."

"Only the best for the both of us."

I followed her from room to room as she decorated to the limits of her imagination. There would be a walnut-paneled billiard room for me and a music room in the solarium at the rear of the house for her.

Upstairs, she peered in each room as she walked down the hall. "Yes, this must be the master—"

I followed her into another light-filled room.

"—it has an en suite bath. Look at the size of this tub!"

"And a sitting room of its own?" I stepped through an archway into a large alcove at the far end of the room.

She glanced my way. "That's big enough to be a nursery."

Her offhand comment left me thunderstruck. She didn't seem to notice and was long gone by the time I repeated, "Nursery?" Nurseries were for babies.

I'd long since written off the possibility of becoming a father, but suddenly the desire to have a child with Mira became an ache that surpassed the pain of missing her I'd known for so many years.

It was ridiculous. We couldn't have a child in a dream.

But what if we could? a voice in my head answered. *What if we could have everything here?*

"Peter!" she called to me from somewhere on the lower floor.

"Coming."

"Hurry! You've got to see this."

I ran down the stairs and met her in the kitchen. "What is it?"

"Out here." She grabbed my hand, pulled me out the back door and led me across the garden to the carriage house. She took the bolt off the double doors and opened them with a flourish. "Look!"

Inside was a gleaming Mercedes roadster—two-tone green with green leather seats. I'd never owned a car—I'd never even been behind the wheel before. This one sure was a honey.

She stepped up on the running board and inspected the instrument panel while I walked around the car. "It looks like it's just off a showroom floor. And it's sure to run, because everything works for us here." As the words left my lips, I swallowed hard. Everything did work for us here. The image of a glowing, pregnant Mira rose in my mind.

"Peter? What are you thinking about? Wake up!" She snapped her fingers to interrupt my reverie and handed me the keys. "Let's go exploring outside of town."

I opened the driver's side door, and just as when I tried to dance and to play the piano, I already knew what to do. I pressed in the clutch, inserted the key into the ignition, and pushed the starter button.

A belch of black exhaust came out of the tailpipe as the engine gasped and choked. Once the oil and gasoline began to flow into the chambers, it purred. A smile spread over my face.

Mira opened the passenger door and climbed in beside me. "Take me for a ride."

I eased the brake off, and the car stalled. Embarrassed, I struggled to shift back into neutral.

She leaned over, trying to be helpful. "Balance the pressure on the gas and the clutch when you ease it into gear." She held her hands out in front of her, palms flat, and pushed down with her right hand while lifting the left. "See? Just do that with your feet."

I tried to shift too fast and the car stalled again. "Why don't you take over?"

"This is your new experience. Not mine." She slid over on the seat and straddled my lap, her back against the steering wheel, and draped her arms around my neck. "Just remember—an automobile is like a woman. You have to finesse it a little. Treat it like a lady."

When she kissed me, I nearly forgot about the car. "We don't have to go anywhere if you'd rather stay home."

"No. We're off on a picnic this afternoon. I know just the place. I'll be ready in an hour and a half." She gave me one more exuberant kiss, opened the door, and let herself out. "Use the time to practice."

Alone in the garage, I clutched the wheel. We had the freedom to go anywhere. What would we find outside Leipzig?

18

I pushed the starter again and the engine roared to life. The gears ground as I searched for first, but this time, I pulled out of the carriage house without stalling, rolled down the drive, and turned onto the cobblestone street.

Over the next hour, I learned the rhythms of the car—how to tell when it was time to shift, how much pressure to apply to the gas and the brake. It was easy to get comfortable behind the wheel when I didn't have to worry about other traffic. The car glided as smoothly as if it was on ice, yet I felt in complete control.

When I pulled up in front of Mira's house at the appointed time, I was grinning from ear to ear. She came out carrying a wicker basket and folded blankets. I hurried to take them from her and tipped an imaginary cap. "Where to, miss?"

"It's a surprise."

I put the blankets in the backseat and set the basket on top of them, then opened her door with a flourish. "Point me in the right direction, then."

We left the city and traveled southeast. As soon as the outer suburbs and villages were behind us, my stomach rumbled. "How long before we get there?"

"Two or three hours, I think."

"That long before we eat?"

She laughed. "I packed plenty. I thought you might need suste-nance on the way." She reached into the back seat to open the basket and brought out cheese and crackers, apple slices, and grapes. The rolling countryside was dotted with farms and villages that looked as pristine as our surroundings in Leipzig. Mira took off her scarf and turned her face to the sun, letting the wind ruffle her hair.

When she pointed out the turnoff, I followed a tree-lined, gravel road for another mile or so until I spied a castle through the trees. We parked and gathered up the blankets and picnic basket, then Mira took my arm and led me in another direction down a forest path until we emerged in a clearing.

"I can't wait to show you! Come see!" She gave a little skip of de-light as she started down a grassy slope bathed in the afternoon sun-light. Stone steps led to a pond, and when I beheld the scene, I caught my breath. "What is that?"

A perfect circle of stone, like a great wheel, seemed to sit in the water, half above the surface, half below, as though some ethereal force had brought it up from the center of the earth. It was a single-span bridge, with abutments surrounded by jagged spires like a stone stock-ade fence. Its reflection in the still water made it look as though it was half-submerged.

"It's a devil's bridge." She clutched my arm, and the determined, hungry look on her face made me shiver. She dropped the blankets. "Legend says only someone who's made a deal with the devil would know how to build such a thing. Isn't it amazing? Come on, let's go across!" A smaller arched bridge bordered with the jagged, sharp stones led to the larger span.

I set the picnic basket beside the blankets and followed her to the water's edge. Surprisingly narrow, the bridge rose at a breakneck an-gle with no handhold or railing, until we stood some twenty meters above the water. I almost lost my balance twice on the climb, but Mira moved with confidence, as if she'd done it a thousand times before.

The sun, already sinking toward the horizon, cast long shadows over the water as we looked out to the surrounding forest. Mira spread her arms, embracing the vista before us.

I put a hand on her shoulder, feeling I should keep hold of her lest she take flight. "That climb was enough to scare the devil out of me. The view is worth it, though. How long has it been here?"

"A prince ordered it built on his castle grounds more than a hundred years ago."

I had never heard of this place when I was a boy, but I assumed asking how she knew of it fell outside the limitations imposed by the dream.

She glanced back over her shoulder as if she knew what I was thinking as she continued across the bridge. "Just imagine the stories this place has inspired!"

"Tell me." I placed each foot carefully on the downward slope.

She reached the bottom of the main span and held out a hand to me. "First we explore. We'll have story time while we eat." On the opposite shore, she led the way through a wooded path until we emerged at the castle's formal garden, with clipped hedges and rose bushes that looked as though they received daily care. There wasn't a fallen twig or a spent bloom out of place.

She sighed as we walked along the gravel path. "I wonder why the prince who lived here wanted the devil's bridge."

"Maybe so he'd have a yard ornament that would make the neighbors envious."

"I'm being serious. Curses and blessings are real. He must have wanted something so badly that he was willing to risk calling on the devil to attain it."

"There are always witches and devils in fairy tales, but witches aren't necessarily evil. You do realize," I lowered my voice to a whisper, "that you've utterly bewitched me?"

She burst out laughing. "Peter, will you ever be serious?"

I had been serious, and even though I laughed with her, I could understand why people would seek out this mysterious place, in the hopes of making a bargain with otherworldly forces.

We skirted the pond and returned to the grassy slope just as shadows began to envelop the clearing. As Mira shook out the picnic blanket, I watched her lithe body bend and stretch and appreciated the gentle swell of her curves through the fabric of her clothes. Tiny flames of sunlight glinted orange in her dark hair. I moved the basket aside and knelt beside her, fingers trembling as I traced the curve of her cheek, down to her neck, and then fingered the heart-shaped locket dangling at her throat.

She covered my hand with hers. "You like it here, don't you?"

"It's perfect." The word faded to nothing as our lips met. As my hands closed over her shoulders, I breathed in her perfume and the scent of her skin. Her hands set my nerves firing as they trailed down my chest and over my stomach. She took hold of my belt and my hands roamed over her body like she already belonged to me. My brain ceded control as my body took over. I wanted her more than I'd ever wanted anything.

Then, out of nowhere, sadness slammed up against my excitement, driving me outside myself. My analytical side protested that this dream would only serve to torture me, for I would never have the life with Mira I truly desired. The part of me that believed in fairy tales and magic sensed Old Peter somewhere in the shadows, like a voyeur intruding on a young couple's passion. I drew back, afraid to look her in the eyes, lest she think the war within me was about whether or not I wanted her.

"Peter," She unbuttoned her blouse, whispering encouragement between kisses. "It's all right. This is what we should have had all along."

Old Peter had waited a lifetime for this. But this moment was mine. Once I claimed it, the energy flooded back into my body and every sensation proved that yes, this was happening. Her breath came faster, and her sweet smile ripened into one that was sultry and fetching

She was the Eve to my Adam, leading me where I'd never been

before. Face just inches away, her gaze held me mesmerized. My chest rose and fell against her hands as she undid each button on my shirt. Then she pulled the tail out of my waistband, and in that simple act, she freed me. I don't remember how we got out of the rest of our clothes, but when we became one it was like a missing piece fell into place in the universe's puzzle. Somewhere, far away, I heard Old Peter whisper, "I've been waiting my whole life for you."

I repeated the words to Mira to make them mine, not his, even as I made her mine. I hadn't truly known her until now. I hadn't known myself, either. When I could speak again, I whispered, "Thank you."

As we lay in each other's arms, the last of my shyness left me. What could be more natural than running my fingers over the curve of her hip or cupping her breast? I would never tire of the wonders of her.

In the gathering darkness, I could feel Old Peter's eyes upon us again as he watched from the shadows. I pitied him, for he did not belong here. I was the one lying with Mira's head pillowed on my shoulder. It might not be fair, but now that I was here, I wasn't giving her up. There was nothing in his world worth going back for.

She was silent so long I thought she had fallen asleep, but then she whispered, "What are you thinking about?"

"About how we can't go back to the way things—"

"Hush." She rolled over and straddled me. Her eyes looked as dark as the water in the pond.

I lost count of how many times we made love on that hillside. Dinner turned into a late-night snack. With our hunger for each other temporarily satisfied, I uncorked the wine and we devoured the rest of the basket's contents before I took her in my arms again.

It was nearing midnight when I felt her leave the warmth of our shared blanket and slip away. I sat up and gathered the folds around me, watching her move with the grace of a doe toward the water. Ripples glittered and spread in the moonlight as she waded into the pond.

Her voice, barely above a whisper, carried back to me. "I know you're awake, Peter. Come, let me tell you a story."

The full moon seemed suspended inside the ring of the bridge. I followed a silvery path of moonlight on the dark water that led to where she waited.

Little currents from the springs that fed the pond ran cool and wrapped themselves around my legs. In the darkness, it was easy to imagine they were tendrils of a mermaid's hair or the long, curling fingers of a water sprite. Except for the touch of those currents, the water felt warm enough for a bath. The sand and pebbles were smooth beneath my feet.

She backed away as I approached, coaxing me closer to the bridge. "It is said that anyone who passes under the arch during a full moon can enter another dimension."

We were already someplace that defied explanation, but she wanted more. I caught up to her and she framed my face in her cool, wet hands. She snared my bottom lip between her teeth, stopping just short of breaking the skin. The kiss that followed felt demanding. "Let's try."

She had to tread water at the center of the pond. As the bridge loomed overhead, I expected the stones beneath my feet to grow hot, and the water to boil and emit the odor of brimstone. Instead, everything grew cooler, and I shivered, imagining I heard a hoarse cry carry across the water. I gathered her close, and she wrapped her legs around my waist.

"Please," she whispered. "Come through to the other side."

Above us, the curve of the bridge's span rose to a dizzying height, and the water came up to my chest. The droplets that clung to her hair shone like pearls in the moonlight. Her breasts, slick and warm, pressed against me. I scanned the bank from which we'd entered the water. Old Peter was too weak to summon me back.

I propelled her to where the arch met the water's surface, and with her back against the bridge, we moved as one, generating waves that slapped against the stones already worn smooth. As I lost myself in the throes of passion, it was easy to imagine the bridge was alive, its heartbeat pulsing in the stone under my palm.

19

Mira woke me with kisses at dawn, and as we made love again, I realized this was the first time that falling asleep didn't send me back to New Jersey. The first golden rays of sunlight, diffused by the mist rising off the water, threw the bridge into silhouette. The scene looked every bit as mystical as it had in the moonlight. Had the magic worked? If it had, what would that mean for us?

We dressed in our rumpled clothes, and Mira twisted her hair into an untidy knot and put on her scarf. The picnic basket, emptied the night before, had replenished itself, and we breakfasted on the slope before making our way back to the car.

On the road to Leipzig, I asked, "Are you game for another adventure?"

"Always."

"Then let's go to Bastei. It's on the way back." I remembered the spot from family hiking trips, and when we drew near, I found the turnoff with no trouble. While the devil's bridge had been tucked away in a forgotten glade, the rugged sandstone crags of Bastei thrust themselves hundreds of feet in the air above deep ravines.

We held hands as we climbed up the trail toward the jagged cliffs. The trail brought us to the Rockfall, an impressive cluster of granite spires striped with horizontal grooves worn by the elements. There we crossed a medieval-style stone bridge and took in the commanding views of the Elbe River, a ribbon of blue that wound through the fields and rolling hills below.

Smaller rock formations and fir trees filled the gorge, and we used the telescopes mounted on the observation platform to take in the vistas. Rolling farmland stretched to the edge of a forest, which was nestled at the base of mountains that looked like the swing of a giant axe had shorn them off into flat plateaus. Farther beyond, individual hills melted into shades of blue and gray on the horizon. The landscape seemed too far reaching and enormous for just two people to occupy.

We sat with our backs against the ramparts. "Mira, how did you know about the devil's bridge?"

She raised an eyebrow. "Don't you know by now not to ask too many questions?"

I locked my lips closed with an imaginary key and tossed it away.

"That's not what I meant, and you know it. You can still speak to me."

I shrugged as though there was nothing I could do now that I'd lost the key.

She fell on me and kissed me until my lips parted in response and we ended up laughing. Her ferocious insistence on testing the legend of the devil's bridge had given way to lightheartedness, and I wondered if her demeanor had changed because she believed the charm had worked.

We remained at the gorge until the sun was halfway down the sky, and though I kept watch, I saw no sign of Old Peter lurking in the forest.

On the way home, Mira dozed with her head on my shoulder, the ends of her scarf fluttering in the breeze. Gas streetlamps sprung to life with a hiss as I drove through our neighborhood, where we found both my house and Mira's dark. I nudged her awake as I pulled up to the curb in front of her dream house. Yesterday, the windows had been bare. Now drapes blocked our view of the inside and lights glowed in every room. "I think we're supposed to stop here."

"Yes, I believe we are." She threw open the passenger door without waiting for me to come around and open it for her and was halfway to the front door before I got out of my seat. As before, it opened at her touch, and as she disappeared over the threshold, I heard her cry out.

I hurried inside. "What?" Then I saw. It seemed as though a team of interior decorators, painters, and seamstresses had descended on the place the instant we'd left. Everything in the sitting room was as Mira had described—the blue and yellow upholstery, the cream draperies, the shiny lacquered furniture. It looked like a feature in a magazine. "Wow." I couldn't think of anything else to say.

She clapped her hands in delight. "It's a fairy tale. The most wonderful make-believe come true."

I put out a restraining hand as she started up the stairs. "Hang on a minute."

"What?"

"This is going to be our home, right?"

"Yes."

"Then let me carry you over the threshold, and we'll make it official."

We walked back outside, and I swept her into my arms with no effort at all. She pressed her lips to mine, and neither one of us seemed to want to break the connection.

Finally, she whispered in Hebrew, so close our lips were still touching, "*Ani leh-dodee veh-dodi-lee.*"

I stepped through the doorway and repeated the phrase in English. "I am my beloved's, and my beloved is mine."

The first thing I saw when I opened my eyes was Mira's tousled head on the pillow. I'd been able to remain with her again. From that time on, the pathway between worlds seemed to close. Was this the bridge's magic at work?

Mira and I had toured a vacant house, just as young couples often did—and I'd watched her spin a fantasy into a home for us. As I lay beside her, I ran my fingers over her bare shoulder. She stirred and rolled over to spoon with her back against my chest. As I wrapped my arms around her, molding her shape more closely into mine, my lips brushed her hair. "What would you like to do today?"

"Let's stay right here."

"Sounds perfect."

We lingered in bed, but only until noon. Mira was too keen to organize our new home, and that afternoon she supervised the moving of our clothes and personal things from our parents' houses. In her childhood bedroom, she emptied her bureau drawers into a pair of heavy cardboard suitcases while I leaned on the doorjamb, watching.

She glanced over her shoulder. "Are you staring at my underthings?"

"Who, me?" I smothered a smile as I looked away.

"It's fine. Look all you like." She gestured to the suitcase's contents like she was presenting a prize on a game show before snapping the locks closed.

I took hold of the handles and lifted both cases off the bed. "Is this all you need?"

"What? No, of course not. There's still everything in the wardrobe, and my cosmetics and curlers."

"Oh." I shifted my grip on the handles. "Do you want me to drop these off and come back?"

"I'll come with you. I'm particular about arranging my things."

After I'd carried her suitcases to our new shared bedroom, I headed to my parents' house and brought my own clothing and personal things back in one trip. Arms full, I looked for a place to set my clothes down, but hers were strewn across the bed.

"Which drawers are mine?"

She bit her lip and then giggled as she pointed. "Well, I guess you could have these two."

"Just two?"

"How many do you need?"

It took the rest of the day before Mira was satisfied, and though I teased her about taking up too much room in the wardrobe and the bureau, I loved to see her clothing mingled in with mine.

If I had come back to our houses after the war, as I'd promised, and reunited with Mira, we could have had seventy years together instead of these few nights of dreams. Still, for however long it lasted, I was forever beholden to her for the gift of her love.

We spent our days making up for lost time, unencumbered by responsibility, making love whenever we pleased, without a care about being late for work or a well-meaning mother-in-law or a nosy neighbor dropping by. Any worry I'd had about being intimate with her was long gone. Her taste and the softness of her skin had become as familiar to me as my own body.

The clothes Mira wore made her look shapely while only hinting at what was underneath. That, I realized, was much sexier than clothes that leave too little to the imagination. Her blouses, skirts, and dresses might have seemed simple, but each outfit was a learning experience, full of hidden pathways to be navigated on the way to the goal, which was, ultimately, their removal. Hooks, snaps, zippers, ribbons, buttons—and especially the lacy garter belts that held up her stockings.

Every room in the house had been decorated to her wishes, but I'd been so wrapped up in her that I hadn't given a thought to the alcove off our bedroom. She'd called that space a nursery. Heavy drapes hung in the arched doorway, and I hesitated, hand trembling, before pushing them aside.

The space was empty except for my toy airplane, which rested on the windowsill. I went downstairs to the kitchen, and when I returned, I raised the window sash in the alcove a few inches and left a lump of sugar on the sill.

We'd been living together for about a week when I woke in the middle of the night to her twitching in her sleep. Before I could rouse her, she said, "No—please! Let me be," and I drew my hand back. Would she reveal something in her sleep that she couldn't tell me when she was awake? I held my breath, waiting for her to speak again, but she only thrashed and whimpered. Then she sat up with a heartrending cry.

I switched on the bedside lamp. Mira looked possessed—glassy-eyed, her hair plastered to her sweating brow. Her unseeing eyes darted to the far corners of the room, near the nursery alcove, and she screamed.

I couldn't see anything. "What? What's the matter?"

She threw herself into my arms and, quaking with sobs, buried her face in my chest. Half an hour passed before she stopped crying. I was at a loss to comfort her.

20

At breakfast the next morning, Mira waved off everything but coffee. Unused to seeing her pale and listless, I cast about for something to restore her good cheer. "Let's go spend the day at Augustusplatz."

"I don't feel like going. I don't have the energy to bike into the city."

"We'll take the trolley and bring your violin." I kissed the top of her head as I carried my dishes to the sink. "Remember? You were going to play a concert. Your finger is healed, isn't it?"

"Yes, but do I really need to play a concert for one?"

"For the most appreciative one."

She was slow about getting ready to leave, but the trolley was waiting to carry us to the city center, where the doors to the Markt were flung wide in anticipation of our arrival. I scanned the horizon and there wasn't a cloud in the sky.

At Coffee Baum, I held the door while she passed beneath the carving of Cupid offering a bowl of coffee to a Turk. Inside, the rich aroma of roasted beans seemed to emanate from the very walls, and we lingered over tiny cups of the deepest black coffee and fruit-filled pastries.

Mira looked around the café. "I could play for you here." Before I could protest, she cut me off. "There's nothing wrong with an intimate concert setting. Especially for a small, appreciative audience."

"Maybe another day. This time, I want to watch you on a big stage." I held out my hand. "Come on, let's walk around for a while first."

We strolled through the shops in the arcade, a narrow alleyway under a soaring roof made of small-paned glass windows. I studied everything, from the merchandise to the shopkeeper's ledgers, searching for a calendar or a check—anything that could speak to *when* we were. So far, I'd seen nothing in the dream world with the date on it.

We were around twenty-two, maybe twenty-five years old at the most. That would place us in the 1950s, but our clothing was no different from the styles our parents had worn in the 1930s. The Mercedes was definitely pre-war vintage, and I'd noticed none of the advances in technology, like record players, radios, and televisions that should have been available to us when we were young adults. The record player at Mira's house was the same one they'd had when we were children, operated with a crank instead of electricity. I looked behind the counter in the stationery shop. "Have you seen a telephone?"

She gave me a sidelong look. "Who were you planning to call?"

"No one. I was just thinking." Without the Second World War, many great minds would have been spared an untimely death. What might they have invented to advance society? What weapons of war might never have existed at all?

I wasn't naïve enough to believe that erasing one terrible chapter in our history would make the world perfect. Time spent in this static version of utopia left me wishing for a little imperfection every now and then, and I itched to accomplish things I'd never done. Mira had called our dream world a fairy tale—and fairy tales always had an element of darkness. Every story revolved around a curse that must be broken, or a task to test the hero's worth, before the players could live happily ever after.

After the arcade, we crossed the square in front of the New Town Hall, bound for the university library. Mira ran lightly up the marble stairs to the music section and made selections from the sheet music on the shelves, stacking it on one of the reading tables. Sunlight flooded the room, and a smile played over her lips as she sat and began flipping through the pages. She glanced up. "You don't have to stay with me."

"It's fine. I don't mind waiting for you."

She shooed me away with a flick of her hand. "Go. I know you're itching to look for something that interests you."

"All right." With a wary glance around the empty room, I headed back into the hall and up one floor, to the history section. Though I checked dozens of books on Europe and Germany, I found no mention of Adolf Hitler, the National Socialist German Workers' Party, or the Nuremburg Laws against Jews. No *Kristallnacht*. No concentration camps. That meant eleven million civilians and twenty million members of the military had not died as a result of war.

As I passed beneath the marble archways in the hall, I pondered the difference between this reality and the one I had already lived. With such a destructive chapter in history erased, who knows what those people whose lives were spared might have contributed to society. Germany would have had unlimited potential for good. But none of those people were here. Only Mira and me.

In the reading room, clusters of leather club chairs and lamplit library tables could have accommodated dozens of patrons. I went straight to the rack on the wall for the most current edition of *Leipziger Volkszeitung*, but none of the newspapers and magazines I found were dated later than 1925, three years before I was born. There were no current events—only history.

Before I could head off to the science section, Mira crept up behind me and whispered my name. She giggled when I jumped. "Are you finished?" She carried an armload of sheet music and her violin case.

"You don't have to whisper just because we're in the library. There's no one to disturb."

"What about you? I thought I'd startle you if I raised my voice."

"How kind of you to think of me."

"I am always thinking of you, Peter."

"And I'm always thinking of you. May I carry those for you?"

She handed over the music and violin with a smile. "Now come." She led the way down the marble stairs and over to the Markt in the center of the plaza. The clock tower chimed the hour as we went inside. Savory smells filled the main hall, and though we could have spent hours shopping for food, clothing, and even furniture, she beckoned me to follow her into the city museum. There we wandered through the exhibits and viewed everything from suits of armor to ancient books to velocipedes. Again, nothing hinted that Germany's history had continued past the 1920s.

It was useless to pry into the secrets of the dream, and pointless to mention my quest to Mira. I let her lead the way upstairs and through the feast hall, paneled in wood darkened with age. Long trestle tables flanked by heavy wooden chairs filled the space, and I tried to imagine people occupying all those seats. She continued into the ballroom, where she ran to the center of the floor and spun around. "Come dance with me."

"You're feeling better. Was it the coffee?"

"It might have been the pastry."

I set her things aside and took her in my arms. We glided around the room, in perfect time, as if we both heard the same music. "We must come back and dance more after you choose your gown for tonight."

"You're making a few songs into a big deal."

"It is a big deal—it would please me, and it would please you, wouldn't it?"

"Yes, of course."

"Good. I'm sure the shops in town have everything you need to be properly dressed for the occasion. You once dreamed of playing a concert in an *haute couture* gown, didn't you?"

She giggled. "Yes, and it's sweet of you to remember. But first, I'd like to get a few things from the market." Though her cheeks were still pale, her energy had returned to normal, and I hurried to keep up, following her past stalls of cooking implements and unfamiliar foods and spices.

She seemed to be searching for something in particular. "What's your favorite food?"

"Anything you cook tastes great to me."

"Well, all right then. I'll surprise you." She plucked up a market basket. Into it went fruit, vegetables, rice, and a bundle of ginger root so pungent it tickled my nose. The cut of meat she wanted was wrapped in paper and waiting at the butcher's counter. On top of it all, she placed a round bamboo basket with sections that stacked together and a woven lid.

"What is that? It looks like an apartment building for birds." I took off the lid. "Robins on the first floor, wrens upstairs?"

She swatted my hand away, pretending annoyance. "No, silly, I need it to cook with. You'll see."

We moved on to the garment shop. I spent the next half hour watching while she tried on one frothy gown after another. When she came out of the fitting room in a midnight-blue strapless with a jeweled bodice, I could tell by her smile she'd found the one she wanted.

The hem swept the floor in back as she turned. "It's perfect. Even for a matinee performance."

At the theater, she paused before the stage door and gave me a lingering kiss. Then she held up a warning finger. "Don't come back to the dressing room. I want to make an entrance." With a wink over her shoulder, she headed off with the garment bag and her violin case.

I set the market basket on a seat in the front row and went up to the control booth. When I'd flooded the stage with light, I found a seat in the center of the vast theater, where the acoustics were best. There I prepared to let the music wash over me.

Mira's dress sparkled as she stepped into the light and raised the bow to the strings. When she played "Muss I Denn," she looked as comfortable and content as the first day I'd seen her in this dream—eyes closed, swaying to the music.

After she drew the final note from the strings, she took the violin off her shoulder. Even without a microphone, her voice carried in the empty hall. "Ever since I was a small girl, it has been my dream to play a concert here, in my home city. All the pieces on the program tonight have special significance. The selection you just heard was the first song I learned to play, when I was six years old. It is very dear to me for many reasons. It reminds me of my guest of honor, who is my oldest friend and will be my dearest love, always, until the end of time."

The folk tunes, classical pieces, and German marching songs were all familiar. But then she surprised me by playing a piece with an Asian quality to the melody. Partway through, she stumbled over a note and made a clumsy recovery. I snapped out of my reverie, wondering if she was ill again. She had rarely made mistakes, even as a child, and I'd not heard a single one since we'd been together.

Violin and bow clutched in her hands, she stormed toward the edge of the stage and jabbed the bow toward the balcony, off to my right. "Go away! I don't want you here!" She collapsed in the spotlight in a puddle of midnight blue satin, rocking as she cradled the violin against her chest. "You're ruining it. This is my time, do you understand? My time!"

I leapt to my feet, rushed up the aisle, and took the stairs to the balcony two at a time. I arrived panting and searched every row, but there was no one in sight.

Since our return from the devil's bridge, I had not sensed Old Peter's presence. He was not with us now. Something else had invaded our paradise.

Though I ran all the way to the dressing room, Mira had changed back into her everyday clothes before I burst in. "What was it? What did you see? Why didn't you wait for me to walk you back here?"

Worry lines etched her face. "I don't want to talk about it."

"Can I help you pack up your dress?" Her lovely gown was draped carelessly over the back of a chair.

She shook her head. "I'm not taking that with me. I never want to see it again."

I followed her out of the theater, blinking in the bright afternoon sunlight. Though I scanned every corner of the plaza, I saw nothing that would threaten her. Mira marched to the trolley stop, eyes straight ahead, and remained silent on the ride home. When we arrived, she took the shopping basket to the kitchen and shut the swinging door. Once I'd set the table, I retreated to the sitting room to give her some space.

Before long, the house filled with good smells that made my mouth water. When she called me to the table, she laid two bamboo sticks beside my plate and took away the forks and knives before she served chicken soup with dumplings and little steamed buns stuffed with meat.

I picked up my sticks. "What do you call these?"

"Chopsticks."

"I know what chopsticks are. I meant those." I used one to point to the buns.

She laughed. "They're called baozi, and they're very popular in parts of Asia. I made them in the steamer I got at the market."

"Oh, the birdhouse thing?" Stabbing one of the baozi off the serving platter with a chopstick, I managed to get it into my mouth on the first try. "They taste great."

Mira wielded her chopsticks like she'd eaten with them a million times, and I tried to copy the way she held them between her fingers as she picked up the baozi without having to stab it.

When she used the chopsticks to fish one of the dumplings out of her soup, I gave up and picked up my spoon. "I'm not quite dexterous enough to eat soup with chopsticks yet."

"I can do it." She fairly sparkled with mischief as she picked up her bowl and tilted it to her lips to drink the broth, and I laughed. She seemed determined to put the afternoon's incident at the theater behind her.

When we were finished, I carried our plates into the kitchen, where Mira was already elbow-deep in the sudsy water. She giggled when I slid my arms around her waist and kissed her neck. "You cooked. I'll do the dishes."

She lifted her hands out of the water. "If you're offering . . ."

"Yes, I am."

"Then I accept." She turned to face me and lifted her lips. I smiled down at her, pretending to consider my options. "The dishes will wait if you'd rather go upstairs first."

She flicked water off her fingers at me. "Sounds like you're trying to renege on your promise."

"Never. I'd do anything for you."

"Would you really?" As she drew back, the smile faded from her lips.

"Yes, of course."

Her face hardened and she gave a derisive snort. "I don't know why you would say that."

"What?"

"Oh, what am I thinking? It's pointless to get angry with you." She was talking to herself more than to me.

"That suggests you are angry with me. But why? And why doesn't it do any good?"

"Never mind."

"What have I done? Have I hurt you somehow?"

"Nothing. That's the problem. It doesn't matter." She said it under her breath, more to herself than to me. "You're not real."

I stared at her, thunderstruck, expecting her to vanish into thin air. When she did not, I protested, "I am too. You're the one who showed up in my dream—so maybe you're the one who's not real."

"That's a laugh. You're just here for window dressing. Peter . . ."

"Yes?"

When her mouth twisted in anger, she looked like her mother. "I'm talking about the real Peter. He's not like you. You're so damned agreeable. He lied."

"Hang on just a minute." I released her and took a step back, and she darted into the sitting room.

When I caught up with her, she was holding the atlas against her chest. "Peter said he'd meet me at home. That he'd never stop trying to find me. That he'd marry me." Tears sprang into her eyes. "You say you'll do anything for me, like none of that ever happened and you haven't let me down before."

This time the earth trembled in warning.

"Why didn't you keep your promise?"

"I—" Cold sweat broke out on my forehead.

"Did you think I would just forgive you? That I would forget?" Tears rolled down her cheeks.

"No, I don't expect you to forgive me." The earth shook again, stronger than the last time. "But if I'm not real, could I do this?" I pulled her to me and kissed her lips. "Could I feel how soft your hair is, or lie awake at night and listen to you breathe beside me? We've both cut ourselves—and bled and healed again—since we've been here. Don't you think we're here because we're supposed to help each other heal in other ways, too?"

I held her chin so she wouldn't look away. "You've been right all along, Mira. We deserve this time together. I have no idea how we got here, but it's like a gift, to make up for the hard stuff and the disappointments. Some power in the universe has granted me my only wish. This is all I've ever wanted."

She pounded her fist against my chest. "But you didn't come for me! And I couldn't find you! You can't help me now, either. Nothing can."

All these years, I'd blamed my isolation on forces beyond my control. But it was my fault that I had spent my life alone, and my fault that my fear had caused Mira to suffer. My anger turned inward. There was only one way to make it up to her.

As the world tilted under me, I gasped, "It's not too late. Let me prove it to you. Tell me where you are, Mira. I'll find you."

Stony silence was her only answer as the negative gravity took hold of me.

21

I woke up back in Weequahic, still stunned by what Mira had said. It wasn't just a dream. She was real. We'd been playing house—and doing a lousy job of processing the pain and trauma we'd suffered.

Somehow, we'd been drawn into another dimension together, an antiseptic, amusement-park version of our old home.

I wanted to slap that younger version of myself for promising to find Mira here, in this world. I had no idea if it was possible to reunite with her in the present, and the task of finding her would fall to me, not him. Where was I supposed to start looking?

My thoughts whirled until I wanted to clap my hands over my ears. Instead, I did the next best thing. I turned on the television to drown them out. *The Price is Right* was coming on at the top of the hour. Maybe if I gave myself time to calm down, I'd come up with a plan. One of the morning talk shows was on, but I wasn't paying attention until the announcer said, "Up next, a miraculous story. Two brothers separated during the Holocaust reunited after seventy-five years."

The brothers in the story were like me—after the war they had filed all the right forms with the Red Cross and HIAS to try and locate their loved ones, but they'd never connected. One brother ended up in Russia, the other in the US. These brothers, with their children and grandchildren grouped around them, had a family reunion over the computer. I could feel my hope surge as my brain kicked into over-drive. Modern technology could help me find Mira.

The reporter who had covered the story explained about DNA profiling, which had been the key to reuniting the family. One of the grandchildren had submitted their DNA sample to a genealogy site—and the results revealed that they had first cousins on the other side of the world. From there, it wasn't long before the families connected.

To my knowledge, none of my family had survived, and I'd had no word about Mira's, either. Even if DNA couldn't help me, maybe there were ways to use a computer to find her—but I was going to need help.

The public library was about a fifteen-minute walk from my apartment. Even though it wasn't far, I hadn't been to that neighborhood in years, and after all I'd been through, I was wary about wandering around by myself. But Mira's voice rang in my ears, urging me on. When I saw her again, I'd be able to tell her that this time, I'd done everything in my power to find her. I headed out the door and down Lyons Avenue.

The library was a redbrick building on Osborne Terrace, off the main drag and tucked in among houses and apartments. It took me a while to get up the steps. The younger me would have run all the way to the door. I guess most old people reminisce about what it was like to be young, but the memory of having a body that could do whatever I wanted was so fresh that my reality was doubly hard to accept.

Inside, I approached the desk clerk. "I am trying to locate someone I was knowing a long time ago." I lowered my voice a little. "I was losing track of her during the war. In the camps. Is there someone here who can help me?"

"Yes, sir. I'm so sorry that happened to you. There are records available online, and we can help you access the Internet. Let me call Jacob, one of our volunteers." She pushed her glasses up and picked up the phone.

Soon Jacob, a nice young guy of around sixty, joined us at the desk.

He was wearing a yarmulke. I didn't see many Jews in the neighbor-hood these days.

I introduced myself, and when we shook hands, I saw him glance down at my arm, where my tattoo was just visible inside my rolled-up sleeve. "Auschwitz?"

I nodded. "Birkenau."

"Did you know that only prisoners at Auschwitz and its sub-camps were tattooed?"

"No, I didn't. But then, I am never talking about it with anyone."

"With transfers from camp to camp, we see the tattoos on survivors from all over."

"I think you are knowing more about it than me, and I lived it."

"You could probably tell me a thing or two. I hear stories from lots of survivors where I volunteer—at the Jewish Museum of New Jersey. I spend a lot of time there helping people research their ancestors."

"It sounds like I am hitting the jackpot. I am hoping you can help me search for my friend."

He led the way over to a row of computers on a long table. "So, Mr. Ibbetz, tell me more. Who are you looking for?"

"Please call me Peter. Her name is Mira. I knew her from where I was living when I was a boy. We got separated in 1944, at Theresienstadt. Later, I was sent on to Birkenau."

He nodded, encouraging me to go on.

"I am for many years doing everything I can to find her. Letters I send to our neighbors, and many postcards to her old address. I am writing to the Red Cross every month and leaving word with the Hebrew Immigrant Aid Society. Every agency I can find knows I am alive and searching for Mira, but I am never hearing about her or any of our relatives, either."

"I'm sorry to hear that. Situations like yours are all too common."

"After a long time of searching, I am giving up on finding Mira and thinking she has died. Then this morning on TV people who survived the Shoah are still finding loved ones after all this time. I am wanting to try again. I am sure—in my heart—Mira is alive. She is so real to me; it is as though I spoke to her only yesterday."

"I'll help you search all the available records online. They're updated frequently, but I don't think you should get your hopes up. Reunions like the one you saw on television are rare after so many years."

Tears welled up in my eyes and I got out my handkerchief. "Still we must try to find the truth. I am thinking I gave up too soon."

Jacob sat at one of the computers, pulled the keyboard closer, and typed something. "Let's start at the United States Holocaust Memorial Museum online. They have a database—a list—of survivors and victims."

A photo of young boys wearing striped uniforms and standing behind barbed wire came up on the computer screen. One glance at their gaunt faces and I started to tremble. What if there was a picture of Mira, or me, being used on a website or in a museum somewhere? People might study our faces and wonder who we were and what had become of us. If I saw such a photo, would I recognize her? Would I recognize myself?

Jacob cut across my thoughts. "Let's start with her name." He tapped a few keys and a new screen asked for information to begin a search.

I touched the screen. "How are we putting her name in there?"

"Easy." He moved a little thing connected to the computer by a wire, tapped it with his index finger, and a flashing line popped up in the box.

"Her name is Miriam. Miriam Schloss. I called her Mira."

"It asks for a married name, too, but we can search with only her maiden name."

"If she married, that I am not knowing." I squinted at the other boxes on the screen. "She was born in 1928 and lived in Leipzig before the war." When Jacob had filled in all the information, he looked to me for confirmation, and then clicked the blue box marked "SEND." Dread twisted my insides as I waited. The dream could not serve as proof Mira was alive. I had gone this long without the truth. If pre-sented with evidence of her death now, would I lose the ability to connect with her in the dream?

Before I could tell Jacob to forget the whole thing, a message flashed on the screen: No Results for Miriam Schloss. I pointed at the message. "Does that mean she's . . ." I couldn't finish the sentence.

"All that means is she's not on any of the lists on this site." He cleared the screen. "What about you? Is your information on file?"

"I am not knowing."

"Let's check. You should set up a profile in case someone is search-ing for you."

He cleared the form and entered my information, and it turned out I wasn't on their list, either. While Jacob set up my profile, I kicked myself for not doing this years ago. What if Mira had been search-ing for me?

Jacob and I spent the afternoon visiting different websites and scouring databases. One of them listed me among those killed in the gas chambers at Auschwitz in October 1944.

"But how is that possible? If Mira is searching for me, and she is finding that record, she will be giving up."

"The Nazis kept records on millions of people. Even they were bound to make mistakes now and then."

Jacob submitted a note to that site to correct my information. Then we ran searches for my parents and the Schlosses, on the chance that one of them had been alive when the war ended. Jacob said if one of Mira's relatives survived, their information might provide a clue to her whereabouts.

Soon the screen read "Search Complete." There was a list, like an index. Multiple records. My stomach churned. I had never known for certain what happened to my parents, and now I wanted to delay the inevitable. So I started talking.

"My father had one brother, Saul, who emigrated to America after the Great War. After he sponsored me to come to America, Uncle

Saul told me he'd urged my father to emigrate back in the early thirties. Even with my uncle to sponsor us, my father balked. My parents didn't speak English, and he must have worried about how hard it would be to give up his career as a university professor and start over." Pinching the bridge of my nose helped me hold back tears. "It would have been better to start over here, shoveling manure, than to end up—" Swallowing hard, I pointed at the screen again. "It is time to see those records."

They were dead. All dead. Mutti. Vati. Mr. and Mrs. Schloss. Even though I knew there was no possibility they could still be alive, I cried like a little boy when I saw in the records that my mother was among those sent to the gas chamber upon our arrival at Auschwitz, and my father was killed while trying to escape. This was not a recordkeeping error, but a lie. I am certain he was murdered by other prisoners in the train car while we were en route.

Hundreds of pages of testimony served as memorials to the dead. They all started the same way: "*I should like you to remember that there once lived a man named . . . a woman named . . . a girl named . . . born in Leipzig, Germany, who was murdered in the Shoah in 1943 . . . 1944 . . . 1945.*"

I found one of my friends from Montessori school listed. Even though I hadn't seen him since we were seven or eight, it saddened me to know his fate. Tears stung my eyes. "It is hard to look at the screen for so long, right?"

Jacob waited until I'd composed myself. "Have you ever told your story to anyone, Peter?"

"No. Never am I liking to talk about it. The past should be buried, but now the memories, they are coming back whether or not I want them. I don't write or speak too good in English—not good enough to be in a book or anything."

"That doesn't matter. If I lent you a digital recorder and showed you how to use it, would you tell the story to me? Even bits and pieces of memories are fine. You can work on it whenever you have time."

It would mean wallowing in sorrow. Without committing, I let Jacob show me how to use the digital recorder, and when I understood, he put it in a canvas bookbag so it would be easy for me to carry. On my way out, I stopped at the front desk and applied for a library card. I had never wanted to know what had happened to Leipzig during the war, for no amount of knowledge could change the past. But what I had learned today had piqued my curiosity.

"Now, maybe I am borrowing some books, right?" Kara, the librarian who'd first summoned Jacob for me, walked me to the sections on Nazism, the Third Reich, and World War II.

The books we brought to the checkout desk made a stack so tall I could not see over it.

"I am not sure I am carrying them all at once, for I am walking to get here." I ran my finger down the spines, prepared to leave some of them behind.

Jacob was still nearby. "I could walk you home and help carry them."

"Thank you. That would be very kind."

He took most of the books in two canvas bags, while I carried the lightest books and the digital recorder. As we headed toward Lyons Avenue, he asked, "Have you lived in this neighborhood long?"

"Since I am coming to America. It is changed much since then."

He nodded. "We have a collection of photos from the first half of the twentieth century, when Weequahic was pretty much a self-contained community."

"Yes, right. When I am first here, I am thinking I never have to leave here—is for sale everything I could need." When we reached my building, I handed my bag of books to Jacob so I could unlock my door. As he followed me inside, I thought about how few people had visited me here. I'd known Benny for years before he'd been over. But I didn't hesitate to let Jacob see into my world. That told me I'd already made the decision to share my story.

He set the bags of books on the kitchen table, and his eyes swept the room, taking in the shabby furniture and my stuff that had seen better days. Then he spoke. "You said you gave up looking for Mira years ago. But you never stopped waiting for her. Did you?"

I shrugged. "I am guessing no."

"You never changed a thing about this apartment, did you?"

"*Arbeit macht frei.* So I worked. And I waited. I could have been having anything I wanted here—except I am not wanting anything but Mira, right?"

"But work doesn't make you free, Peter. It might have helped you survive, but from what I've seen, it's love—and truth—that do the most to set you free." He shook my hand. "I look forward to hearing your story."

"Yes, yes."

He paused at the door. "Sharing has a transformative effect on many people. You may be surprised how free it makes you feel."

Alone in my apartment, I read all that afternoon and evening, until my vision grew blurry and I had to stop. Then I started again the next morning, reading parts of one book, then another, until I had a clear picture of my home city's destruction. There really had been nothing left in Leipzig for me.

Benny had said I needed to open up and share my pain. In those hours at the library, I had told Jacob more about my life than I'd ever told anyone. Though it had been difficult to revisit those memories, I already felt lighter inside. If I recorded the worst of my memories—the ones I still had not told anyone, ever—I would benefit from the telling even before anyone listened to what I had to say.

I stared down at the machine for a long time. When at last I laid my finger on the record button, I did not push hard enough to turn it on. I wasn't ready. Loneliness swept over me and I hurried out to the bodega.

Benny was busy with a customer, so I walked the aisles with my little basket, like I always did, but it was still empty when the door finally fell shut and we were alone. I made my way to the front.

"Hey, Benny—ever am I telling you about Frau Bressler's café in my hometown? Her lemon cookies were Mira's favorite."

He looked at me like I was crazy. "What did you—are you speaking German?"

"Was I? I did not notice." I laughed nervously. "Even with no one to speak it to, it is still in my brain. Maybe it was far in the back, in the discount bin."

"Pete, if you don't mind me asking—where have you been, anyway?"

"What do you mean? I am here yesterday. And the day before. Just like always."

"No, you haven't been in regular, and I was afraid you were sick or something. Are you sure you're all right?"

"I am getting my days mixed up sometimes. I am forgetting."

"You used to be as regular as clockwork." He looked at me like he was trying to figure something out.

"I am lost, Benny. Lost in memories. I am not knowing how to leave them behind. My family, my friends—they are all dead, but they are in my mind like they are waiting for me in the next room."

I wasn't expecting the tears that came to my eyes. I didn't think I had any left. Benny hurried around the counter and held me while I cried.

22

That evening, after supper, I made my first recording for Jacob. When I played it back, I didn't like the way my voice sounded. As I'd feared, it was difficult to express myself in English, and my halting, fractured thoughts were not at all what I wanted to present to Jacob.

My head felt so full of memories that Mira was just a heartbeat away. But could I find my way back to her? I used my relaxation breathing to fall asleep, hoping that when I opened my eyes again, she'd be glad to see me.

Sunlight flooded our bedroom. I rolled over and reached for her, but her side of the bed was empty. Then I heard her heave and vomit. The toilet flushed, and water ran in the sink. When she came out of the bathroom, she looked pale, with dark smudges beneath her eyes. I turned back the covers and helped her into bed, and when she shivered, I chafed her cold hands. "Are you ill?"

"No." Her voice sounded forlorn as a lost child's.

I pulled the duvet closer around her and drew her shaking form close, sharing the warmth of my body until she relaxed with a sigh. "Then what's the matter?" When she didn't answer, I took her face in my hands, afraid to hope. "You're pregnant." I glanced down at her middle. "Aren't you?"

A single tear slipped down her cheek as she nodded.

"That's the best news I've ever heard! Oh, Mira. I didn't know you could be."

"I didn't know either." She shuddered in my arms. "I was afraid you were angry with me and weren't coming back."

"You were aware that I left?"

"Yes of course."

"Nothing you could do would make me want to stay away from you."

A tear slipped down her cheek. "Don't be so sure. I think I made a mistake."

"No, no this wasn't a mistake. I want to be a father. You'll be the best mother in the world—"

"Not that kind of a mistake."

The hair on the back of my neck prickled. "What do you mean?"

"I was greedy. I wanted too much and I think I pushed too far. Now I can feel something—I don't know what it is but it's watching me. I don't know how to escape it."

I took both her hands in mine. "It happened to me, too, when I first came here. You need to stay in the moment. Be here, with me, in the now. That's how I got rid of mine."

"Truly?"

"Yes. Mine hasn't been back since the first time we—"

She didn't let me finish, and as we made love, she clung to me as though I was the only thing tethering her to this place. For the next few days, I didn't leave her side. We spoke only of the now and the future. But instead of growing stronger, she grew pale, and at night she woke screaming.

When I coaxed her out of the house to sit in the garden, she wrinkled her nose. "Can't you smell that? There's something rancid nearby."

To me, the air smelled of lilacs and sunshine, just as it always had. "Maybe it would be good to take a trip. Visit someplace else for a few days."

She didn't answer.

"Where would you like to go on holiday, my love?"

"Nowhere. I'm so tired." She squeezed my hand but turned her face away.

I went inside and retrieved the atlas. "The automobile and its driver are yours to command." She looked over my shoulder as I turned the pages, and soon she was game to discuss an itinerary.

"Not Poland. Not Berlin, either. I'd rather go west."

I kissed the tip of her nose. "Whatever you choose." None of the motorways built to facilitate Germany's invasion of its neighboring nations existed in the 1900 atlas, and I assumed they would not exist here, either. I traced my finger along routes to the west. "Salzburg, Munich, Amsterdam, Brussels, Lyon, Turin . . . take your pick."

"You know that all roads lead to Paris." As she got up off the garden bench and headed inside, she tossed a fainter version of her old saucy smile over her shoulder. "You're wearing me out just thinking about all those places. It's going to take me forever to get ready. I have a million things to do."

I planned to pack only my shaving kit and a change of clothes, because the dream catered to our every whim. With no need for money or travel documents, we might leave as soon as we liked.

Mira did not share my attitude about packing. Long after I was ready, she brought out one outfit after another to compare in the mirror and tried to decide which shoes she should leave behind. She was packing as though she did not intend to return.

Would we now live as nomads, one step ahead of the dark presence? It saddened me to think that the nursery alcove in our bedroom would never welcome our child. I packed the toy airplane in my suitcase. No matter when the baby arrived, we would be alone, without a doctor or midwife, and I could only hope the dream would continue to provide what we needed. The thought of being Mira's only attendant during our child's birth was both terrifying and exhilarating. I would be husband, father, and my family's sole protector.

I brought my suitcase and the atlas down to the car and returned for her suitcase and the violin. I caught a whiff of perfume as she closed the lid and snapped the locks closed. "That smells good."

"My mother always put a sachet doused with Evening in Paris in her luggage. She said that way, no matter where she was, her clothes smelled like home."

When we drove off after breakfast, Mira looked back at our house until it was out of sight. Then she faced forward and did not mourn what we were leaving behind. In this she reminded me more of my mother than hers, and it made me glad that she was holding fast, rather than crumbling under the strain.

As we traveled, it was hard to imagine that anything malevolent followed close behind. All day, the sun shone down on us, and as before, each new vista was worthy of gracing a picture postcard. We passed thatched-roof cottages, clusters of homes nestled in the shadows of castles perched on hilltops, curving rivers, and the snow-capped peaks of the Alps.

The terror and destruction wrought by Hitler's dozen years in power had not touched this pristine version of Germany. There weren't even any soot stains on the buildings.

But even though it looked like the fairy-tale locale Mira sought, my initial suspicions about this place had been spot on. It was too good to be true.

As the car nosed forward, I sensed that it was our energy that sparked the lovely tableaux to life, and once we passed by, the land turned dormant and gray.

Mira slept much of the drive, and the fresh air brought color to her pale cheeks. She awoke midafternoon, just before we arrived in Salzburg. We ate in a café and strolled the cobbled streets past elegant buildings in the historic section of town. On the Getreidegasse, the main street, Mira pointed out the district's famous wrought-iron signs, formed to show what was for sale inside each shop. Of course, they didn't all match the current proprietors' wares, but I craned my neck to see them, nonetheless. The shop doors were all open wide, inviting us in. When I suggested we browse in a jewelry store, she shook her head.

"I need nothing."

"But you could have whatever you want."

"I want nothing in the shops. I know why Salzburg is on the itinerary, though." She hummed the opening bars of "Eine Kleine Nachtmusik," conducting with one hand. "We're going to see Mozart's violin!"

I took her hand and kissed her fingertips. "We must pay tribute to my second-favorite violinist of all time."

"I shall play for you at the museum."

She did, and she came to life, as always, when her bow touched the strings.

After, her energy surged, and she insisted we go up to the Hohensalzburg Fortress. As we walked around, she read from a placard, "'Salzburg was never taken by force, but surrendered to Napoleon. The fortress was never used for defense.'"

I looked around at the inner courtyard, ringed with shops for artisans, blacksmiths, butchers, and bakers. "They could have moved the city up here and survived a siege."

Inside the main building, Mira squealed with delight when we happened upon a marionette stage. "I've always loved these." She stepped up behind the curtain and unhooked a furry, horned goat from its place on the wall. As she worked the strings to make it dance across the stage, she yodeled in a raspy voice.

"Is that what a goat sounds like?"

She laughed at my puzzled expression. "You never heard that song?"

"What song?"

"Never mind. Come be the lonely goatherd."

I took the puppet and found that, like everything else I'd tried, it was easy. I made the little guy trip over his own feet. Mira brought out a girl puppet with yellow braids and pulled the strings to make her swish her skirts and blow a kiss.

I didn't understand why she kept giggling as she said in a sing-song voice, "I'll take the girl in the pale pink coat. She'll make a bride for the lonely goatherd." She paused and looked at me expectantly.

"Yodel-ayee-yodel-ayee-yodel-oo?"

She laughed so hard she had to sit down. "Close enough."

When we'd had our fill of playing with the puppets, we hung them back in place and walked out to look down on the city from the fortress's lower bastion. I scanned the horizon and the winding streets below. The fortress could hold off a hostile army but could offer no protection for us. I must do it alone. When the dark presence returned to threaten Mira, I would be ready, and I'd welcome something to fight for—and to fight against.

That night, we dined at St. Peter's Stiftskeller in St. Peter's Abbey. When we arrived, I read from a placard on the wall in my best tour guide voice. "This is the oldest known restaurant in Europe, visited by Charlemagne himself in eight-oh-three A.D."

Mira looked up from the menu board. "Hmm. What did he order?"

"No idea."

Though she remained lighthearted and the meal was exceptional, there were too many dark corners in the restaurant, and my imagination conjured centuries' worth of ghosts flitting just out of sight.

When she opened her suitcase in our hotel room, a hint of Evening in Paris wafted out. It was she who reached out to me, and we made love as though it was a tune we alone could hear. She fell asleep immediately after, and when I dozed off, I dreamed I saw her walking ahead of me toward the sandstone hills at Bastei. I ran to catch up with her, but I couldn't close the distance between us. I called to her and she turned, smiling and waving.

"Wait for me!" Rooted to the spot, I woke up, confused. I'd never dreamed while I was in the dream before. As I lay in the darkness, musing over the dream within a dream, my scalp prickled. For the first time, I sensed the dark presence. I rolled over and woke her with kisses. At first, she turned her face away sleepily. Then she noticed it, too.

"Oh, no—"

"Don't give in to it." I positioned myself to block her view of the room. "Don't give yourself to it, Mira. Give yourself to me. Stay with me." I ran my hand up her thigh, pushing her nightgown higher, and defying the thing that terrorized her. She climbed on top. As we moved as one, I thought, *Take that, whatever you are. If you lurk in the shadows, we'll give you something to watch.* The heat of her body, the thrill of her touch, and the taste of her mouth were real. Would our love and our bond be enough to keep the shadowy figure at bay?

The next morning, sun streamed into the room and Mira stretched like a lazy cat. "Where are we going next?"

I snapped the clasps on my suitcase closed. "It's a surprise. Just a few hours by car." I hoped that by keeping our destination a surprise, Mira would not unwittingly draw the dark presence after us.

Breakfast was ready in the hotel café when we came downstairs, and I took heart when Mira ate nearly as much as I did. I drained my coffee and held out my hand. "Come, my love. The rest of Europe awaits."

In Munich, Gothic spires marked the Town Hall on Marienplatz, the colorful square dominated by the Rathaus. We arrived in time to witness the Glockenspiel chimes at eleven, and then spent an hour window shopping before lunch. Around two, Mira played another concert on stage at the National Theater, uninterrupted except by my applause.

Before dinner, we took a sauna and swam at the Müllersches Volksbad. Until we entered the cavernous room that housed the indoor pool, I'd had no warnings from my heightened intuition, no indication that the dark presence had followed us to Munich. But in this echoing space, where the water's ripples reflected off the walls and ceiling, my eyes kept darting toward the shadowy corners. When we finished swimming, we changed in the same bathhouse by tacit agreement, neither of us wanting to be alone. As we strolled out in search of dinner, a beer garden strung with bright lights beckoned to us from the street. That night, it was Mira who woke me with kisses and whispered, "Stay with me."

Each day of travel brought new sights and new experiences. We arrived in Strasbourg in time for a late lunch and wandered the narrow, cobbled streets of La Petite France, with its half-timbered houses, cantilevered waterways, and canal locks. Here we sampled Vin d'Alsace, a sparkling white wine, and found a case waiting for us in our hotel room that night. In Luxembourg, we explored the Casemates du Bock, tunnels dug in natural fortifications used to hide soldiers, horses, and munitions from ancient times until the mid-nineteenth century. As we stood on the fortifications, I looked out over the city center and my scalp prickled. It was time to move on. The thing that pursued us was out there somewhere.

Mira slept in the car, saving her strength for our arrival in Bruges, where we walked the cobbled streets, watched the swans on the canals, and ate chocolates. The next day, she rose with dark circles under her eyes and wore an extra sweater in the car, hiding the gold locket she'd worn around her neck throughout our trip, though I found it warm enough to roll up my sleeves. I crossed any remaining destinations off my list, and after a brief pause for lunch in Lille, we headed straight for Paris.

When we reached the city late that afternoon, I nudged the dozing Mira at my first glimpse of the Eiffel Tower. She stirred, and when she saw it, a blazing smile swept over her face. "It's just as beautiful as it was the last time I saw it."

She gave no sign that she recognized her slip.

23

Though I was in favor of taking her to the hotel to rest, Mira roused herself and insisted we begin the visit as we'd planned when we were seven. Our first stop was the Eiffel Tower. We rode the waiting elevator to the first observation platform, where she leaned her elbows on the railing. "When I was little, I imagined we could ride a single elevator straight to the top of the Tower."

How changed she was since we'd reunited in this dream world. Then, she had been the picture of health. Now, she was thin and pale, her hair dull and brittle. Could pregnancy really take such a toll, or was something else causing her to waste away before my eyes?

"Are you ready to go up to the next platform?"

She nodded and leaned on me on the way to the elevator. Two more levels up, we reached the top. The wind ruffled her hair as we looked out over the pristine city, silent, yet vibrant with color.

Back down at the base, market stalls were ready for Mira's perusal, scented with the lavender, milled soaps, and fresh flowers on display. She started toward them, and when I hesitated, she pulled at my arm.

Worried about her and on edge lest the dark presence reveal itself again, my words came out grumpier than I intended. "Another market?"

"I know I don't need anything—but I want to see everything."

"All right." She sagged against me, and I walked slowly to accommodate her. "Can you imagine this market full of people?"

"Why? Do you miss seeing other people?"

"Sometimes."

Her face fell. "Aren't I enough?"

"Of course, you are." I passed my hand over her middle. "You are enough, and when we are three, it will be an even bigger blessing. We shouldn't think about what could be different. We're in Paris—and there are no crowds of tourists. We can go anywhere we like."

She smiled, her good humor restored. "Where shall we stay the night?"

"The Ritz. Wasn't that what you said?"

"You remembered."

"How could I forget?" I escorted her back to the Mercedes and piloted it across the bridge that spanned the Seine and through the uninhabited streets, slowing as I turned onto the Champs-Élysées. Mira leaned on the passenger door, absorbing all the sights on the grand avenue and in the gardens near the Louvre. When we parked in front of the Ritz on Place Vendome, the hotel's delicate grillwork gates and inner doors were open wide, as though an unseen host had anticipated our arrival.

Inside, we crossed the red carpet into the lobby. "I expected something grander."

She giggled. "It is really small, isn't it? I read once that they made the lobby this way on purpose to discourage loitering."

I laughed as I looked around the empty room. "Looks like it worked."

At the desk, I signed the register Mr. and Mrs. Peter Ibbetz. Proof that we existed, somewhere in the universe.

Then I picked up the waiting room key and dangled it in front of her. "Shall we go up?"

"Not yet." Her energy had returned, and she smiled in anticipation and took my hand. "Don't you want to see every inch of this place?"

I did. Everything in the hotel gleamed, from the soaring ceilings to the polished cream-marble floors. We strolled down long hallways past arched windows hung with heavy silk draperies. Dining rooms stood ready to receive dozens of guests. While the décor was too feminine for my taste, Mira adored the pastel furnishings. I enjoyed watching her eyes dart about as she tried to take in everything at once.

I caught a faint whiff of cigar smoke as we strolled past the Hemingway bar, a dark-paneled room filled with tufted leather furniture and heavy oak tables. In such a lavish hotel, that bar was intimate and cozy, the perfect place to hunker down as the only people on Earth. But there was more to see, and Mira pulled at my hand to lead me outside.

Under the striped awnings in the terrace garden restaurant, we came upon trays of fruit, a three-tiered stand of pastries covered with a glass dome, and a pot of tea. Mira sighed blissfully. "It's perfect."

I held her chair for her. "If we could stay here, would you care to live like this all the time?"

She poured two cups of tea. "No, not really. This is marvelous, and I'm having a wonderful time, but I'd be just as happy at home with you."

"I'm glad you feel that way, too. With the entire world laid out for us, and anything we want at our fingertips, it would be easy to . . ."

"Get greedy?"

"Yes. That's not who I am. I'll stay in Paris for as long you want. But it doesn't matter where we are. Being with you is what makes me happy." After tea, we rose and I tucked her hand into the crook of my arm. We strolled through the gardens, but as the shadows grew long, her energy faded again.

There was a note of apology in her voice. "Perhaps we should go up to the room and rest awhile before dinner."

On our way back through the grounds and the endless hallways, she needed to stop and rest twice before we reached the lobby. I left her on a settee while I went to fetch the bags from the car. "Come, we should take the elevator and save your strength."

She eyed the cage with distrust. "No thank you. The elevators at the Eiffel Tower were much more spacious. This one is too confined for my taste. I'll take the stairs."

The stairs went up and up and up, around the forty-foot crystal chandelier suspended from the soaring ceiling. The thick, red oriental carpeting muffled our footsteps. Our suite on the top floor should have made Mira squeal with delight. It was furnished in a perfectly coordinated palette of cream and blush, with gold leaf on the crown moldings. Red accents in the accessories and the floral arrangements exactly matched the cord around Mira's neck, but she seemed too tired to notice. She crossed immediately to the bed, slipped off her shoes, and burrowed under the covers. I lay beside her while she napped, wondering how long we would stay here, and how long before the baby would be born.

The sun was low in the sky when she stretched and rose. "I must get up and start my hair and makeup or we'll miss our dinner." She rummaged in her suitcase as I lounged on the bed.

She caught my eye. "Don't you need to get ready, too?"

"It'll take me fifteen minutes. I'd rather watch you."

Restored by her nap, she tossed her head, flirting. "Do you want a private show?"

She looked surprised when I laughed. Her reaction made what she'd said even funnier, and I kept on laughing until I was holding my stomach and gasping.

"What in the world is so funny?"

"You said a private show. Is there any other kind here?" I wiped my eyes and sobered. "You're beautiful without makeup. Don't go to the trouble if you don't want to."

"But I want to. When a woman takes the time to primp and curl and put on lipstick and rouge, she's treating herself well. I do it as much for me as you." She leaned across the bed to tap me on the nose with her powder puff. "Even though you're the last man on earth, I still want to look my best."

I sat up and brushed off the powder before it made me sneeze. "I wasn't kidding when I said you don't need makeup." I got on all fours and crawled to the edge of the bed.

With a coy smile, she twisted up a tube of lipstick, gliding it on in an alluring performance. As soon as she put it away, I grabbed her around the waist and pulled her onto the bed with me. "You're feeling better, aren't you?" I kissed away her carefully applied makeup.

She rubbed a smudge of lipstick off my cheek and struggled to sit up. "See what you've done? Now I've got to start over."

I pinned her beneath me and kissed her some more. "They'll hold our dinner reservation."

When she left the bed an hour later, she stood out of arm's reach and pointed a warning finger. "If you want to leave this room tonight, you've got to let me get ready."

"Don't tempt me."

"I'm serious. I'm not missing dinner in Paris." She brandished her hairbrush at me, and I held up my hands in surrender. I quickly threw on some clothes.

"Then I'll leave you in peace for a while. I'll be back." Before she could ask where I was going, I hurried out. I had an errand to run.

When I returned, Mira looked like a fashion plate. Expertly applied rouge hid her pallor. She'd swept her hair into an elegant chignon and dressed in a red silk gown.

"You look amazing." I touched the heart locket, which gleamed against her creamy skin.

As promised, I got dressed in my evening attire and was ready to leave in a fraction of the time she'd required. We watched the sunset from our balcony, and though the lights that winked on all over the city created the illusion that it was throbbing with activity, the silence from below told the truth.

She turned to face me and straightened the knot in my tie. "What shall we do after dinner and dancing?"

"How about a river cruise?"

"That would be lovely."

"Let's bring your violin."

I'd never eaten in such an elegant restaurant before. The first course was on the table when we arrived. When we finished the soup à l'oignon, I led Mira to the dance floor, where an invisible orchestra played from behind a screen of potted palm trees. Upon our return to the table, the soup dishes had been cleared and plates of duck confit, haricots verts, and herbed mashed potatoes awaited us.

After the meal, we walked to the dock, and she squeezed my hand. "We forgot to stop at Le Mans."

"I don't mind. We'll go another time."

She nodded, but without enthusiasm. I kept my arm around her as we walked up the gang plank to the boat.

As an unseen captain piloted us down the Seine, the melodies she drew from her violin drifted across the water and through the silent streets. I smiled as I closed my hand over the velvet box in my jacket pocket.

When the boat docked as though guided by invisible deckhands, I tucked Mira's arm through the crook of my elbow, and we walked down the gang plank. There, on the banks of the Seine, I dropped to one knee. "I asked you once before, a long time ago. Now, will you make me the happiest man in the world and marry me?" I brought the velvet box from my pocket and opened it.

Tears welled up in her eyes, but as I took the ring out to put it on her finger, she shook her head no.

No.

My shoulders sagged. "Mira, you know this is what we've always wanted. Don't turn me away. Say you'll marry me." I got to my feet, as awkward as a boy angling for his first kiss.

"Peter." Her tears spilled down her cheeks. "You know this isn't—I mean, you remember where we are, right?"

"Of course, I remember!" I had to check myself to make sure I didn't slip away from her now. "But why does it matter? No one really knows how much time they have. We could be here for years and years." When she remained silent, I burst out, "Don't refuse me without a reason. That's not fair."

"Life isn't fair."

I took her face in my hands so she couldn't turn away and searched for answers in her eyes. "I've loved you my whole life. I'm in your bed every night. You're carrying my child. What more reason do you need to marry?"

She laid her hand on my heaving chest. "I told you I would marry no one but you, and I meant it, Peter. My heart has belonged to you since we were children. But look around. The light is growing dim."

"What do you mean?" The sun had set hours ago, but all the districts around the waterfront were ablaze, pushing back the darkness. The City of Light lived up to its name.

"Nothing." She stood taller, as if bracing herself for something unpleasant.

I held her palm to my lips and then turned it over. Her hands were delicate, but strong, and a hundred percent real.

I took the ring from the box, and when she didn't protest, I guided it up over the knuckle on her fourth finger.

A tear slipped down her cheek. "I want to make you happy."

"You do. And I want to make you happy, too—so we will be. We're going to have a family. We'll have everything we wanted." I held her hand out, so the ring caught the light.

As we strolled past the storefronts, I paused in front of a bridal shop's window display and envisioned how she'd look in white satin with a lace-covered bodice and a sweeping train.

"What kind of gown do you want? If you like, we could be married here, on top of the Eiffel Tower."

"I was thinking of something a little simpler." She put her arms around my neck. "Maybe a garden wedding under an apple tree. With a hand-picked bouquet."

"If that's what you want, you shall have it."

"As soon as we get home, then."

"Yes. When we get home."

A moment later she gasped and pointed. "Did you see that? Across the street." I looked where she pointed, but I saw nothing in the shadows. The wind shifted, and even though it blew warm, she shivered. "Let's go." I took her arm, and though we hurried, the ten-block walk back to the hotel seemed to take forever.

When we rushed into the building and across the red carpet, the brightly lit lobby felt like a haven. Mira's heels clicked on the marble floor as she pulled me past the elevator.

"I can't ever go inside that tiny box. We have to take the stairs."

I followed her up the curved staircase. The round globe of the light mounted on the newel post on the ground floor illuminated the stairs as far as the landing but the cheery lights from the lower floors faded into gloom as we climbed. The wall sconces, which had shone bright when we'd arrived, now gave barely enough light to see by as we ran down the hall. She clutched my arm, watching the hall behind us as I fumbled with the key.

In our cozy, romantic room, the invisible hotel staff had left a bottle of champagne on ice, chocolates, and a bouquet of roses on the table. I locked the door, and Mira sank into one of the upholstered chairs and slipped off her shoes. After a moment, she sighed and smiled. I felt safe inside the room too. I popped the cork, poured into the waiting crystal flutes, and raised mine. "To my wife."

"Just a taste for me. It's not good for the child." Tears brimmed in her eyes again as she sipped. Then she set down her glass and opened the balcony doors. I joined her, and as we looked out over the lights of Paris, the eerie silence pressed on my ears. We would never be carefree here. When I could stand it no longer, I put my arm around her shoulders to draw her back inside.

As she let go of the railing, her ring flashed in the light. Then the reflection faded. One by one, the districts of Paris went dark, until only the streets in our immediate vicinity remained alight. The stars glowed bright, close enough to reach out and touch, and then they, too, winked out, as if someone had drawn an inky curtain across the sky.

Mira buried her face in my chest and my arms closed around her automatically. Was this a not-so-subtle hint that our time, as she had feared, was running out? If this was our last night together, we must make it a night to remember so we could carry the memory with us into eternity.

I unzipped the back of her dress, kissing her neck as I eased it off her shoulders. This was the last step on the way to forever, where she would always be my wife. The dress rippled to the floor and I ran my hand up her stocking to the clip on her garter belt. She trembled as I caressed the curve of her hip. As we swayed, almost dancing, I spanned her waist with my hands, and my fingertips met at the base of her spine. I walked her backward, and she gave a little shriek as we fell onto the bed.

My pulse quickened as she loosened the knot in my tie and unbuttoned my collar. The locket rested in the hollow at the base of her throat and felt warm in my hand when I picked it up.

She lifted the red cord over her head and fashioned it into two slipknots, leaving the gold heart dangling between them. She put one loop around her wrist, and the other around mine and pulled the cord taut. "Promise me . . ."

"Anything, Mira."

She laced her fingers with mine, and I pressed our hands into the pillows, over her head. Our kiss was so deep that I sank into her very core. Then she turned her lips away and whispered close to my ear, "Come to me. In Shanghai. I need you."

The knot around my wrist constricted, cutting off my circulation.

Her fingertips slipped from my grasp. The red silk cord was all that tethered me to her. Lightheaded, I watched as the fibers of silk pulled apart, snapping one by one until the locket slid off the cord and fell. Mira's face, racked with grief, faded from view. As I blacked out, I heard her whisper, "Goodbye, Peter."

24

Drenched in cold sweat, I gasped for breath in the darkness, the pain in my chest so intense I thought I was having a heart attack. I couldn't get out of bed to reach the phone. But I couldn't die alone. Not now.

Mira had sacrificed whatever time remained for us in the dream and sent me to find her in the real world. She'd said she needed me. But Shanghai? She might as well be on the moon.

My legs trembled as they carried me into the kitchen, where I flipped on the light and sank down at the table with the atlas. I'd just promised never to leave her again. *Oy vey.* It was lunacy to even consider a trip like that. But what choice did I have? Cradling my head in my hands, I spoke aloud. "I'm coming as soon as I can. Wait for me, Mira. Wait for me."

In the hours before dawn, I paced my apartment like a caged animal, anxious to take action but not knowing where to begin.

I left for the library right after breakfast and was waiting outside when Kara unlocked the door. "Good morning, Mr. Ibbetz. Nice to see you again so soon. Jacob isn't volunteering today."

"That's okay. I am needing to learn about Shanghai, and my atlas is a hundred and twenty years old."

She laughed. "We have recent books about China, but you can get the most updated information with an online search. Would you like me to help you get started?" Kara taught me how to use a search engine on the computer and left me to read on my own. When I learned Shanghai had a population of twenty-six million, I couldn't believe it. How would I find Mira in such a large city?

I returned home several hours later, my head reeling with new information. The knock on my door caught me by surprise. I looked through the peephole and saw Benny holding a paper sack of groceries. I slid back the bolt and took off the chain.

"Hey, Pete—are you all right, man? You ain't been around like usual. Are you getting enough to eat?"

Stifling a yawn, I motioned him inside. "Yes, yes I am fine. I am just losing track of the time. I have been busy."

"Busy? Like how?"

"Reading. Planning. I am thinking of taking a trip."

"Is that right?"

"You and Valeria, you are doing traveling?"

"Nah. I'm tied down to the business. Most I can hope for is a few weekends at the shore. You ever go to the shore, Pete?"

"Once. In 1949, I am thinking. With my uncle's family."

He opened the fridge and looked at the empty shelves. "You planning to leave soon? You ain't got much to eat in here."

When I didn't answer, he put the groceries away. "Where you gonna go? New York? Florida?"

"I am not knowing anybody in either of those places. I am thinking maybe China. Shanghai."

Benny's eyebrows shot up so high they disappeared into his hair. "Shanghai?"

"An old friend is there—Mira. I am telling you about her sometimes. We are reconnecting."

"How long ago?"

"A few weeks ago, maybe."

"So how did you get back in touch? By phone? Or did she send you a letter?"

"I have spoken to her."

"Pete, how can you be sure it's really your friend? You said you haven't seen her since you were teenagers. I don't want nothing bad to happen to you."

"Benny, you are worrying, but there is no reason."

"Did she ask you for money?"

"No! Nothing like that."

"You know what a scam is, right? When crooks try to trick people out of their money?"

"Trick old people, you mean?"

"Not just old people. Good people, trusting people. Promise me you won't send her any money."

"Yes, yes. I promise. Mira is not tricking me. Is under control." I waved away his concerns as I headed for my worktable. "Finally, I am finishing repairs on the music box. You can take it home to Valeria now, right?"

I wound the key, proud of the fact that the tune again played perfectly. Benny held the box gently in both hands. "We'll treasure this, Pete. Thank you."

"I am happy you like it." I patted him on the shoulder. "You are good boy to worry about me, Benny. I am being fine."

He bit his lip as he nodded. "I sure hope so."

After he left, I heated up a can of soup and made a sandwich using the groceries he'd brought over. As I looked at the atlas on the kitchen table, I slapped my forehead. *Oy vey*. In the dream, I'd left Mira in Paris. Would she try to return to Leipzig in the car? How could I let her know I was on the way?

Then I remembered the locket was here, in my apartment, and also there with Mira. So was the atlas. I scribbled several coded messages. If I left them between the pages, perhaps she'd receive them.

Feeling hopeful, I carried my dishes to the sink and turned on the water. As I washed and dried, I was so lost in thoughts of Shanghai and how to get there that the next knock on my door really threw me for a loop. Remember nosy Miss Richter from Elder Services? This was when she and Benny showed up and nearly foiled my plan to find Mira.

25

Benny, Mrs. Simmons, and Miss Richter had their powwow about me downstairs in the hall, and after Benny and Miss Richter left, I watched to make sure she had driven away before I cut open my mattress. I never trusted anyone else with my money. I had always cashed my paychecks and my Social Security checks and hidden what I didn't need, either in the mattress or under a loose floorboard in my closet. The canvas sack in there was stuffed with cash, a nest egg for emergencies. Until now, I'd never had an emergency, and I'd planned to leave the money to Benny when I was gone.

But he had violated my trust, and I might need every cent of my savings to find Mira. I had no idea how much a plane ticket to Shanghai would cost, so I zipped stacks of bills into my jacket pockets.

In the kitchen, I opened the atlas and put the coded messages near maps of the places we'd visited—Salzburg, Munich, Bruges, Lille, Paris. I hoped it would work like dropping a leaflet bomb, and she'd find a sheaf of messages telling her I was headed to Shanghai to find her. Then I went downstairs and out to the corner, where I signaled for a taxi. When one pulled up, I asked, "How much is it costing to the airport?"

"About sixteen bucks. Plus tip. You got any luggage?"

"No." As I got in, I saw Benny outside the bodega. When he saw me, he did a double take and hurried toward me, but the cab pulled away before he crossed the street.

The roar of airplanes was part of the ambient noise in my neighborhood, but I had never realized the airport was so close. I watched the planes take off as we drove down Bergen Street, just a few blocks from my house. In a flash we were on the highway heading past the golf course and the park. In another few minutes, we were there.

"What terminal, buddy?"

"I am thinking to just pull over here." Sixteen bucks seemed like a lot for such a short ride, but I gave the cabbie a twenty and told him to keep the change.

Inside, the place swarmed with people wearing backpacks and dragging suitcases on wheels. Overwhelmed, but determined, I spotted a clerk at a service desk and headed over. People around me grumbled, and the clerk stopped me before I could ask my question.

"Sir, you need to go to the end of the line." She pointed over my shoulder. I turned around and saw about twenty-five people behind me, waiting in a queue.

Mumbling an apology, I moved to the rear of the line, where another clerk asked for my ticket.

"I am not having it yet. I am wanting to buy it now."

She gave me one of those looks young people sometimes give the elderly—like we've got no idea how to manage the simplest of tasks. "What is your destination, sir?"

"Shanghai."

Her surprise showed I'd made an even bigger blunder. "But sir, this airline doesn't fly to Shanghai. You'll need to go to United's international terminal."

"Can you show me—"

"First may I see your passport, please?"

"What for? My passport is expired in 1958." Then the light bulb came on. I'd gotten ahead of myself. "Perhaps I am not ready to be leaving yet."

"Do you need help to get home? Do you live nearby?"

"No. Yes. Please do not worry about it. I am taking a cab."

"What's your name, sir?"

"Never mind. My mistake." This was more than being a *forgetsik*. I must have seemed like I'd lost my marbles. I was going to need help.

Exhausted by my interactions with people, the voice inside my head asked how I expected to make it to Shanghai when I'd been turned away at the airport. *Button it*, I told the little voice. I needed to think without anyone interrupting.

Like a prisoner planning a jailbreak, I would need help on the outside. I followed a group of people through the sliding doors to ground transportation and got another cab. I sank into the seat, and when the cabbie asked me where to, I said, "Where's the nearest whatayacallit, where they are helping you plan a trip?"

"Travel agent?"

"Yes—that's it."

The cabbie was a young guy, and he chuckled. "I didn't know they had those anymore. Hang on a sec and I'll see." He started messing with his phone. "There's one about six miles from here."

"That far?"

"Yeah. Takes about twenty minutes. You wanna go? They're open till five."

"How are you knowing all that?"

"It's on my phone. Ain't you ever heard of GPS?"

"No. That is very good thing to have."

"Sure is."

The travel agency was located in a narrow slice of a storefront. Inside, the posters advertising destinations like Greece, London, Paris, and Sydney seemed larger than life in the tiny space. The woman behind the desk hurriedly stubbed out a cigarette, waving at the smoke to clear the air. Flustered, she pushed back a lock of dyed-red hair.

"Sorry! I know I'm not supposed to but I hardly ever get walk-ins here. What can I do for you, sir?"

My mouth felt dry. "I need to go to Shanghai right away."

"We have some lovely tour packages that include Shanghai. How many in your party? When would you like to depart?"

"I am wanting to leave today. But first I am needing a new passport."

"I see." She tilted her head to the side as she studied me. I glanced down at my cardigan, with its fraying cuffs and missing button, my faded slacks, and my scuffed loafers. She probably didn't believe I could afford a subway token, let alone a plane ticket.

"It is an emergency. A matter of life and death."

"Life and death, you say?"

"Yes. My friend—a girl I am knowing a long time ago—needs me. If I am not leaving right away, I am afraid I will be too late. I am missing the chance to see her and tell her I am never forgetting about her."

"A long-lost love, huh? How long ago are we talking?"

"Seventy-five years."

Her expression softened. "That's so romantic." Then her eyebrows flew up. "Holy mackerel! What are you gonna say to her after that long?"

"I am never running out of things to talk about with my Mira."

"Honey, I'm a sucker for a love story. You can count on my help." She extended her hand. "I'm Lucille."

We shook. "Peter."

"Pleased to meet you, Peter." Elbows on the desk, she put her chin on her hands. "Now tell me all about your lady friend Mira. And don't worry. I'll get you to Shanghai lickety-split."

Relief washed over me and I ended up telling Lucille everything—except the part about finding Mira in the dream. I fibbed and told her I'd located Mira's name on a list of survivors, letting her think I'd been in contact with Mira and she was expecting my visit.

By the time I finished my story, I felt like Lucille was an old friend. She got two seltzers out of the mini fridge behind her desk and held hers up for a toast. "To reuniting long-lost loves. It's one of the perks of this job." I clinked my bottle against hers, and we each took a sip.

Then she attacked the keyboard in front of her with her lacquered nails. I traced my finger through the condensation on the seltzer bottle until the clicking noises stopped.

"Pete, I can get you an expedited passport, but even expedited it's going to take eight days. The travel visa's a bigger issue, but with a little luck we'll find a way around that." Her fingers flew over the keys in more rapid-fire typing. "Bingo! I can book you on a ten-day cruise to Okinawa."

"No, no cruise. I am needing to get to Shanghai."

"Listen to me, I know the ropes, and I'll get you where you want to go. The only way I can get you into China is as a Transit Without Visa—for tourists who are traveling through to another final destination."

"So I must say I am going to Okinawa to get to Shanghai?"

"Yes—but you'll go to Shanghai first. It's like a free pass into the country—and it's good for a hundred and forty-four hours. Six days. Clock starts at midnight the day following your entry into the country."

Six days. I rubbed my chin. Could I find Mira in only six days?

"That will give you a good long visit with your lady friend. If I book everything today, I can have you on the ground in Shanghai by the end of next week, Pete."

"Well, in that case, a cruise it is. Please."

"I can get you on a nonstop out of Newark to Shanghai. Do you fly often?"

"Never have I been in an airplane. In former times I am coming here to America on a ship. Since I was being a teenager, I have not been anywhere but New Jersey."

"You're sure about doing this? If you've never been anywhere . . ." She scratched her head and stared at the screen. "Definitely the non-stop option then."

"Whatever you are figuring out is fine with me. I will do whatever I must."

"All right." She looked as though she was about to break bad news to me. "The total—including the expedited passport, flight to Shanghai, a hotel for six nights, and the cruise—comes to five thousand two hundred and eighty-four dollars."

I'd never spent that much money at one time. My chest felt so tight I had trouble breathing from the excitement. I was on my way to find Mira! I pulled a stack of bills out of my jacket pocket, and as soon as Lucille spotted the cash, she jumped up from her chair, locked the door, and closed the blinds.

"Pete, you didn't really walk over here carrying that much cash?"

"No. I am coming in a cab."

"Either way you must have lost your mind!" We fell silent. I think we were both wondering if I really had lost my mind.

I counted five thousand three hundred dollars onto the desk. Her hand trembled as she picked up the stack and counted it again. She had to get her purse and give me the sixteen dollars change out of her wallet. "Most people use credit cards these days."

"Never had one."

"You should get one for this trip. It's easier to carry a card than cash." She didn't call me a relic and make fun of me the way my landlady did. I appreciated that.

"Yes, I am thinking so. There are many things I am needing before I'm ready to go. Can you help me making a list?"

Lucille grabbed a notepad off her desk and a pen from the mug by her computer and started writing. "Okay, first things first, you'll need a debit card. Also a cell phone, a money belt"—she eyed my outfit—"and some new clothes for traveling."

When we finished, Lucille called a cab to take me home. Outside, I caught sight of my reflection in one of the few shop windows that wasn't boarded up. Mira wouldn't know this old, withered version of me. Would I recognize her?

Overhead, I watched a plane bank as it approached the runway and felt a rush of fear sweep over me. What if flying made me feel sick? How long would it take to get to Shanghai? I'd read about how planes stay up in the air in my physics textbook, but the knowledge did little to quell the nervous flutter in my stomach.

26

The eight days before I could leave stretched in front of me like an eternity. After the cab dropped me off at home, I went to see Benny. I hadn't forgiven him for siccing Miss Richter on me, but I was going to have to ask him for a favor. He looked up when the bell jingled and blew out an angry breath as he came around the counter.

"What's going on with you, Pete? Where did you go in that cab?"

"To ask Miss Richter on a movie date."

"Quit kidding around. I'm worried about the way you've been acting lately."

"I am needing to get new clothes."

"What for?"

"What are you meaning what for? To wear on my date with Miss Richter."

"All right, fine. Don't tell me if you don't want to. But you ain't gonna find the kind of suit you'd want in this neighborhood." He considered for a moment. "Out on the highway, there's a place. It's too far to walk, though. You in a rush?"

"Soon. Tomorrow maybe."

"You plan on going somewhere?"

"Yes. I am already telling you."

His voice lost its humorous tone. "Hang on, man. Did you go to the doctor? You get some bad news? You're not checking out, are you?"

"I'm not dying. *Oy vey*, it's just time I am buying new clothes. That's all."

"I can drive you tomorrow. Valeria can watch the store for a while."

"Yes. Very good."

"You come by about three, huh?"

That night, I dreamed I could hear Mira calling me, but I couldn't find her. Our dream world had vanished, but her voice stretched out to me through the darkness, repeating my name, over and over. I woke up anxious, wishing my trip wasn't still a week away.

The next afternoon at quarter to three, I left for the bodega. Benny's wife, Valeria, had come in to run the store, and I bought two chocolate bars from her. "I appreciate you letting me borrow Benny. I am sorry to be causing trouble. Where is your little boy?"

"Benito is spending the afternoon with my mom. We're glad to be able to help you out, Pete." When she smiled up at Benny, I saw the same light in her eyes I'd seen in Mira's. "The music box is beautiful, by the way. Thank you for such a thoughtful gift." She squeezed my hand.

Benny kissed her on the cheek. "We'll be back in a few hours, babe."

On the way to the car, I wondered if he felt the same surge of love I'd felt for Mira when he touched Valeria.

Benny's car wasn't new, but it was clean on the inside. He pulled the seatbelt around me and clicked me in before starting the engine, as if I were a child. I wished I could show him my Mercedes and take him for a ride.

"How far is it?" I raised my voice over the noise on the radio.

He grinned and turned it down a little. "Half an hour, maybe a little more."

I passed him a chocolate bar. "For the trip."

He tore off the wrapper. "Thanks, man."

He finished his before we reach the highway. I nibbled mine, using it to distract myself from my fear of being in traffic. Cars and trucks rushed through my neighborhood all the time, but I don't like to go that fast. My scalp prickled and my hands and feet started to sweat as Benny accelerated up the ramp and cut over into the high-speed lane. I shrank away from the vehicles that whizzed along inches from my window.

I took another bite of chocolate and closed my eyes. The next time I opened them, the car in front of us was so close I let out an involuntary yelp.

"I got you, man. No worries."

"I am not being used to so much traffic."

Benny barely touched the brake as we took an exit ramp and merged into traffic on the Garden State Parkway. I'd just started to believe I was going to die before I could leave for Shanghai when he slowed the car and turned into the menswear store's parking lot.

Inside the store—*oy vey*—I didn't know how to choose from so many clothes. One of the salesmen greeted us, and as he glanced from Benny to me, he seemed to be wondering about our relationship. I suppose I could have been Benny's great-grandfather.

"I am needing new clothes for a trip."

Benny, in his fatigue jacket, T-shirt, and faded jeans, looked as out of place as I did in this store, and he stayed out of the way, arms folded, as the salesman measured me with his eyes and pulled trousers and jackets from the racks.

"Shirts?"

"Long sleeve, please."

"Neckties?"

"Two."

"Shoes? Socks?"

I threw up my hands. "Sure."

When I finished shopping a few hours later, I stood in front of the triple mirror in a pair of khakis and a blue button-down shirt, leather belt, and a new pair of socks and shoes, too. I looked like the kind of grandfather who takes the whole family out for brunch, not some lonely old *schlump*.

I asked the salesman, "I am thinking I will wear this home, all right?"

"Of course, sir." As he clipped the price tags, I looked at the tattoos covering his forearms. Seemed like everybody had tattoos these days, but mine wasn't the kind I'd want to show off. I kept my cuffs buttoned instead of rolling them up, as he did.

"Should I put the clothes you wore here in the shopping bag?" He folded my threadbare pants and shirt neatly, but they looked like rags next to my purchases on the counter.

"No, I am thinking you can just throw those out, please."

Benny's eyes widened when I counted out the cash to pay. That was when his cell phone rang. After a few seconds of rapid-fire conversation in Spanish, Benny disconnected the call. "Pete, we gotta go." He gathered up my shopping bags and was halfway to the door before the salesman gave me my change.

"Benny, what is wrong?" I shoved the money in my pocket as I hustled after him.

He held the door for me with his elbow. "The bodega got robbed again. Valeria, she—they took her to the hospital." He loaded me into the car and shoved the bags in after me.

"Is she going to be all right?" I struggled with the seatbelt as the tires squealed.

"I don't know. I just need to get to her." He drove so fast I couldn't do anything but hang on. We were flying around the exit ramp, just minutes from home, before I had the courage to say, "I am very sorry. It is being my fault she was there."

"No, it's not your fault. Bad stuff happens." We screeched to a halt in front of the bodega. Two cop cars were out front, and crime-scene tape blocked the door. Benny hurried around to open my door and gather my shopping bags. I was barely out of the car when he thrust them into my hands.

"I can be going with you to the hospital if you need me."

"No, thanks. This is a family matter."

"Yes, yes. I understand. You go to Valeria. My best wishes to her." He ran back around the car and took off. My shoulders sagged as I watched him go. No matter what he said, I felt responsible for what had happened, and I was ashamed of the surge of envy I felt. Benny had only to drive a few miles to be with his love when she needed him.

I unlocked the door to my building, and as I headed for the stairs, Mrs. Simmons poked her head out of her apartment. "Excuse me, Sir? Can I help you?"

"It is just me." I turned around.

"Well excuse me, Mr. Ibbetz. I didn't recognize you."

"Is all right." I plodded upstairs.

The robbery got a mention on the news that evening, and the next day, Benny wasn't around. The bodega remained closed, with the crime-scene tape across the door.

When I got out the cardboard suitcase I'd had since leaving the DP camp to pack my clothes, I realized the fragile, crumbling case would never stand the trip.

I called Lucille for advice, and she offered to come by in an hour to take me shopping for a new one. I was waiting outside when she pulled up in a car that was a rusted-out piece of junk.

As I hesitated on the sidewalk, she called, "Don't worry, honey. It may not look like much, but it gets me where I need to go." When I got in, she reached across me to slam the passenger door closed. "Takes a special touch. But I never worry about it getting damaged. People drive like maniacs in the city, you know."

She hit the gas, and I held on as the car rattled down the street. I breathed a sigh of relief when we pulled into the parking lot of one of those department stores that advertise brand name merchandise at discount prices. When we went inside, Lucille headed straight for the luggage section.

"I am liking this one." I pointed out a black canvas suitcase on an upper shelf.

"Let me get it down for you, honey." She reached for it.

I felt bad to have a lady lift something off a shelf for me, but it was surprisingly light. "How much clothes will I fit in here?"

"You'll be surprised how much. Look, this zipper expands the space." She demonstrated, and then pushed a button on top of the bag. "And here's the handle. You should get a smaller one to carry on the plane, too. It's a good idea to take a change of clothes, a book, and your toothbrush with you on a long flight." She picked a matching bag and handed it to me. "*Voila!*"

I liked the new bags so much I took them for a spin up and down the aisle and executed a fancy turn that would have made Mira proud.

She put her hands on her hips. "Pete, don't get carried away. You're not done until you've got a new wallet and a money belt. And compression socks. Follow me."

It all added up to two hundred and fifty bucks. Money was slipping through my fingers like water.

When we finished shopping, Lucille insisted I open a bank account and get a debit card. "You need to be able to access your money while you're overseas."

"This I am never doing before."

"Do you have some cash on hand you could deposit?"

"I am not trusting the banks—this money might be stolen."

"No, honey. They changed that a long time ago. Your deposit is insured up to two hundred and fifty thousand."

"Dollars?"

"Yeah."

I nodded. "All right. Then that is all I will deposit. Not a penny more. The rest is staying hidden."

I thought Lucille's eyes were going to bug out of her head. "But you don't have to put in that much. In fact, you shouldn't. Banks have to report deposits over ten thousand dollars to the government. There are forms to fill out. It's kind of a pain."

"Oh. Are you thinking nine thousand is being enough?"

"Sure, Pete. That should be plenty for a two-week trip." She drove me back to my place and carried a tire iron upstairs to guard the door while I counted out stacks of bills from under the floorboard.

When we left the bank an hour later, I had a plastic charge card in my wallet instead of that bag of cash. Lucille made me practice using the card at the automated teller outside the building until I learned to key in the numbers and make it spit my money out. She said that was how I would get money to spend in Shanghai. *Oy vey*, so many things to remember.

Once I could go through the steps without her prompting, we went inside the bank and got in line to redeposit what I'd withdrawn.

"What's the money in Shanghai called? Deutsch marks and dollars are all I am knowing."

She whipped out her phone, keyed in something and squinted at the screen. "Renminbi. Heck of a thing to pronounce, ain't it?"

"I used to think Weequahic was hard to pronounce, too."

"So, what are you going to do when you lay eyes on your Mira?" She gave me a conspiratorial nudge with her elbow.

"When I see her, I guess I will know."

27

Jacob's recording device sat on my kitchen table, surrounded by all the things I'd bought to take on the trip. Mira had once predicted I'd be a sound engineer and work in broadcasting. Even though I liked repairing old radios, I hadn't cared to learn about more recent technology. It was amazing that a tiny recorder like this could preserve the stories I'd never been able to share.

When I turned it on, I made believe I was speaking to Mira, though in reality I'd never want to burden her with these memories. Perhaps it had been for the best that we could not speak of what we'd experienced during the war.

The memories were snapshots, flashes. My voice shook as they spilled forth like black bile from the depths of my soul.

"At Theresienstadt, the SS is telling parents of young children that the Allies will exchange German prisoners for Jewish children. Many parents jumped at the chance to give their children freedom and sent them off to be traded. But it was a lie, and the children were taken to extermination camps instead. Shortly after, the parents of those children were also silenced, so no word of this cruel deception would spread. Perhaps they did this over and over."

I turned off the tape and wept at my memory of the faces of those parents, so hopeful as they waved goodbye to their little ones. I blew my nose and turned the recorder back on.

"When I was arriving at Auschwitz, suddenly I am an orphan, no longer with my father to protect me. I am at the dangerous age between child and man. I did not want to be perceived by the SS as too young to be useful, but neither did I want to be worked to death."

In my mind, I walked the train platform, jostled by the crowd, mindful of the SS who herded us forward with billy clubs and rifle butts. To the left, to be gassed. To the right, to be worked to death.

"Inside the gates, when I first caught sight of the half-naked, living skeletons that inhabited the camp, I could not stop trembling. I had never been taught of hell, but I knew I had arrived by the corpses strewn everywhere. The smell, I cannot describe. Never was I getting used to it.

"Some had died where they fell, too exhausted to take another step. The bodies of those who were electrocuted as they tried to escape through the barbed wire were left there, tangled and dangling, to remind the rest of us that there was no way out."

I wished I could remember it in black and white, like photographs or newsreel footage, instead of in color.

"Anyone with gold teeth was shoved to the left and gassed right away, and their teeth harvested as trophies. I was knowing one man in my barracks whose job it was to pull the teeth before he put the bodies in the crematory. Even though he was getting extra rations and special treatment, just before the liberation, he went mad—and they shot him dead."

I stopped the recorder again, wishing I had names or dates to share to prove these things that sounded too awful to be true.

"When battles went badly for the Germans, they are raising the quotas to kill us more quickly. And when the Allied bombers came, the Germans are hiding inside our camp, knowing the Allies would not purposely drop bombs on us. For this I am knowing German soldiers were not brave. They were bullies, monsters, and cowards."

My throat was dry, so I turned off the recorder. My hand trembled as I filled a glass with water. I had not been brave or defiant. I had merely survived. Maybe I had always been ashamed of that, but now a small flame ignited deep inside me. There was power in the telling.

"Many of the strongest men who arrived at Auschwitz with me, the ones I am thinking the SS would prize for slave labor, were sent to the gas chamber straightaway. The Nazis wanted to keep their prisoners weak. The strong would be a threat in the event of rebellion or revolt.

"We were marched, sometimes miles each day, to and from our work assignments. Work went on even in bad weather, and often we had to sleep in wet things for we had no change of clothes. To find lice and fleas on ourselves would have been humiliating in our former lives, but in the camps, it was a matter of course."

As I went on, I tried to hold my emotions in check. I clenched my fists to stop my hands from shaking, but I could not hide the tremor in my voice as the memories of the things I had seen spilled forth.

"The guards pushed little children into the latrine pits and let them drown in the filth. Those who had been in the camp longer than I had no body fat to protect themselves from cold or from sunburn. Every sickness and contagious disease became an epidemic, because there was no medicine.

"It would have been bad enough if the gassings had been quick, and random, but the Nazis are making lists and schedules for extermination. Once someone was on the list, they are no longer being given food or water. And they waited, sometimes for days, for the end to come."

I forgot to turn off the recorder and the howl of agony that escaped my throat became part of my testimony.

"Once your name was on the list of condemned, someone could intercede on your behalf, but offering bribes could backfire. Also, there was guilt, knowing if you were spared, someone else is taking your place. The SS was not caring who they killed—only that they were fulfilling their quotas."

Punching the off button, I got up and paced. As hard as it was to recount the horrors I'd seen, I didn't know if I could talk about what had happened to the women without breaking down.

But I recalled the leering faces of the Hitler Youth boys who played master to the stock cars full of women and girls, and I had to speak. I must tell that even young people were part of the evils. I turned the recorder back on.

"Sometimes guards who were barely into their teens forced the newly arrived female prisoners to run naked along the camp road to the gas chambers. The women were frightened and humiliated by the way the young guards laughed and prodded them with their rifle butts. I couldn't help but think those boys were so brainwashed they'd do the same to their own mothers and sisters if they'd been ordered to."

When I finish speaking, I turned off the recorder and pushed it away. Now it carried the memories that had festered inside me for so many years. I felt exhausted, but lighter—and cleansed.

Jacob was there when I went to the library to return the recorder.

I handed it to him. "Here are some things I am remembering. I am hoping it is good enough."

He received the machine with reverence. "Thank you, Peter. Every story is important. I know it must have been difficult."

"It was, but everything is being alright now."

"Good. I'll transcribe this. Can you come back to go over a written transcript in about a week?"

"I think maybe I am not available next week. I am traveling to Shanghai."

Jacob laughed. He thought I was kidding. "Oh, really? You're serious? Well then I'll get to work on it right away."

28

With four days to go, I packed my new suitcase, then took everything out and packed it again. Mira still called to me from the darkness in my dreams, and I was antsy to get going.

To keep myself from climbing the walls, I cleaned out my apartment, taking everything out of the closets and cabinets and sorting it into piles. Most of it could be thrown out, but there were a few things worth saving. I made a pile of stuff for Benny and wrote a note, giving him my kitchen table.

Benny and I hadn't spoken since the day of the robbery, and I didn't want to leave without saying goodbye. Once I found Mira in Shanghai, I was certain I wouldn't want to come back home. It took me hours to write everything down, but I wanted Benny to know the whole story—even the part about how I'd reunited with Mira in my dreams.

I packed the library books in the canvas bag and headed out to return them. Kara was working at the front desk, and she greeted me with a smile. "Hello, Mr. Ibbetz. Jacob and I were just talking about you." She picked up the phone to page him, then turned back to me. "Your books aren't due yet. Are you finished already?"

"Yes. From them I am learning a great many things." I pushed the bag across the counter as Jacob came out of the volunteer office. "Are you finding anything about Mira?"

"No. Nothing yet."

"Okay. I have been thinking about it, and I will also do interview on video if you would like."

"Yes, that would be great."

"Can we do it now? I do not have much time left here."

"Of course. Come on back."

He set up the video camera in the office, and when he patched my image through to a monitor, I couldn't believe how old I looked and sounded. But once I made the recording, I didn't plan to watch it again.

With three days to go, Lucille and I made a test run to the airport. She gave me a tour of the arrivals area first, so I could see how the baggage carousel worked. She was great at explaining what to expect, and she laughed at how much I enjoyed watching the suitcases sliding down the chute onto the carousel.

"It is being like assembly line—so fast."

She chuckled. "You might not think the bags come up fast once you've got a few trips under your belt. Oh, and another thing. Look how many black bags came off just one flight. You need to tie a ribbon or something around the handle on yours so you'll recognize it."

On the way home, Lucille pulled into a shopping center. "Come on. You need one more thing before you're ready to travel."

"What is it?"

"Trust me. It's time to get you out of your comfort zone." She slammed the car door and headed toward one of the stores.

"Again?" I was outside my comfort zone nearly all the time now. Half an hour later, I walked out of the shop with a cellular phone. In the car, it started beeping. I touched the screen, but it didn't stop. "What? What's wrong with it?" I held the phone out to Lucille.

"Nothing, honey. The phone is fine. That's your seat belt beeping. Put it on, already."

Believing I would never need to use the phone, I stuffed it in my pocket. Later that day it rang, but I couldn't remember how to answer it. Whoever was calling rang off and called again four more times. Then my real phone rang.

It was Lucille. "How come you didn't pick up your cell?"

"I was not knowing it was you."

"I'm gonna call you again on it. This time, answer it, already."

"Yes, yes, all right. Can you remind me how?"

Lucille chortled. "Just tap that green circle with the handset in it."

Like a *meshuggeneh*, she called me not once, but three more times. After all that, she told me why she'd called in the first place—my passport had arrived.

I took a cab to her office, and she did a double take as I came through the door in a creased pair of khakis, striped button-down shirt, and loafers. I'd been saving my new clothes to wear on the trip, but I wanted to surprise her.

"May I help you sir?" I saw the twinkle in her eyes and knew she recognized me.

"Very funny." I turned in a circle. "So, am I ready to go?"

"You look fab." Lucille handed me the passport and I opened it up. *Oy vey*, the photo! That was not the face of a man about to embark on the biggest adventure of his life. It was more like a mug shot. But it would have to do.

Next, she gave me the envelope with my plane ticket and cruise itinerary. I glanced at the cruise information without interest. I had no intention of actually going.

"I booked you a room at the Crowne Plaza. It's easiest to take a taxi from the airport." The hotel reservation confirmation she tucked into the folder with the cruise itinerary.

I waved the airline ticket at her. "This gets me home, too?"

"After the cruise—but you can change the date if you need to."

I looked at my date of departure, just three weeks after I'd begun to have the dreams about Mira. I put it back in the folder.

"Pete, I hope your dreams all come true and you find who you're looking for at the end of the rainbow."

"Oh, she is still being the same girl. I know she is."

"I'm rooting for you. Call or stop by when you get back. I'll want to hear all about it."

I waved on my way out. "See you."

When I got home, I found a red bandana in my bureau and tied it around the suitcase handle.

The day before my flight, I put the things I had set aside for Benny in a box and bundled up the donations. As I set the stuff out in the hall, Miss Richter came up the stairs. One look at her fake smile and I ducked back inside my apartment.

She didn't take the hint and go away. She called through the door, "Mr. Ibbetz? It looks like you're getting used to the idea of downsizing. Do you have time for a chat?"

Oy vey. If I let her in, she'd see my suitcase, the passport, the tickets. She'd know I lied about my trip. "No. Not today."

"It won't take long. I brought you some brochures for assisted living facilities in the area. Maybe we could go over them together?"

"No thanks."

There was a long pause. "All right, Mr. Ibbetz. I can see you're busy. I'll stop by another time. Would it be better if I called first?"

"No."

"All right, then. I'll just leave these here." She shoved the brochures under the door.

I stood at the window and watched her leave, knowing I'd be long gone before she came back for another visit. Then I took a deposit to the bank and added to my balance, in case I needed more to tide me over once I found Mira.

Sometime in the night I woke up in bed in our dream house. As soon as I realized I was back with Mira, I rolled over to take her in my arms, but her side of the bed was empty. As I threw back the covers and reached for the bedside lamp, my back seized up. Stretching those last few inches to turn on the switch left me in agony. Light flooded the room, and I gasped at the sight of my hand, knotted and veiny, marred with age spots and purple bruising. In disbelief, I touched my face and the sagging flesh on my belly and legs.

I had gone back to her as Old Peter.

"Mira!" My voice came out so raspy I feared she wouldn't hear me. "Mira."

Her light footsteps sounded on the stairs, and she hurried into the room. "Peter, what is it—" Her scream rose above my hoarse cry. One hand flew to her mouth, the other to her pregnant belly.

I startled myself awake and lay there panting, clammy with sweat. I was still in Weequahic. I hadn't left yet. I sat up, testing my back, but it hurt no worse than usual. It was all systems go. I sank back against the pillow and tried to go to sleep.

29

My flight left at 10:45, but I was up at six. I had cleaned out the fridge and wiped down the bathroom by seven and was ready to go at eight, my packed and repacked suitcases waiting by the door. Mira's locket was safely hanging by its red cord around my neck, hidden by a new shirt. I wanted plenty of time to get through security. But I still had a few minutes to go by the bodega and check if Benny was there so I could say goodbye.

The sign on the door read closed, but inside the lights were on. Benny was behind the counter, his back turned. I knocked, and when he saw it was me and opened the door, he looked a wreck—dark circles under his eyes, stains on the front of his sweatshirt.

"Hey Pete."

"Hi. How is Valeria?"

"She's on the mend. They roughed her up pretty bad." Tears welled up in his eyes. "It's going to be a while before things get back to normal."

"I am so sorry, Benny. I am still feeling like it is my fault."

He didn't deny it. "You need to come in and get a few things? I'm not really open, but—"

"No, it is fine. I am here to say goodbye."

He passed a hand over his face. "Oh. You heard. After what happened to Valeria, I can't stay in this neighborhood anymore. She'd been bugging me for a while to move farther out, to a better location. I should've listened to her. Maybe the new owners will keep the stuff you like in stock. I can talk to them if you want."

"I am sorry for your trouble. But it is me who is saying goodbye."

"What do you mean? Did Miss Richter talk you into moving to assisted living?"

"No, I am leaving for Shanghai. Mira is needing me to come to her."

He looked at me for a long moment before he spoke. "Are you coming back?"

"I am not knowing." I shook my finger under his nose. "But I am knowing what I'm doing—and it is no different from the way you are making sacrifice for Valeria. I was writing down everything that happened, so you are knowing the whole story. You are my best friend in Weequahic, Benny. I will miss you."

I handed him the envelope. "Is long story. You should read it later. While I am searching for Mira, I am making new friends, Jacob and Lucille. They are both helping me get ready for this journey. Now I am going."

"Who are Jacob and Lucille?"

"Jacob volunteers at the library. Lucille is my travel agent. I know I will find Mira because the truest things are strange, and the strangest things are true."

He shook his head like he was clearing out the cobwebs. "You have a travel agent?"

"Yes, yes. Booking this trip was trickier than I am expecting. Now, come here so we are saying goodbye." I wrapped my arms around his middle, and my head fit under his chin. "You are good grandson, Benny."

His arms tightened around me and he sniffled. "I wasn't expecting you to take off like this. At my new place, I'll still be looking for you to come through the door."

I took out my handkerchief and blew my nose, nodding because I couldn't speak.

"You were a great granddad, too." He wiped a tear off his cheek. "Without you, who's going to tell me about Weequahic's glory days?"

"Maybe you are making new glory days in the suburbs, right?"

"Yeah. Hey, will you stay in touch? Let me know how your reunion goes?"

"Yes, yes. And if you get lonely for stories about the old days, you must call my friend Jacob at the library."

"Will do. Pete, you're one in a million. I hope you and Mira will be happy together."

I checked my watch: 8:25 a.m. "We are. Now I must to call the cab." The bell on the door jingled on my way out, and I walked quickly, not wanting to look back.

I was halfway down the block when I saw Miss Richter get out of her car and march into my building. I ducked into a doorway, thinking it was lucky she didn't recognize me in my new clothes.

Then my blood turned to ice. My bags and my passport were upstairs. How was I going to get past her? I waited a few minutes and she didn't come out. Even though I'd made up with Benny, I couldn't be sure he wouldn't gang up with Miss Richter and try to talk me into staying if I went to him for help.

I fished my cell phone out of my jacket pocket and called the one number in the memory. "Lucille?"

"Yeah honey—what's up? You should be on your way to the airport."

"I am knowing this, but Miss Richter, the social worker from Elder Care, she is staking out my apartment. I am in the street, and my bags and passport are inside. She is thinking I am too senile to live alone. If she sees me, she will not let me leave for Shanghai. How am I getting rid of her?"

"Did she drive there?"

"Yes, I am seeing her car on the street."

"What's the make and model?"

I told her.

"Hang on, Pete. I'm texting you the number for a cab. You call it, alright? I'll be there in five."

30

I stayed huddled in the doorway, keeping watch for Miss Richter and trying to remember how to call the number Lucille sent in her text. My fingers fumbled on the screen, and when it went dark, I forgot how to bring it back. Just as I started to panic, the facial recognition feature unlocked the phone.

I touched the phone number in the text and the call went through. The dispatcher said my cab was four minutes away.

Lucille's car must've lost its muffler on the drive over, because I heard it long before it came into view. Her red hair blew around her face as she barreled down the block and plowed right into Miss Richter's car.

As the car's alarm shrilled, Miss Richter dashed out of the building. Lucille waved a hand to shoo me inside while Miss Richter wasn't looking. As I climbed the stairs, I heard Miss Richter say, "What's the matter with you? Were you even looking where you were going?"

Inside, I put on the money belt and gathered my bags. Though I wasn't leaving much behind, I was still leaving the place I'd lived most of my life. I gave the faded linoleum and the dingy walls one last look. On the way out, I dropped a goodbye note in Mrs. Simmons's mail slot. My hand trembled, but from nervousness, not fear.

Lucille should've been an actress or maybe an air traffic controller instead of a travel agent. As I tiptoed out of the building behind them, she was hollering at Miss Richter about parking too far away from the curb. My cabbie pulled around the accident scene and got out to collect my bags. With a last wave at Lucille, I shut the door. Miss Richter's head snapped around, and she recognized me too late. I was free.

When the cabbie asked, "Which terminal, pal?" I read what Lucille had written on the envelope. "United Airlines. International departures."

"You going on vacation?"

"Yes. I am going to visit a friend."

"Good for you, pal." When we reached the airport, he pulled up to the curb and hopped out to get my bags from the trunk. "Safe travels."

Inside, the terminal teemed with people, just like it had when I'd first tried to buy a ticket. Even though I'd practiced with Lucille just days before, I was a nervous wreck. The signs confused me and I couldn't remember where to go. A crowd of people swept me along as I was trying to read the departures board, and before I could dodge all the rolling suitcases, everyone surged forward, taking me with them. My heart jumped into my throat as the crowd constricted, and I saw the reason for the bottleneck. We were boarding a train. Inside me, something snapped. I wouldn't be forced onto that train. I didn't want to go.

A wailing sob burst from my throat. I thrashed around and would've tripped over my suitcases if I'd had room to move. Before I could catch my breath and calm down, the crowd backed off, flowing around me like I was a rock in a stream. The train's doors slid shut, leaving only a few people on the platform. My breath came in gasps.

"Sir?"

I jumped when a young man touched my arm. He was wearing an ID badge for one of the airlines.

"Are you all right, sir? Do you need a doctor?"

"I was afraid." It took so much effort to speak that I gulped to get the words out. "Afraid I am getting on the wrong train."

"Do you have your ticket?"

I brought the envelope out of my breast pocket and found the ticket. He glanced at it and motioned for me to follow him. "This way, sir. We'll get you straightened out."

I trailed after him, pulling my suitcases like a kid with a toy wagon until he handed me off to a woman in a similar uniform.

"This is the line to get your boarding pass, sir." She gestured toward a long line of people snaking through one of the roped-off queues. When it was my turn, the man behind the counter fired off a bunch of commands. Before I knew it, one of my bags was on the chute, I had a new piece of paper in my hand, and he pointed me toward another line.

"Security is over there. Then on to the B Gates."

"Thank you."

In the security line, I followed a new set of commands. They let me keep my shoes on, I guess because I looked too old to take them off without sitting down, but my cell phone and jacket had to go in a bin. One by one, the guard motioned us through the little doorway. I was next in line when something beeped, and the guards took a woman off to the side. Heart pounding, I watched as they patted her down.

"Hey buddy—next!"

One of the guards motioned to me, and as I walked through the doorway, I avoided eye contact with him. When I heard the beep, cold, clammy sweat started in my armpits. My hand shook as I wiped my brow.

When the guard held up a hand to stop me, I flinched.

"Do you have any metal on you?"

My hand reached for Mira's locket, hidden beneath my shirt.

He made an impatient sound like I should know what he meant. "A belt? Or change in your pocket?"

"Oh—yes. A belt." I took it off and we began again.

This time, I passed through without any problem. The bin with my jacket and cell phone was waiting for me at the end of the conveyor, and soon my belt slithered down beside it.

I was sweating too much to want the jacket, so I folded it over my arm and pocketed the phone. More people swarmed past me as I stared up at the signs for the departure gates. Lucille and I hadn't been able to practice this part of the journey.

By the time I got to the right place, I felt like I'd walked halfway to Shanghai. Lots of people were already there waiting, and I took a seat where I could look out the windows. The plane was bigger than I'd expected. I'd never seen one up close before.

Everyone else waiting at the gate was either looking at their phone or reading. There were lots of business travelers, and four or five families with kids. I think I was the oldest of all. When they called us to board, I watched and copied what the other passengers did. On the way down the ramp to the plane, my heart pounded with excitement.

An attendant helped me find my seat, and boy, did Lucille set me up right. I had a little cubicle with a TV, a seat that reclined into a bed, and a tray table. I hadn't expected this much privacy.

The last time I'd crossed an ocean, it had taken five days. On this trip, I'd reach the other side of the world in a fraction of that. I buckled myself in with my blanket and pillow, got the atlas out of my carry-on, and opened it to Shanghai. The coded messages I'd left between the pages were no longer there. When the plane backed up and turned toward the runway, I felt a shiver run down my spine. I hoped Mira knew I was on my way. I whispered into the pages of the atlas, "I'll be there soon."

We rumbled along on the ground until I grew impatient and began to wonder if we were going to drive partway. Then the sudden acceleration and takeoff set my heart pounding all over again. I remembered telling Mira how objects traveling at a high rate of speed experience time differently than objects standing still. I hoped that meant the trip would pass quickly.

Once we were off the ground, flying wasn't frightening at all. In fact, it was boring. Nothing much happened for half an hour or so, until the attendants passed out hot towels, and then food and drinks. I was amazed to be presented with five courses, ending with a cheese plate and an ice cream sundae. Though I was too excited to feel hungry, I ate. I had learned long ago never to refuse food when it was offered.

After the meal, when the attendants came back for the trays and dimmed the lights, most of the people around me put on headphones and started watching their little TVs. I got up and walked the aisle a few times. Lucille made me promise to do so because it would help keep my legs from swelling. Already I was wearing the compression socks she'd made me buy. I hoped Lucille's parents realized they raised a good daughter.

A few rows up, I passed a family whose youngest daughter was asleep in her father's arms. My own arms had always been empty, and I felt a pang of envy so sharp I had to force myself to give him a pleasant nod as I went by. I had grown used to the idea of becoming a father. I wondered if the child Mira carried was a girl or a boy.

I dozed through much of the flight, and every time I awoke, I checked the screen that tracked where we were. The little airplane seemed so small as it moved across the map of the world. Those of us inside it were specks too tiny to be visible on the screen, just as Mira was a speck in the vast landscape of Shanghai. As I drifted off, I tried to send my thoughts winging ahead of the plane so she would know I was almost there.

A huge jolt woke me, and at first, I forgot where I was. When I realized I was on the plane, I thought we'd hit something in the air. One of the flight attendants bent over my cubicle and touched me on the shoulder.

"Sir? Are you all right?"

I passed my hand over my face, trying to calm my galloping heart. "Yes, yes, I am fine."

"You were shouting in German."

"I'm sorry. I am thinking I am having a nightmare."

She nodded. "Unexpected turbulence can be frightening. Can I get you some water, sir?"

"No, thank you. I am all right now."

Sleep eluded me for the rest of the flight, so between my trips up and down the aisle, I turned on my reading light and looked at the atlas. Even after getting up every few hours, my joints were stiff and my shoes felt too tight. Travel at my age was a lot harder than I had realized it would be, and I was more than ready to land by the time the attendants turned on the cabin lights and brought more hot towels and breakfast trays.

31

When I arrived in the terminal, to my surprise, all the signs were in English. At the baggage claim, I spotted the red bandana on my suitcase with no trouble. I thought I'd be asleep on my feet in the immigration line, but there was so much to see I got my second wind. While I waited in line, I got out Lucille's list of instructions. She'd said to get a thing called a SIM card for my new phone so it would work outside the US. I must've heard at least ten different languages before it was my turn to have my new passport stamped.

Once I was through customs, I found an ATM and put my card in the slot. Just like when I'd practiced at home, it spit out a stack of bills—renminbi.

There was a shop selling phone accessories a few feet away, and the young guy who sold me the SIM card even changed it over for me. I felt like I was getting the hang of traveling.

He handed me back the original card in a plastic envelope. "Are you taking a taxi to your hotel, sir?"

I nodded.

"It can be difficult, because many of the taxi drivers do not speak English. If you like, I will write the name of your hotel in Wu so you can give it to the driver."

Distrust welled up in me. "No, thank you. I am fine." I wasn't sure if there really was a language called Wu—and I began to think this guy was running some kind of a scam. Benny had worried about someone taking advantage of me. But what if I got to the taxi line and couldn't communicate? My confidence evaporated and, stalling, I joined the line at Starbucks, hoping a coffee would help me think.

When I emerged, I looked like a genuine tourist, with a venti latte in one hand and my Rollaboard in tow as I headed for ground transportation.

Contrary to the young man's warning, the taxi stand captain spoke English. He quoted the fare at twenty-eight renminbi for the forty-five-minute cab ride into the city. As my driver pulled away, I settled back in the seat and congratulated myself for getting the cab by myself.

Out the window, Shanghai looked huge—even with half of it shrouded in smog. I didn't tear my eyes away until we'd pulled into the Crowne Plaza, which had to be the toniest place I'd ever been, except for maybe the dream version of the Ritz.

My cabbie pulled up beside a golden two-humped camel statue in the porte cochere and handed me my bags. I was determined to act like a seasoned traveler, but as soon as I entered the lobby, I stopped to stare. Lucille had been right when she'd said, "Honey, if you're only going to do something once, you might as well pull out the stops." Everything in the lobby was shiny, from the marble floors to the lacquered furniture. Fresh flower arrangements in gleaming vases four feet tall flanked the reception desk.

There was just one couple ahead of me in line, and though the coffee had perked me up for the cab ride, I was so exhausted, I nodded off on my feet once or twice while I waited to check in.

At the desk, I handed over the reservation confirmation Lucille had put in my envelope. The clerk, whose nametag read Tao, typed my information into the computer and wrote down my room number. He handed me a plastic card with both hands, like it was a tiny tray, and bowed. I accepted the card with one hand and wasn't sure if I should bow in return. I ended up doing a strange halfway job of it. The clerk signaled for a bellhop.

"It is okay. I can manage without help." Then I stumbled and nearly lost my balance as I turned away from the reception desk, bumping into the man behind me. The bellhop took my bags and put his free hand under my elbow as he guided me to the elevator.

We joined a group of people waiting in front of a row of glossy double doors. I wondered what everyone would think if they knew I'd only ridden one once before—when Mira and I had visited the Eiffel Tower in my dream. The one in my building at the DP camp had always been out of order, and all of my apartment buildings in Weequahic had been walk-ups. Mira's claustrophobia had forced us to avoid the one at the Ritz.

A set of doors opened, and as we filed inside, someone asked me what floor. At first, I didn't want to say because I was afraid of someone following me to my room to rob me. Then I realized he was pushing buttons for everyone, and that was how we'd all get where we were going. He'd already pushed the number for my floor for someone else.

When we got off the elevator, the hallway looked like it went on forever and my heart sank at the thought of walking that much farther. Thankfully, the bellhop went only a short distance before he stopped and showed me how to hold the plastic card to a sensor on my door. A green light came on.

Inside my room, he tapped a screen on the wall to turn on the lights. Shiny, pale paneling—bamboo, maybe—covered every wall. I started to worry when I didn't see another door. At these prices, I should get a private bath, not a shared one at the end of the hall.

He bustled around the room. "Sir, let me show you how the lights and the window shades work."

"My bladder's about to bust. You can be showing me in a minute. Which way to the can?"

The paneling camouflaged the bathroom door so well I never would've found it on my own, and the bellhop turned on the lights for me as I went inside. The toilet looked like a big white trash bin, the kind with the foot pedal that opens the lid.

I was two steps away when the lid popped up on its own, startling me so much I almost peed myself. When I yelped in surprise, there was a discreet knock on the door.

"Sir? Is everything all right?"

"Yes. Is no problem." He was waiting right outside the door when I finished my business, so I felt like I had to say something. "I am never seeing a contraption like that toilet in my life—and I was a plumber. For a second I am thinking it was trying to bite me. Are all the toilets in China like that?"

"No, sir. The Crowne Plaza prides itself on having all the latest technology."

"I'll say." I held out my hand. "My name's Peter."

"I am Hongqi." When he took my hand and bowed over it, I felt like I was a prince or something.

Hongqi showed me how to work the lights and the shades and explained that because of the smog, the view was better at night. It made me wish I'd gone up in the Chrysler or the Empire State Building at least once to get a birds-eye view of New York.

He bowed again at the door. "Please let us know if we can do anything to make your stay more pleasant."

After he left, I went back into the bathroom and approached the toilet a few more times just to watch the lid pop up. It worked with a sensor, like one of those automatic doors at the supermarket.

There was a row of buttons on the control panel next to the toilet for all its functions. One had a lady on it, and another had a baby. I had no idea what they were for and left them alone.

When I pressed one of the buttons on the wall beside the sink, a television came on inside the bathroom mirror. If I needed to watch the news while I was brushing my teeth, I was all set. I couldn't figure out how to turn on the faucet until I realized it had a sensor, too. I ended up pressing nearly every button in that hotel room. It was fun. Why had I waited so long to travel?

Just like the bathroom, I never would've found the closet if I hadn't noticed a groove between two of the boards, but when I pressed it, the closet door opened like a secret passageway in an old movie. I unpacked and hung up my clothes. Then I sat down on the bed just for a minute to slip off my shoes, and the next thing I knew, I woke up and it was dark outside. The TV was still playing in the bathroom mirror.

My wristwatch, still set to New Jersey time, was useless. Then I remembered my cell phone had a clock. I turned it on, and when the screen popped up it read 4:35 a.m. Even though I couldn't have gone searching for Mira in the middle of the night, I felt time slipping away. I had fewer than 140 hours left to find her before I was supposed to board the cruise ship.

Then I thought of something I could do while I waited for daylight: look her up in the phone book. There couldn't be too many Miriam Schlosses in Shanghai. I searched the room for a phone directory but came up empty handed. Maybe they had one at the front desk.

Down in the lobby, there was no one around but the young woman at the reception desk, who bowed as I drew near. She made me think of Valeria. Why did they have just one woman working in the middle of the night?

When I asked for a phone book, she shook her head. "You can look up telephone numbers online, sir."

I nodded. "All right. Thank you." I was embarrassed to say I didn't know how. It was another thing I'd have to learn how to do.

When I walked past the door that led outside, it opened with a whoosh and a rush of air. Wide awake and with nothing else to do, I went out under the lighted portico, where the heat and humidity took me by surprise. I stared up at the gold camel.

The doors whooshed open again and the desk clerk came out. "Do you need something, sir?"

"No. That's some camel, right?" Standing outside in the middle of the night like that, I couldn't think of anything else to say.

"Ah, yes. Do you know the camel's significance?"

When I shook my head, she seemed eager to share.

"The two-humped camel is an important symbol for the traveler. Finding one upon your arrival means that you will have success in your endeavors."

"How interesting. I was never knowing this about the camel."

"Do not forget to treasure your opportunities. Be grateful." She bowed again and headed back inside.

After she left, I looked up at the camel with skepticism. Everyone who stayed at the Crowne Plaza saw it when they arrived. It couldn't be a sign of good fortune for everyone—could it? Though I dismissed the story as nonsense, I knew Mira would find it charming.

Back in the lobby, a male clerk stood at the front desk. "Where's the other clerk?" I asked him. "The young lady?"

He shook his head, puzzled. "I'm sorry sir, I'm the only one on duty tonight. You walked past me when you went outside."

"That cannot be. I am remembering she is a young lady working alone. And I am speaking to her about the telephone directory and the camel."

He nodded as if it was his duty to be agreeable. "Jetlag is very common among travelers. Did you come from the US?"

"Yes. I am having trouble sleeping."

"That is to be expected, sir. It will take you a few days to adjust."

I raised my eyebrows. "Apparently." But I suspected that now I was getting closer to finding Mira, I was experiencing more of the magic that had brought us together.

32

Back on my floor, I stood at the railing and looked down into the lobby. It had come to life around five o'clock, and members of the cleaning crew, maintenance workers, wait staff, and clerks scurried about like ants on an anthill. Their hurried preparations matched my roiling thoughts. How was I going to find Mira?

Around six, I stood at my window, watching commuters throng the streets below. Too nervous for a big breakfast, and homesick for my morning routine of coffee and a bagel, I decided to find a café where I could get a cup of coffee and a pastry. When I left the hotel, I headed for a park I'd seen from my window. It was just a few blocks away, close enough that the Crowne Plaza's distinctive silhouette still dominated the landscape. I was certain I could not get lost.

The air was already hazy with pollution, and I didn't blame the many people wearing surgical masks. I wondered how much of the haze was from vehicles and how much from cigarettes. It seemed like everyone in China smoked. Lucille got me a non-smoking room, but the pungent scent of tobacco was everywhere and already it clung to my clothes.

At the park, I spotted a vendor selling baozi. Mira must have learned to make them here in Shanghai. No one queued in a line, like at home. Instead, they jostled each other and crowded close to the window. When two men pushed to the front, no one called them out. People say New Yorkers can be pushy sometimes, and I'd certainly seen a few like that over the years. I'd also lived where personal space was nonexistent, and Shanghai reminded me of both, combined. But at least we weren't fighting over the last of the food.

When it was my turn, I bought an order of buns and a cup of tea and carried them to a nearby bench. Suddenly starving, I ate one of the buns right away. It seemed like a very long time since I'd eaten, and I realized my last meal had been on the airplane.

Closing my eyes, I took a sip of tea and reminded myself to treasure my opportunity to connect with Mira in the dream, and to be grateful for this adventure in Shanghai. While I was at it, I gave thanks for Jacob, Lucille, and Benny. I hoped Miss Richter wasn't too mad about my getaway and the damage to her car.

Someone burped, and when I opened my eyes, my gaze fell on a man sleeping on a bench a short distance away.

"It's not unusual for people to nap outside." A woman was sitting beside me with her own order of baozi and tea.

I chuckled. "I was thinking that is the best-dressed bum I am ever seeing."

She inclined her head in the customary bow and smiled. "I hope I might ask your help, sir."

"Yes, yes, if I can."

"You are from the United States?"

"Yes."

"My name is Mei Qiang. My daughter married an American and lives in Boston. They are expecting a baby, and when it is born, I will go stay with them. May I practice speaking with you?"

"Absolutely." I offered my hand, and we shook. "I am Peter Ibbetz. Your English is sounding very good to me."

"Thank you. Perhaps I should have asked for the opportunity to listen while you talk. The regional accents in America are sometimes difficult to understand. When I first met my son-in-law, I did not know what he meant when he said he had to 'pahk the cah.'" She giggled at the memory. "Where do you live in America?"

"New Jersey, by way of Germany. I was emigrating when I was a young man."

"What brings you to Shanghai?"

"To visit a friend. An old friend, from long ago."

"How lovely. Does your friend live nearby?"

"That's the thing. I am not sure. We are having kind of a . . . communication breakdown, I guess you'd say."

"But you can reach this friend by telephone or perhaps by email?"

"The way we are trying to set up our meeting, the details are being fuzzy."

"Fuzzy?"

"Unclear." The look when someone thinks you're crazy is the same in any language. In desperation, I pulled the locket from inside my shirt and showed it to her. "My friend gave me this, a long time ago. She'll know me when I find her."

"A red thread!" Mei Qiang nodded. "Now I understand."

"You do?"

"Of course. If you have the red thread, you must have heard the . . . what you might call folk tale. Fairy story."

"Maybe the camel legend I heard about yesterday and the red thread go together somehow. Please, tell me."

She laughed. "I do not know if the camel fits into this story, but legend says a red thread connects soulmates, linking them forever so they can always find one another. Yue Lao, the matchmaker god, ties an invisible red cord around the ankles of those destined to be lovers, regardless of place, time, or circumstances. The cord may stretch or tangle, but it will never break."

She patted my hand. "You possess a locket on a red thread. Even in modern times, many people here believe the old legends and fairy stories. Remarkable and unexplained things happen all the time, don't they?"

"If you only knew." I took another sip of tea. "But how is that help-ing me find Mira?"

"You must trust the magic, but I would not rely on it alone. Have you tried to find her telephone number?"

"Not yet. I was planning to start there."

She took out her phone. "Would you like me to try for you?"

"Yes, please."

We bent our heads over the screen, with me telling her how to spell Mira's name. The search came up empty.

"Are you certain she lives here?"

"Yes." Though I wasn't as certain as I'd been before I'd arrived.

"And you are certain this is the correct name?"

"It is possible she is using another name."

Mei Qiang tapped her chin with her finger. "I must introduce you to my friend. She may be able to help you."

"Is she a detective?"

"No, she works at the Information Office. Please wait just one min-ute." She dialed her phone, held a brief conversation, and then stood up. "Come. I can take you to her now."

Why I chose to trust Mei Qiang I cannot say, but I followed her out of the park, where she hailed a cab. She gave the driver an ad-dress on Century Avenue, and we joined the flow of traffic. When we merged onto a highway heading away from the city, only then did I consider I might have made a severe error in judgment, driving away with someone I'd just met. The minutes ticked by, and I started to sweat. I could feel my cell phone in my pocket. But even if I could dial it without her noticing, who would I call for help?

"How far is it?"

"About eighteen kilometers."

I settled back against the seat and closed my eyes for a moment, breathing slowly to calm my racing heart. When Mei Qiang shook my shoulder, I blinked blearily. "What? What happened?"

"You dozed off for a little while. Here we are."

The cab had stopped in front of a soaring office building. The sign out front read "Information Office of Pudong New Area People's Government."

Mei Qiang patted my arm. "Pay the cab driver. Inside, ask for Yu Yan. She will help you."

I shifted to get my wallet out of my pocket. "Aren't you coming in with me?" When I turned back, she had vanished. I looked out the window.

"Where did she go?" I asked the cab driver.

He looked at me blankly. "Who? You got in the cab alone. Thirty renminbi, please."

I paid him and got out. Camels and magical red threads jumbled in my mind as I went inside.

At the reception desk in the lobby, I asked to speak to Yu Yan.

The bespectacled clerk wore a microphone headset. "Who may I say is here to see her?"

"My name is Peter Ibbetz. I am being . . . referred by Mei Qiang."

"One moment, please." I stepped back while she dialed, but I couldn't have eavesdropped, since she did not speak English during the call. Then she waved me back over. "Yu Yan will be down shortly."

When the elevator opened, several people got out. All the women were dressed in conservative, dark suits, but the one who approached me seemed to sparkle, despite her drab attire.

"Mr. Peter?"

When I nodded, she bowed. "Mei Qiang sent you to me?"

"Yes. But she couldn't stay."

"She is not one to linger. Please"—she gestured toward a sofa in the lobby— "let us talk for a few minutes. How can I help you?"

"I am looking for my friend, Miriam Schloss. Mira. She is not in the telephone directory, and I only have five days to find her before I must leave."

"I see. Mei Qiang told you I could search the records here?"

"She didn't say exactly what you could do. If I need to pay you—"

"No, that is not necessary. I will do everything I can for you and your Miriam."

She studied my face for a moment, and then took a pad and pencil from her handbag. "Where are you staying?"

I told her the name of my hotel.

After she wrote it down, she put Mira's name on the next line. "What is her age?"

"She'd be ninety, almost ninety-one." Even as the words left my lips, I pictured the young Mira, whose hair had blown in the wind as she rode with me in the Mercedes. Who danced the Charleston. Played the violin. Defied the heights on the devil's bridge. Carried my child.

When I found Mira, she would not be the laughing little girl with the curly hair or the young woman who loved me and wanted me even though I had let her down. She would be old, like me. Approaching the end of her life. She had said she needed me—but would I find her in time?

Yu Yan's voice penetrated my thoughts. "Might she have another surname?"

"I don't know." There was so much I didn't know—and I wasn't sure how I would take it if Mira had married someone else. Unexpected tears welled up in my eyes.

Yu Yan laid a calming hand on my arm. "Everything will be as it should be, Mr. Peter. You must trust your path, trust your love for Miss Miriam, and trust the power of the red thread to reunite you."

"How did you know about the red thread?"

She pointed at my open collar, and I glanced down. The frayed silk cord showed inside my shirt.

"Also," she said with a smile, "Mei Qiang told me. I will be in touch when I have news. What do you plan to do today?"

I hadn't thought about it. "I was going to look for Mira, but if you're on the job . . ."

"There is little you can do until I complete a records search. What are you interested in seeing while you are here? Maybe you could take a tour of Yu Garden?"

"I guess I could. I hadn't given sightseeing much thought. Mira—Miriam—was all I was thinking about when I planned my trip."

"The red thread has a strong hold over you. Have faith that we will find your Miriam. You should visit the gardens and the Old City Temple today. It's not far from your hotel. I'm sure the concierge can help you plan your time."

She stood. "I'll leave word at your hotel when I have news."

33

When I left for Yu Garden, I wasn't sure what to expect. I thought I'd find a nice bench near some plants and sit for a few hours watching the crowd go by.

Instead I stepped into an exotic world, in which every rock, plant, and structure had been carefully placed to create perfectly composed vistas. I melted into the crowds that walked along the covered walkways over slow-moving streams. Schools of koi swim past, and willow branches dipped low enough to touch the water. When I looked up, I noticed delicately painted panels in the ceilings.

The buildings were painted in reds, whites, and blacks, with gold-leaf Chinese characters on the walls, and curving pagoda roofs made of tile or timber. Swaying paper lanterns hung between buildings in the row of shops. Even here, I found a Starbucks.

I sipped coffee as I continued walking, and a round archway that framed a carved and lacquered door reminded me of the devil's bridge. I wondered what was on the other side. Though Mei Qiang and Yu Yan seemed to believe folk tales, like the one about the red thread, I had no sense of foreboding here. It felt peaceful.

Carved stone statues of lions and dogs posed on the paths and in front of some of the buildings, while bronze warriors with bows and arrows and undulating dragons perched on the rooftops. The curving tips of the pagoda roofs seemed to be smiling, and I smiled too.

They reminded me, just a little, of the dormer windows on City Hall Leipzig. It was fascinating to consider that people of different cultures, who lived on different continents centuries ago, could have influenced each other's architecture. Even after driving across Europe with Mira, I never imagined such a beautiful place.

My father would have loved to take photographs here. I found myself wishing I'd bought a camera for the trip, until I realized people all around me were taking photos with their cell phones. I pulled out my own phone and poked around on the screen.

When I'd bought the phone, I'd thought I'd never need it, but the camera was easy to use. I got detailed shots of the temples, rock carvings, and the round door. If I lived in Shanghai, I'd come here every day. Did Mira? With a jolt, I wondered if I might find her before Yu Yan.

In my ignorance, before I made the trip, I had assumed I'd be one of only a few non-Asians in Shanghai. But I was wrong. An elderly white woman wouldn't stand out, either in this crowded tourist destination or on any street in the city. A red scarf caught my eye, and I studied the wearer's face as she walked by with her grandchildren. It wasn't Mira, and a wave of bitter disappointment threatened to overwhelm me.

"Get ahold of yourself," I muttered aloud. "You were knowing it would not be easy." In the dream, I got whatever I wanted with little effort. Here, it was up to me to make my own luck. I spent hours walking through the park, watching people pass by, and straining to hear Mira's voice or glimpse her smile.

When the crowd thinned near the dinner hour, I had trouble getting a cab, and it was nearly dark when I got back to the hotel. Tao, the clerk who had checked me in upon my arrival, greeted me when I returned. "Did you enjoy your visit to the gardens?"

"Yes. I am thinking if I go there every day, I will not run out of new things to see. It was the most beautiful place I have ever been."

Tao bowed, pleased.

"Are there any messages for me?"

"No, sir. I'm sorry."

My shoulders sagged. I wasn't ready to go up to my room, so I ambled over to the restaurant off the lobby, where a young man in a white chef's uniform attended the buffet.

I decided to embrace the new experience and picked up a plate. "What is it you are recommending? I am not knowing this type of food, but everything smells very good."

"If you like, sir, I'll select a variety of things for you to try."

Just as I'd enjoyed the gardens, I sampled the unfamiliar flavors with gusto. The chef had given me a cup of shark fin soup, steamed crab, some pancakes he called Cong You Bing, and Xun Yu, which was a spicy smoked fish. I washed it all down with a bottle of Tsingtao and had a couple of little pineapple buns for dessert with tea. When I finished my plate, I was the only diner left in the restaurant. I flagged down the chef from the buffet line as he passed my table. "Thank you. This was all very good."

"Why are you here alone, grandfather?"

I motioned toward the empty chair across from me. "Please—have a seat. I came to meet a friend of mine. A friend from long ago."

"How long since you have seen them?"

"Seems like all my life. But I've been here for a day and I think—I think I'm getting close. It's a long story."

The bartender brought me another bottle of Tsingtao and joined us as the chef said, "Tell us about your journey and your friend."

"Well, once upon a time, there was a girl. A beautiful girl. I wanted to marry her. During the war, we lost track of each other. But then I was getting another chance, and it was like a miracle, until I lost her again. I came here to find her. With a little help, maybe I will."

The next day, I asked Cheung, the concierge, to book me on a tour of the Jade Buddha Temple. It was another peaceful refuge from the crowded streets of Shanghai. The Grand Hall in the main courtyard was painted mustard yellow with tall, varnished wooden doors. Fringed red paper lanterns swayed in the breeze as the guide spoke to our group about four noble truths, which made me think about how Mira and I had asked questions that would keep our conversation going without venturing into taboo subjects.

After lunch, we continued on to the Shanghai Museum. As I wandered among the exhibits of ancient Chinese bronze, ceramics, and calligraphy, I realized how much I was enjoying having new experiences. It felt great after so many years of shutting myself away.

When the tour gave us free time to shop, I found a park and walked around, studying the faces of the other old people. My time in Shanghai was half-spent, and my search was like looking for a needle in ten haystacks.

The following day, with still no word from Yu Yan, I went back to the Yu Garden and spent the morning people watching, hoping I'd hear someone speak Mira's name.

That afternoon, I found an open-air market where street musicians entertained the crowds. The sweet strains of violin music filled me with hope, but no one played "Muss I Denn."

When I got back to the hotel that evening, Tao gave me a message from Yu Yan. It said she didn't want to tell me what she'd discovered over the phone. She would meet me at the hotel for breakfast.

Yu Yan wore a fringed red scarf when we met in the café in the hotel lobby the next morning. As the waiter poured our coffee, my hands were shaking so badly I didn't try to take a sip.

Yu Yan did not smile. "I am sorry to tell you I have had trouble locating your Miriam. There are a number of women of European descent of the right age in Shanghai, but none with the right name."

"Now what do we do?"

"Are you certain she lives here?"

I thought for a moment, and Mira's whispered last words to me echoed in my head. "No. She only said she was *in* Shanghai." How could I have made such a journey without being sure?

"Do not lose hope. If she is here, we will find her."

"I only have two days left, and if you think we can find her in that short time—don't take this the wrong way—but you're as *meshuggeneh* as I am."

"That just may be, Mr. Peter." She smiled broadly. "Aren't you glad the fates brought us together? Now come. I will take you to the homes of the women on my list, and we will see what we shall see."

What other choice did I have?

34

Outside, I gazed up at the camel statue as Yu Yan gave the valet the ticket to bring her car around. I muttered to the camel, "If you're going to bring me good fortune, how about you hurry up already?"

On our way to Hongkou District, she filled me in on its history. "This area was a major sanctuary for Jewish refugees from Europe, and Russian Jews who fled the Bolsheviks. By the mid-nineteen-thirties, over thirty thousand Jews lived side by side with the Chinese in Shanghai.

During the war years, when Japan invaded and took control of the city, including the international districts, they forced restrictions on Shanghai's Jewish population. By 1943, nearly all of them lived in a Jewish ghetto, created in response to pressure from Germany."

"Mira and I spent time in a ghetto, too," I chimed in, "in Leipzig, before they deported us to a camp. I was not knowing the Jews who fled Europe to Shanghai are facing the same persecution we did in Europe."

Yu Yan turned to me and nodded, as she pulled off a major arterial and weaved her way onto a street lined with apartments. "Yes, but here the Chinese and Jews united against their common foe—the Japanese. After the war, many Jews chose to emigrate someplace else. During the

Chinese civil war in 1945, most of the Jews who had remained here fled to the US, Israel, or Australia, until only a few hundred remained."

"I am wondering if she is coming here after the war and staying, but that is seeming unlikely, right?"

"It does, but over the last few decades, the Jewish population in Shanghai has resurged, with many older people coming back to the home of their youth. But Miriam's situation is still a mystery." She parked the car. "Now, our detective work continues. Maybe it is better if we ask if they ever knew a Miriam, or a Mira, rather than focusing on the name Schloss. It is possible she did not use that name."

"I don't know if she ever married."

"She could have changed her name for a number of reasons. Now come."

Yu Yan had a list of names and addresses, mostly apartments in the old Jewish section of the city. The first woman who answered our knock was far too tall to be Mira. Even as I shook my head and started to turn away, Yu Yan spoke to the woman in Chinese and introduced us before launching into her inquiry. As the woman listened, her curious expression brightened, and she nodded.

My heart thumped as the two women continued their rapid-fire conversation, and Yu Yan produced the list of names and addresses for the woman to see. When she bowed her thanks, the woman shut the door, and Yu Yan took my arm.

"Come, Mr. Peter. We may have a lead."

"What was she saying? The suspense, it is killing me."

"She is acquainted with a woman of the right age, who she believes lived in Germany as a girl. It is one of the names on our list, so we shall go there next. It is not far."

My trembling legs carried me down the street while my thoughts roiled in my head. Would Mira be surprised to see me? Whatever she needed—whatever had prompted her to summon me here—would it be within my power to help her? I thought of the money in my bank account, knowing I would give her my last dime without hesitation. I could only hope the way we'd loved each other in the dream was as real for her as it was for me.

Yu Yan paused before a cozy-looking apartment building. "This is the address."

When we reached the door, I rang the bell. The woman who answered was petite and dark-haired—and much too young to be Mira. Confused, I stepped back and let Yu Yan do the talking.

After a moment she murmured to me, "This woman's mother used to live here." She pressed her lips together before continuing. "She died last week."

My vision clouded and I felt like I might pass out. Yu Yan gripped my arm to steady me. "We do not have all the facts yet, Mr. Peter. Let me learn more."

Again, I stood back while the women conversed in Chinese. After a moment, the woman beckoned us inside. She brought a framed photo from the console table in the sitting room and held it out to me. I accepted it in shaking hands and looked carefully at the smiling face.

The smile was wrong, the eyes too deep-set. I drew a shaking breath. "No. This is not her."

I turned to Yu Yan. "Please tell her I'm sorry for her loss."

We took our leave, and though my nerves were nearly shot, we continued our quest. None of the women on the list knew Mira, but one suggested we inquire at the Shanghai Jewish Refugee Museum in the Ohel Moshe Synagogue.

When we'd exhausted the names on Yu Yan's list, it was almost lunch time, and we drove to the museum.

The museum wasn't far, and after we found a place to park, we walked through an iron gate into the courtyard, where Yu Yan spoke to the clerk at the ticket counter.

While I waited, I turned in a slow circle, looking up at the striped inlaid brickwork, the arched windows, and the gallery porches that ran the length of the synagogue's second and third stories. A bronze statue of six people dominated the other side of the courtyard, and I walked over to get a closer look. A series of memorial plaques adorned the long wall behind the sculpture. My heart beat faster as I reached out to touch the raised letters. There were thousands of names. Though I knew Mira might not have used her maiden name after the war, I hurried past the first half of the alphabet. By the time I reached the names that started with S, my breath was coming in sobs. I couldn't look. Had all these people died in the Jewish ghetto here during the war? Had I come this far, only to find Mira in some cemetery?

Yu Yan caught up and laid a calming hand on my arm. "Do not despair if you find her name here. The woman at the ticket booth said these are names of Jewish people who sheltered in Shanghai during the war. It is a tribute—not just a list of the dead. Some of these people are still alive."

Together we scanned the names. Mira's was not there.

I blotted my forehead with my handkerchief. "I don't know how much more suspense I can take."

"Come, let us make inquiries. Maybe Miss Mira made a donation or signed the guest register at one time. Maybe inside there is a clue." She encouraged me with a smile. "Take heart, Mr. Peter. We are not finished searching. The red thread remains unbroken."

We had arrived during the lull between guided tours, and while we waited, we walked through the museum. The first floor was set up as a synagogue, and upstairs housed various exhibits. In a glass display case, another sculpture caught my eye. I hurried across the room and stared at the likeness of three round-eyed children. The girl in front carried a violin and wore a locket shaped like a heart.

I pressed my palm to the glass as tears streamed down my cheeks.

"Mr. Peter. Mr. Peter!" Yu Yan shook my arm.

"I'm sorry. It's just—I was not knowing it would be so hard to be here and to be seeing—" I mopped my face with my handkerchief and blew my nose.

"No, not that. Come. Look over here." Hand under my elbow, she led me away from the statue and stopped triumphantly in front of a poster in the stairwell. It advertised the season's scheduled programming and lectures.

She pointed to a photo of an elderly woman playing a violin. It was Mira. As soon as I saw her face, I realized I would have known her anywhere. I didn't have to read the caption under the photo.

"When? When is the performance?"

"It was last month."

My knees threatened to collapse, and Yu Yan caught me under the elbow to hold me up.

"Are you the ones asking about Mira Schloss?"

I turned toward the voice. It was a woman, maybe in her sixties. "Yes. I'm an old friend of hers. A very old friend. Peter Ibbetz."

I held out my hand to shake and she clasped it with both of hers. "You're Peter? Mira's Peter? What a surprise! Oh, it's such a pleasure to meet you." Tears sprang up in her eyes. "I'm Marjit Warner."

"Where is Mira? Did I miss her? Did she leave before I could get here?"

Her chin trembled. "You don't know?"

"Know what? I am told she was here."

"Please, come with me where we can have some privacy and I'll explain."

She gestured Yu Yan and me into a cluttered office with a worn sofa and chairs. "Make yourselves comfortable." We took seats on the sofa, and Yu Yan gripped my hand as Marjit sat opposite us. "I was once Mira's student. I'm a member of the museum's board of directors, and I invited her to come for our program celebrating Jewish culture in Shanghai last month.

"Mira performed all over the world during her career, as you probably know."

I glanced at Yu Yan, who asked tactfully, "Where did you first meet her?"

"In Copenhagen, where we both lived after the war. She taught me, and all her students, folk songs from her childhood. Music connected the Jewish refugees who fled Europe and spread to all corners of the globe. Life in Shanghai was hard, but my parents had happy memories of their childhoods here. That is why I returned as an adult.

Mira came planning to stay at my home for a few weeks, because there were other events in Shanghai she wished to attend. When she played across the street in the White Horse Café, our Viennese-style coffee house, she took requests for all the old songs— 'Muss I Denn,' 'Lorelei,' 'In Stiller Nacht'—and the happy songs, too. And then, the day before she meant to leave for home . . .''

I swallowed hard. "What? What happened?"

"She had a stroke."

Yu Yan gripped my hand as she asked, "Is she alive?"

Marjit nodded. "She has been in a coma since April third—for almost a month now."

I thought back. April third. That was the day of the first robbery at the bodega when I had the first dream. Mira must have found herself alone in the dark and reached out until she found me.

I gave in to my disappointment, frustration, and exhaustion, and as I sagged against Yu Yan, my sobs threatened to tear my heart from my chest. Marjit hurried to sit on my other side and put her arms around me. The three of us cried together for a long time.

How terrifying it must have been for Mira, falling ill in a strange place. No wonder her subconscious searched for mine, until we connected in our dreams.

Marjit left us for a short while, and by the time she returned bearing coffee on a tray, I had composed myself. I was ready to face whatever came next.

She set the tray down. "I telephoned the hospital. Mira's condition is unchanged, but she is resting comfortably. I told them we will be coming by for a visit."

I nodded. "Before we go, are you knowing what is happening to Mira when she did not play in the concert at Theresienstadt? That was the last time we were together, and all my life, I have wondered."

Marjit looked surprised, but what she knew filled in many of the gaps for me. "At that time, the detainees were allowed to send and receive packages, and Mira's music professor was smuggling out messages on sheet music. When the authorities learned what he was doing, the professor was transported to Auschwitz and gassed, and Mira, who was often with him, was taken to the Gestapo's headquarters in the Small Fortress, across from the main Theresienstadt compound."

"She was fifteen years old. How much could she have known about what her professor was doing?" Even as I spoke, I remembered Mira's resolve not to let her circumstances break her. She would have been her professor's willing accomplice.

Marjit continued. "They held Mira in the Little Fortress for several weeks, torturing her for information. She remained there after all the other musicians who had performed for the Red Cross visit had been transported. One of the officers of the camp who had heard Mira play admired her skill. After she provided no useful information, that officer got her released and made sure she received medical attention at the camp hospital. She was very weak, as she had also been deprived of food, and it took her a while to regain her health. After she grew stronger, that officer was transferred to Krakow, and he took her with him, obtained papers for her, and had her play for Nazi officers at his parties. He gave her decent food and clothes. He even rescued her violin from the rehearsal hall.

"Though he was German, Mira once told me, he was not a terrible man. He did not leave her to the fate suffered by so many others. Before the war ended, she became his mistress, not for love, but because she knew staying in his favor would help keep her alive."

Though my stomach heaved at the thought of her in the keeping of a German officer, I knew how it felt to be vulnerable and alone. I could not disparage her for doing whatever was necessary to survive. "Then what happened?"

"She was still in Poland when the Allies came. Her officer was captured. Mira once said to me that, at first, she believed her survival was a punishment. She was doomed to live when everyone she loved had left her. Music saved her, and she made music her reason to live."

Though I wanted to go straight to the hospital, Marjit pressed us to have lunch first at the White Horse Café. We crossed the street to a turreted three-story building that looked like it belonged in Europe. In the front garden was a fountain with statues representing a Chinese woman holding an umbrella over the head of a Jewish girl.

I stared at it, seeing Yu Yan sheltering a ten-year-old Mira.

Inside the dark-paneled coffee shop, we ordered and sat at one of the marble-topped tables. Yu Yan asked, "What was Miss Miriam like as a teacher?"

Marjit's smile reflected her happy memories. "She was the kindest, most understanding teacher, but she expected the best from her students. No exceptions! She told us nothing should stand in the way of us becoming the very best we could be. But as I said, she was not harsh or impatient."

Yu Yan asked, "Did she have children of her own?"

"No. She never married."

I cleared my throat. "She would have been a wonderful mother."

"She would indeed. I believe she thought of us all as her children." Marjit patted my hand. "Mira told me she grieved for you all her life. She believed you were lost to her forever. What a pity you were not reunited sooner. She was so brave, so kind. One could not help but love her."

I cleared my throat. "I also have grieved for her."

When the meal was done, Marjit shepherded us back to the museum. "I have more things for you."

In her office, she handed me a compact disc. "This is a recording of Mira's concert last month. I am sure you'll want to listen to it."

I had to wipe my eyes again. "Yes, yes. Very much."

"All right. We can play it whenever you're ready. She brought some mementos with her, to share at the performance. Shall I leave you with everything? It will be almost like she is speaking to you and you are getting to know her again before you see her at the hospital."

When I nodded, Marjit brought out Mira's things—a satchel, a suitcase, and her violin case—and started the recording before she and Yu Yan left me alone.

Mira's voice, old and shaky, but still the same, came through the speakers. "These songs remind me of the joy I felt as a little girl, when I was first learning to play the violin. They also remind me of the sad times, when I played to cheer those around me, and of the darkest times, when music was all that kept me from losing my sanity. Most of all, these songs are my tribute to my dearest friend, Peter, my one great love. Wherever he is, I hope he has not forgotten the warmth of my feelings for him. Love does not end. It goes on for all time."

The music followed, one tune after another, just as she had played for me, her audience of one. But this time, she told stories between the songs, some that Marjit had told me, and other moments from her life I never would have otherwise known.

While I listened, I looked through a box of programs from concerts and photographs of her with her students. A much younger Marjit was present in several.

The next thing I drew out of the satchel was a book of Chinese folk tales, with a red ribbon marking her place. I opened it to the tale of The Red Thread of Fate.

At the very bottom, I found the leather-bound album I'd seen just recently in the dream. There were photos of us, as children. Somehow, they'd been saved, and she'd gotten them back. Tears blurred the images as I reached out to touch the snapshots my father had taken.

On another page was a photo of Mira, at the age she might have been in our dreams, but instead of glowing with good health, she had sunken cheeks and dark smudges under her eyes. Her hair, which was short and still growing out, was held back by a ribbon tied around her head.

She was arm in arm with a young man, who also bore signs of time in the camps—skin stretched tight over angular cheekbones and close-cropped hair. He was smiling with his lips closed, probably to hide damage to his teeth. It was not her German officer.

I flipped through the rest of the album, but there was just that one photo of her with the young man. I pulled the crumbling snapshot gently from the album page and put it in my shirt pocket.

When I opened her suitcase, my toy airplane lay on top of her clothing and the scent of Evening in Paris cologne wafted out. Mira's violin played on in the background as I clutched the airplane to my chest and broke down all over again.

35

At the hospital, I carried the compact disc player as Marjit led the way to the long-term care unit. Marjit and Yu Yan chatted while we waited for Mira's doctor to meet with us. I paced the hall and looked into the closest rooms, hoping for a glimpse of Mira, but all the patients in sight were Chinese.

When the doctor arrived, I prayed she would offer some glimmer of hope, some change in Mira's condition. Instead, she was matter of fact. "Ms. Schloss suffered a stroke and has been in a coma for almost a month."

"What is the chance she will wake up?"

The doctor's face was expressionless. "We expect no improvement. We're keeping her comfortable, but there is little we can do. I'm sorry, sir, but she is dying. You may sit with her if you wish."

I picked up the compact disc player. "Yes. Please take me to her."

Yu Yan and Marjit stayed in the waiting area while I followed the doctor down the hall to a dimly lit room. The figure in the bed was so tiny it could have been a child. A monitor beeped softly.

I thought I was prepared until I saw her face. Though it was lined with age and drawn out of shape on the right side, I could see her at every stage of her life—the little girl and the young woman were still there in the curve of her brow, the tilt of her nose, the faded rose of her lips.

"That is my wife." I wept. "That is my wife. Oh, Mira."

The doctor bowed and quietly shut the door behind her as I sat beside the bed and took Mira's withered hand in mine. It was the same hand that had touched my cheek, picked flowers, and coaxed music from the strings of a violin. Now her bones felt fragile beneath her papery skin, and she didn't return the gentle pressure when I squeezed. I rubbed my thumb over the scar on the knuckle of her index finger. It was just a faint, white line, well healed, as though it had been made many years before.

The words spilled easily from my lips in German, just as they had in the dreams. "Mira, I'm here. Everything's all right now. I found you, just like I promised."

I leaned closer. "You've known about the legend of the red thread since we were children, haven't you? That's why you gave me your locket that day at Theresienstadt. I don't know if it was magic that brought us together in the dream. Maybe it was like Einstein said, and objects that travel at a high rate of speed experience time differently than ones who stand still. I wish we could have stayed together longer, but I feel like we've jumped forward seventy-five years, practically overnight. When we jump again, I don't know where we'll go, but I'll find you every time—no matter where you are."

Mira had suffered, survived, and defied those who had tried to destroy her. She had found a way to thrive and to make the world a better place, while I'd stayed hidden in my apartment, living in fear. She had lived a full life, traveling and performing into her nineties. Now she was lying here waiting to die. I wished I could trade places with her. Tears rolled down my cheeks and splashed on our hands. "I'm sorry I didn't get here in time."

But for the beep of the monitor and the whoosh of the machine that was helping her breathe, there was no sound in the room. The murmur of voices in the hall seemed so far away, they might as well be on another plane.

"I brought you something." I plugged in the compact disc player and set it on the stand beside her bed. "Listen, Mira. It's a recording of your concert. That's you talking." As I held her hand, I remembered waltzing with her around the living room. In the dance hall at Augustusplatz in Paris.

She didn't react, and I begged silently, *Please, Mira. Come back to me. Just for a moment.* Then the sweet, simple violin solo filled the space and I felt her hand twitch in mine. Was it just a reflex? It happened again, and again, until I was sure she was moving in time with the music.

"You are here, aren't you? Move two times for yes. One for no."

She twitched twice and was still. I hit the call button, and when a nurse came in, I pointed at Mira's still form. "She can hear me! She moved her hand."

She shook her head, but unlike the doctor, she was sympathetic. "I know you'd like to believe that, sir, but we've monitored her. She hasn't responded to stimuli since she went into the coma."

"That's because she was waiting for me to get here."

"Sir, it's hard to accept, but—"

"No. Listen to me. What about dreaming? Can she dream?"

She hesitated before answering. "I should summon the doctor and let you speak with her—"

"Please, tell me what you think."

"Dreams could be an early indicator of a return to life, but we can't be sure because we can't ask the patient. People who are deep in a coma don't dream." She looked at me sadly. "I would like to give you hope, but she has shown no signs of waking up."

"But she did. Just now she is moving her hand in time to the music. I am asking her to squeeze twice for yes if she could understand me and she did." I turned up the volume. "Stay here a minute and watch. Please."

"Sir, we have cared for many coma patients here. It was good of you to come to visit, and I hope it comforts you to know she's resting peacefully." She turned the music down and put a hand on my arm. "But I must be frank. There is no chance she will regain consciousness and speak to you. Her vital signs have weakened over the past week, and we don't expect her to live more than another day or two."

"Please do not talk about her like she cannot be hearing you." I waved the nurse away and turned the music back up.

When visiting hours were over, the nurse returned to usher me out. I kissed Mira's forehead. "Goodnight, my love. I'll be back in the morning."

I cradled the compact disc player as I plodded down the hall. As I came into the waiting room, Yu Yan and Marjit rose to their feet.

Yu Yan hurried to my side. "Mr. Peter, I'm so sorry. I'm afraid we found your Mira too late. Are you all right?"

I looked down. My hands were shaking, but I nodded. "Yes, yes. I'm okay. It is difficult to see her like that, when I am remembering her so clearly as young and vibrant and funny. She is still my Mira, the love of my life. I kept my promises—to her and to myself. I found her."

Yu Yan wiped away a tear. "I'm afraid your red thread stretched so far across the ocean that it took too long to reunite you."

"It is my fault. I am not blaming the red thread or the gods or Einstein. I had thought that keeping to myself was keeping me alive. But living in fear wasn't really living, and I am learning this too late." I turned to Marjit. "Thank you for telling me stories about Mira so I am getting to know her again. I will treasure the recording. May I borrow the player until I am leaving for home?"

"Of course. Maybe you'll come back and take part in some of next season's programming. You'll always be welcome here."

"Thank you. It has been a very long day. I am ready to go back to the hotel now."

I held Mira's locket tight in my fist on the drive back to the Crowne Plaza. When we arrived, Yu Yan parked beside the camel. "I will come and take you to the hospital again in the morning. You should spend her remaining time together."

"My time in Shanghai is almost up. I have only tomorrow." I took a deep breath. "But I am not going. I am staying with Mira until they are finding me and kicking me out. You will not be telling on me, right?"

She shook her head. "I will not tell a soul."

"I will take a cab to the hospital tomorrow. You are doing so much for me I can never thank you enough." I didn't know the customs or what was proper in Shanghai, but I was glad that she hugged me good-bye before I got out of the car.

"You do not need to take a cab, Mr. Peter. I will be here first thing in the morning. *Míng tiān jiàn*. See you soon."

36

Tao hailed me from the reception desk when I came into the lobby. "You were out late, Mr. Peter. You look tired. Did you eat?"

I had to think about it for a moment. "I had lunch. But I am not hungry." I fought back tears. "I found my friend."

Tao nodded sympathetically. "Yu Yan telephoned earlier to tell us your friend was in the hospital. I'm very sorry she is not well. Please, Mr. Peter, come sit down and tell me about it."

He took my arm and led me to one of the sofas in the lobby, and I poured out the whole story. When I was done, he stood.

"You must eat to keep up your strength. I will bring you room service. Anything you want."

"Thanks, Tao. I suppose I could maybe be eating soon. But first, I am wanting to play this for you. It is my Mira."

I plugged in the compact disc player. As we listened, the music drew the chef and another of the night clerks out to see what was going on, until several of the hotel staff had gathered in the lobby. As we listened to "Lustig ist das Zigeunerleben," Tao stepped out in front of the reception desk, took one of the waitresses by the hand, and they began to waltz. I imagined Mira was smiling.

When the music ended, everyone applauded, and I realized I was hungry after all. "Tao, could you see if the guys in the kitchen can make me a turkey sandwich? If you are not having rye bread it is okay. Maybe with a dill pickle?"

"Right away, Mr. Peter."

I unplugged the disc player and took the elevator up. Alone in my room, I felt the full impact of my exhaustion. It was all I could do to slip off my shoes before I lay back on the bed and closed my eyes.

Mira shook my shoulder to wake me. She was sitting up in bed beside me, the blanket clutched to her chest. "Please wake up, Peter. I'm afraid to be alone. The darkness never leaves me now."

Something was waiting in the shadows on the far side of the room. "I know."

"I'm glad you're here. There are things I must tell you while there's still time."

"Are you sure? I don't want to risk—"

"Yes. I'm ready to talk now." She didn't look at me. "Thank you for bringing the music to me. It was so good to hear all the songs one last time."

"Marjit gave me the recording of your concert. She filled me in on a lot of things, so you don't have to—"

"There are things she doesn't know. I want to tell you the rest."

"None of it matters. Mira, all that matters is that I love you."

"And I love you." She took my hand. "The last time I saw you, before the concert, I couldn't tell you that I was helping my professor smuggle information out of Theresienstadt. No matter what you may have thought, I was not an innocent. I kept on with Resistance work after they released me, after I went to Krakow with the German officer. I kept notes, encoded in my music, the way my professor had taught me, but with a different code that escaped detection.

"At the war's end, I had a great deal of information that I passed on to the Allied authorities. It was I who made sure the German officer who'd saved me was arrested. I had no pang of conscience. I wanted to avenge everyone I'd lost during the war. If I'd had the opportunity, I would have shot that officer myself. I was a different person then, and you could not have protected me. You probably would not have liked me much. That time is over, and I have no regrets."

I must have looked shocked, for she smiled as she touched my cheek. "Now show me the photo in your pocket."

I reached into my pajama pocket and brought out the picture of her and the young man.

She studied it with a sad smile. "His name was Lev. I met him after the liberation, in Poland. When we got settled in one of the DP camps and made inquiries about survivors, we both learned our parents were dead. You had been sent from Theresienstadt before they released me from the Little Fortress, and I didn't know where you'd gone. Lev and I applied for visas, thinking it would be months before we heard anything. We weren't too far from Leipzig, and I believed you would come home if you could, as we had promised. Lev traveled with me.

"At home, everything was in ruins. Our tree had been shattered by a mortar shell and our homes were nothing but rubble. Lev wanted to go back to the DP camp right away, but I insisted on waiting. We camped in your father's workshop.

"I carved my initials and the year into the bark of the tree, so when you came, you'd know I'd been there. Lev was kind and understood what I was going through. I wanted to believe you were on your way to meet me, and I insisted we wait."

"Stop. Don't tell me anything else."

"Please. I need to finish. It was almost more than I could bear, to be at home without you, but I pressed Lev to stay, even after we ran out of food. When we went foraging, we came across gangs of men roaming the ruins, looting, and we hid from them. If they had found us, they would have—you know. I would never be safe there. Finally, I had to admit you weren't coming. Lev made me promise we'd go back, and we left the next day."

"That was the night I let you go, Peter. And when I let you go, I had to let someone else in. Otherwise I'd have been nothing but a shell. We went back to the camp and waited for our futures to move forward. Within days, Lev got a visa to Palestine. I thought he'd wait for me, but he didn't. He was gone before I realized I was with child."

"Oh, Mira. I'm so sorry."

She wiped away a tear. "It's all right. It's been all right for a long time. I wasn't the only girl who got pregnant after the war. But the baby was stillborn. My body wasn't healthy enough to nurture another life. A couple I met had just had a baby, and they took me in as a member of the family and a nanny. They were kind to me, and eventually I went with them to Denmark. I still had my violin and began to give lessons. Soon, I had more pupils than I could handle." She looked up at me. "I kept the music, Peter. I had a good life. The only thing that was missing was you."

"I'm not missing anymore. You don't have to wait around, feeling afraid of the darkness. In fact"—the idea was unfolding as I spoke— "I think we should go."

"Where?"

"Back to Bastei. The sandstone hills. Right now."

"In the middle of the night?"

"Why not?"

I found a kerosene lantern and matches in the kitchen and she carried folded blankets in her arms. The lantern cast a wide circle of light as we made our way to the car.

Wrapped in one of the blankets, she slept with her head on my shoulder as I drove through the night. When we reached Bastei, she leaned on me as we climbed the path through the woods to a small clearing near the looming silhouettes of the craggy peaks. There, I spread one blanket on the grass and drew the other one over us, and we lay side by side, looking up at the starlight that filtered through the tree limbs.

I needed to make my confession too. "I let my fear drive me deep inside myself, and it ruined my life. I didn't take chances in my adult life. I didn't give anyone a chance to love me." I bit my lip before blurting out, "Fear kept me from looking for you, but I'm done being afraid. Mira, I can help you face your fears now that the darkness is closing in. You don't have to run from it anymore."

She nodded. "I couldn't let go until I knew you were all right. Then, once we were together, I couldn't bear to let you know the worst of me."

"There is no worst of you. You are good and kind. You've taught me so much." I pulled her closer. "The energy and the love—the part that is you—doesn't end. It has to go somewhere—if you believe in physics, that is."

She kissed me. "At the hospital today, when I felt you touch my hand and heard your voice, and realized we were together, both here and there, I wasn't afraid anymore. I can let go and you can live. Promise me you'll travel and give talks to share our stories. Go to *shul,* even if it's just one time, and observe *yarzheit* for me and for your parents so you can finally have closure. Leave nothing undone in the time you have left."

I tightened my hold on her and felt the hair on the back of my neck prickle. I didn't tell her I could feel the dark presence eyeing me, too. "Let's take one thing at a time and wait for the dawn together."

Even a week ago I would've made love to her in panic and desperation, terrified of the impending loss. But instead, as I held her, I savored the experience, memorizing every curve of her body, and the way her touch burned and cooled my skin at the same time. When it was over, I knew we were bound together for all time, in defiance of anything that that might try to separate us.

The first rays of sunlight that appeared in the cleft of the sandstone rocks lit her face and her skin glowed, as if with health and vigor. She ran her fingers through my hair, combing it back off my forehead, and kissed me gently, first one cheek, then the other, then on the lips in farewell.

When she left the warmth of the blankets and started toward the prism of light that shone through the rocks, I threw back the blanket.

"I'll walk with you."

Together we climbed toward the gap in the rocks. Squinting against the glare, I saw silhouettes moving as they gathered near the cleft.

Mira froze for a moment and called, "Mutti? Vati?" Then she broke into a run, moving lithe as a deer toward the light. The figures held out their arms, and the light fragmented into prisms that filled the sky as more figures joined the ones already waiting there.

I ran after her. "Mira—wait!"

She turned, her smile as bright as the sun behind her. "Peter, everything's all right. Look!" She pointed toward the growing group of figures.

"I know. Wait for me. I'm coming, too."

When I had almost caught up, she reached back and squeezed my hand. Then her fingers slipped through mine as she disappeared into the light.

Mist, thick as the smog over Shanghai, slowly cleared. I saw the red thread, frayed but unbroken, stretching before me. It led across the ocean, back to the apple tree in the garden of our childhood.

The sweet sound of Mira's violin drifted out her open windows. I picked an apple and polished it on my shirt, knowing that no matter how much time looped and coiled on our way to wherever we were headed, eventually, when the music ended, she would be there to greet me.

Rebekah Pace Collection

(Faith, Inspirational, and Christmas)

ISBN: 978-1-646300-28-0

When the daughter of a materialistic man prays for God to heal her disintegrating family, a fire destroys everything they own, forcing them to rediscover each other and their faith.

ISBN: 978-1-646300-36-5

When a postal manager is transferred to rural Appalachia as punishment, she discovers the importance of helping others.

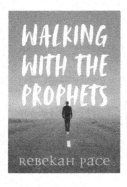

ISBN: 978-1-646300-50-1

A hedge fund manager and quant in NYC receives enlightenment and is commanded to walk across the United States with nothing but a walking stick and begging bowl.

ISBN: 978-1-646300-32-7

When he learns that his wife is thrilled at the prospect of divorce, a man decides to make her fall in love with him again so that he can punish her by leaving.

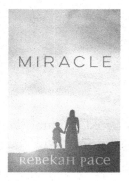

ISBN: 978-1-646300-34-1

When the decision is made to stop life support for their mother, a daughter must justify that decision to her siblings and reconcile her own feelings of guilt.